MW01415502

REBIRTH

A SCI-FI ALIEN INVASION ROMANCE

CAPTURED EARTH
BOOK 5

A.G. WILDE

PETRONIE

Copyright © 2023 by A.G. Wilde

All rights reserved.

No part of this book may be used or reproduced in any manner whatsoever without written permission except in the case of brief quotations embodied in critical articles or reviews.

The characters and events portrayed in this book are fictitious. Any similarity to real persons, living or dead, businesses, or locales is coincidental and is not intended by the author.

This story is intended for adult readers and it may contain elements not suitable for readers under the age of 18. All sexually active characters portrayed in this book are eighteen years of age or older.

To our tiny dot in this vast universe. Even as we teeter on the edge of oblivion, love endures.

REBIRTH

HE'ROX

I stand on the edge of a world reborn. My purpose fulfilled in eradicating our enemies. But a deep emptiness remains, an abyss within me. There is nothing left to offer this new world rebuilding from the ruins.

I must return home.

Her arrival is ordinary. A hyu'man like the others. But one I did not expect to change the core of my very existence.

Soh'fee arrives at the site of this new Er'then city, at the same time that I sense a disturbance that will change our paths forever.

Small, unsuspecting hyu'man, she comes along with me on a journey that brings horror, violence and chill into her world.

As we track a nightmarish menace, blood is spilled and lives hang in the balance. And it is not long till I realize one thing.

This little hyu'man has come to mean more to me than she should. Soh'fee has become my world in this place, fueling hope I'd thought lost.

She gives me a reason to stay and fight. And I discover my true purpose lies not in destruction, but in fiercely protecting what has been reborn from the ashes...

This new world, and Soh'fee who has become my own

BEFORE YOU READ!

This note is a trigger warning.
When writing this series, I decided not to put a block on the things the books will cover.
That means there might be topics that some readers might not want to read about.
I will try to give adequate warning of this beforehand (in the text below), and if you decide to pass on this book/series, that is completely okay!
This is not meant to be a light, fluffy read. If you've read the rest of the books in this series, you'll already know this will be filled with terror.
The only thing is, He'rox's story in particular, has some elements of horror as well (okay, *more* horror than the others maybe. I'll let you decide).
Let's face it. A reality where the Gryken are real and arrive to eradicate us all is a reality I'd willingly say "no, thank you" to. So just a fair warning with this one.
There is death. Torture. Graphic scenes.
Violence. Terror.

Raw emotion and raw, hot sex.

It's the apocalypse and it hasn't ended, but I hope that if you do continue to read, you will enjoy the story as much as I enjoyed writing it.

Happy reading!
 AG

CHAPTER ONE

HE'ROX

For five thousand years, we traveled to this world. Five thousand years away from our home.

Five. Thousand. Years.

In silence.

Locked in stasis. Our bodies frozen. Our aging suspended.

We left our home to save a world we did not know. And we have succeeded. Our sole purpose, achieved.

The dust from the war with the Gryken has begun to settle. Er'th begins to rebuild. Cities lie in ruins. Billions of hyu'mankin are dead. But the hyu'mans, so fragile yet so fiercely defiant, will continue their era on this planet. They have earned the right to endure. To forge a new age from the ashes of their near-destruction.

And yet...

I stand on the bridge of our mother ship as if I am on the brink. The controls, the walls that surround me, all disappear as I stare out at this planet's blue sky.

Calm.

It is calm now, this section of the planet mostly liberated. Wherever the war still rages does not affect here, and one can almost imagine what this world was like before we arrived.

Bright star. Blue skies. Crisp air.

Warmth.

So different from Edooria.

Gazing at this world from this viewpoint, I wonder if we Vullan did the right thing. In our thirst for revenge, we saved this planet. But saving this world has come at great cost. Not only to myself but to every Vullan who came here on this ship.

While hyu'manity rebuilds...we are left with nothing.

Our home is long gone. Five thousand years... We may tell the hyu'mans we will travel back...but we know there is nothing left to return to. Our clans. Our nests. Long gone. Through time. Through the war, our extinction event, when the Gryken came to our world.

To return to Edooria would be to lose everything all over again.

And yet, it is a trip we must take.

For Er'th is saved. But it is not our home.

We wanderers have no place here.

I have no place here.

"He'rox." The sound behind me doesn't pull my attention from the viewscreen, but the edges of consciousness that create this space I've walked into slowly return.

I become aware of the lights on the control panel before me. The walls that enclose the bridge.

I am back.

Down below, small dots move like insects across the surface. Our Vullan-kin and their mates, alongside the hyu'mans they've rescued and brought to this place.

This new beginning. This *rebirth* is the start of a city the hyu'mans have called Unity.

"The drones have picked up a new set of hyu'mans heading this way," Dri'ro says. "They require your presence on the surface."

I do not miss the slight shiver that goes through his ba'clan as he comes to stand by my side. The way they ripple to move away from my own, while mine don't react. And despite how he tries to hide it, standing by my side while his ba'clan rear back for self-preservation, it is a reaction I've come to expect. Another thing I've adjusted to.

Another effect of sacrifice.

For this has all been sacrifice. A constant giving. For revenge. For life. For survival.

And for some of my brothers, sacrifice for that thing the hyu'mankin call...love.

My attention remains on the outside, only my head tilting slightly at Dri'ro's words.

"I have nothing more to offer."

My technology, the weapons I developed to kill this scourge that infested Er'th, has been my life's work. Revolutions of research on Edooria. All paid off. My obsession. My intent. Fulfilled.

I have succeeded.

"What more..." I begin.

What more can I give? What more am I worth?

For I have given my all.

I have given *myself*.

Dri'ro releases a breath, his ba'clan shivering, and I commend him silently on his control. For not all of my brothers can remain composed in my presence. And even those that can, have trained themselves to do so over what feels like eons, while I tried to accept the one thing that sets me apart from the rest of my kin.

That I am now *Other*. Not Vullan, but something else altogether.

"A meeting," he says. "The females think one of the arriving Er'thkin was important in the Before." His gaze slides to mine, all darkness with no light. I can see myself reflected in those eyes. Like a white shadow.

Strange.

Unnatural.

An aberration.

Such a sight should make my hackles rise. But those instincts? Dimmed. Memory of such responses is a fading mist in the back of my mind.

"Hyu'mankin no longer have castes," I reply. "They are now all equal. Now they rebuild. Together."

Dri'ro's lips pull back in a hyu'manlike grin that shows how much we've adapted since arriving here. His fangs bare as he speaks. "If you spent more time observing them, you would know they are not like us, brother."

He turns his attention back to the viewscreen and I sense his words bear twice the meaning.

But he is wrong.

I've spent many cycles observing the very beings he thinks I ignore. The females. The ones who've mated with my kin.

Their differences, their intricacies, their desires...all of it fascinates me.

But it is not something I can indulge in.

Ever.

I've seen them inside out. Yet, they surprise me.

"There," Dri'ro says. Far below, a vehicle pulls into the settlement, dust rising in its wake. "They'll be waiting for you."

Why?

My brethren all know there is a reason I restrict my movement to the surface. A reason I keep to the ship.

"I must remain on the ship."

Dri'ro clicks. No words. Only a sound. One of understanding... and pity.

"It will only be for a short while."

My attention moves from the convoy of arriving vehicles, and I slip back into my mind's space once more. The control panel disappears. The lights. The walls. And once more, I stand at the brink.

I had one goal for surviving this long. One reason for embarking on this journey across the cosmos.

And I have realized that purpose.
There is nothing left.
"Very well," I say.
It has all...come to an end.

CHAPTER TWO

SOPHIE

Inhaling deeply, I release a breath as the vehicles head toward the camp. Pop-up buildings, structures, and tents appear in the distance, the first signs of a thriving settlement in what is still a damaged wasteland.

There are people there. More than I can count. More than I've seen in what now feels like forever.

Glancing at the males seated alongside me in the transport, their hard faces don't reveal much, but I can tell they're all thinking the same thing.

It's the singular thought that ricocheted in my head after I braved it outside my bunker. The singular thought that struck me in the aftermath. That silence.

Is it really over? Is Earth really...saved?

It's been a while since I've seen one of those towering machines. Heard the bone-chilling sound they make as they traverse the landscape, crushing everything beneath their feet.

The silence says it's over. That we're saved. But we couldn't have done it alone.

And now I know we didn't.

"Looks like that's the place," one of the men says, long hair whipping in the breeze as we jolt over the uneven ground.

I don't know any of these men. Long ago, I came to terms with the fact that everyone I know is either dead or safe somewhere. The latter being highly unlikely.

I am alone.

These men and I have only three things in common.

We're human. We're survivors of the end of the world.

And we saw the flyers.

Ones that spoke of a brand new home. A settlement where all was welcome. A new place called Unity. Where humanity was beginning to rebuild.

"See any of them?" the guy that spoke continues, eyes pointed as he searches what he can see of the camp set out before us, right before his gaze returns to the heavens.

"Nah," another answers.

Because that's where all of our gazes have been pointed ever since that...thing became visible.

Hundreds of feet above the camp floats a vessel unmoving. As if in suspended animation, it sits there, everything about it looking inhuman. Unreal. Because it is.

The sleek dark metal that covers every inch of the vessel, hiding its angles and edges, is so dark it soaks up all light from the sun like a hungry black hole.

"What if it's a trap, man?" The man in the front passenger seat speaks, his voice coming through the small window that separates the bed from the cab.

I grip my pack tighter, pulling it between my legs at the same time that the guy beside me taps a finger against his leg at a pace that tells me he doesn't even realize he's doing it.

"We won't know until we get there."

The tension in the van is only heightened the closer we get, and I wonder if this was the right decision.

I could have stayed in my bunker. Waited till all my food ran out. Waited it all out in a place that still smelled like home.

"And then what?" another one of the men says.

I know they aren't speaking to me, but the question comes at such a perfect moment that I huff a mirthless laugh through my nose. Eyes still on the object in the skies, the question repeats in my head.

And then what? If I'd stayed, what would I have done? Starve to death? Do the very thing my body, my *mind*, protests against?

I'm one of the survivors of a massacre of my species. The day I stepped out of my bunker was the day I decided I wasn't going to hide away in a hole anymore.

And it was the day, like a message from the universe, I bumped into that flyer.

"Look, man," the first guy says. "If it's a trap, then we're fucked. We should have a backup plan. In case we see one of 'em, you know?"

They say no names.

But regardless that I don't know these men, I don't need inside information to know who they're talking about. Or rather...what.

Living in the bunker my father built years ago, locked away from everything else, *safe*, I'd wondered if the thing that would bring my death was time. There'd been no way out. I would stay in that bunker, time slowly ticking, slowly aging while the world above me was torn to pieces.

I would stay there forever, until my time ran out and I no longer existed.

The small radio I had rarely picked up any signals, but when it did, when I heard what was happening above ground, it only solidified the fact that my fears were coming true. I would either die in that bunker, or I would die at the hands of the strange beings that fell to Earth.

Either way, my time was up.

Either way, Sophie Seltzer's time had come.

Until...it didn't.

I grip the flyer in my hand so tight, I almost rip the worn paper.

On one side, the invitation to Unity is written in big bold letters. And on the other...

I turn the paper to that side now as the van slows down. Eyes still on that thing in the skies, there's a feeling in my gut that isn't fear.

Because if this is a trick, a trap, they don't need to spring one. The beings that came in that ship are clearly more advanced than we are.

The van grinds to a halt, a cloud of dust floating up into the air, and the men bunched in with me glance at each other. It takes a moment before they start moving, each hopping out of the vehicle to stand on the earth below.

"Thanks for the ride." I force a smile and the males nod.

Their movements are slow. Hesitant.

Not the type of reaction you'd expect after arriving at what should be a haven. And as I hop down from the bed of the van, that paper I'm gripping in my hand crumples as I grab my pack and stand, for the first time, on the ground that is now Unity.

"Maybe they're not here," I hear one of the men say. "Maybe they're in that thing up there." He gestures to the massive ship floating above us, a shudder going through his shoulders as a gust of wind whips around us.

But as the sun shines down, the blue sky calm and so beautiful I'm afraid to trust its stillness, I see something they do not.

I see...*life*.

The camp is busy. The people on the ground are without fear as they hustle about the camp. Everyone is doing something, and those who aren't working sit together. Chatting.

There's the sweet scent of food, and children play.

Children...

Children that survived.

And there is...*laughter*.

"You there! Welcome to Unity!" A woman dressed in what looks like black, shin-tight spandex heads our way, pulling the attention of the males behind me. Not because of the outfit that melds to her like a second skin but because, behind her, like a dark shadow, stalks something I couldn't have ever imagined was real.

Except, it's right before me now.

"Hi, I'm Mina!" Her jovial demeanor does nothing to soothe the sudden stiffness that goes through the group of us. Her countenance falls a little, only slightly, before she glances over her shoulder. "Ah, sorry. Didn't intend to introduce you to our allies so soon. We have an onboarding process and everything, but I suppose the sooner you get used to them, the better." She grins again, turning and gesturing to the alien at her back. "This is San'ten."

The Vullan.

At least, that's what they're called on the flyer. Aliens who liberated our world. Aliens who *helped* us.

Ones we can trust.

Their ship looms like a silent threat above what humans have built. And yet, the humans below it are safe.

It is almost too much to believe. And yet, it appears to be true.

We were advised. Every single soul who found a flyer would have seen the message, the warning on the back. A depiction of the saviors of our little planet. What they've done. How they saved us.

But the image on the back of the flyer was but a crude sketch compared to the creature before me now.

Bipedal with ridges running over its entire frame, it looks like a shadow taken form rather than something real. And yet, it moves so fluidly, head tilting upward in a way that makes me realize it had been holding me in its gaze but has now dismissed me, focusing on the males at my back.

"San'ten?" Mina pastes a smile on her face, eyes widening slightly as she communicates something unsaid to the creature.

Black, soulless eyes pull away from her, the suit the creature's wearing rippling like a wave as he focuses once more on the males at my back.

"Welcome to Unity."

Deep. Gruff. A voice I never expected.

They speak like us.

"Fuck," one of the men behind me whispers.

A growl erupts, vibrating the air immediately.

"*That* female, maybe." The creature leans forward over Mina and points directly at me with a hand with dark nails so long it looks like a claw. "*But not mine.*"

"What?" the guy behind me asks and the alien steps forward, so close to the small human standing before it that her back presses into him. The males at my back retreat, jumping backward, and I must be stupid or frozen, because I do not move.

This…thing…whatever it is, is incredible.

I am witnessing something my species only ever hypothesized. Dreamed of. Yet, here, it stands before me, as real as myself.

A low rumble comes from its chest and vibrates over my arms.

The alien inhales deeply, nostrils flaring as its mouth opens to reveal fangs.

"Allllrighty then, I think that's enough introductions for you, big guy." Mina chuckles, but her laughter doesn't transfer to any of us.

I am enraptured, staring at the impossible, while the men at my back stand afraid.

"He wanted to mate with you," the alien growls.

"San'ten, that's not what he meant." Mina gives us an apologetic grin before turning and bracing both hands against the alien's chest. "Please forgive him. As you will notice with the other Vullan, they might speak our language, but sometimes things still get mistranslated." Her grin widens. "Come, there's food being served."

Bracing both hands against the alien's chest, she pushes it backward. With her size compared to the beast, she shouldn't be able to move it an inch. Yet, it obeys. It watches us…or rather, it watches the men at my back, but it obeys her.

It takes a few moments for the men I traveled with to gather their bearings.

"Fuck, what do we do now?" one speaks. "Do we cut our losses and leave?"

Another scratches his head, inhaling through his teeth with indecision. "Man, I don't even know, dude. That thing's fucking scary, and there's more of them. Did you see its teeth?"

They continue to mumble together, trying to decide what to do, before I suddenly grip my pack and throw it over my shoulders. I follow in the wake of the human, Mina, and her...friend, San'ten. And the indecisive chatter behind me suddenly halts.

"Hey, lady, you sure about this?" one of them calls.

A huffed laugh brushes through my nose as I glance over my shoulder and shrug, my legs taking me into what feels like a new era of my life.

Every step that I take pushes me further into the unknown.

"Fucking crazy," one of them says, and I turn toward the camp at my front, a surge of adrenaline coursing through my veins as I take my first steps into the unknown.

CHAPTER THREE

SOPHIE

Onboarding wasn't what I expected it to be.

I sit in a circular area at the center of the camp. Children playing around me, and humans chatting together.

The mug of hot chocolate in my hands feels like some sort of treasure.

Never thought I'd be drinking something so luxurious again.

The people around me talk and chatter as if they're long-time friends. Gone is the strain of what's happened to us, our planet. It's all in our nearby past.

Gone is their fear.

And still, I wonder if this is the place I should be. If I should have followed those men who brought me here. Take my chances of surviving somewhere else and leave.

I don't know those men, but we came here together.

And I'm the only one who stayed.

"Hey, it's Sophie, right?" The woman who plops down on the seat beside me grins at me as she offers her hand for a shake. Mina.

"Oh, yes. Yes, I am." I return her smile, not sure if it reaches my eyes, as something moves under my hand the moment her suit touches my fingers.

She's dressed in that same dark suit as before and I'm beginning to wonder if it's some kind of tactical gear from the government or something the aliens brought with them.

There are soldiers here. A few. And among their ranks, working alongside them, going over strategy maps and the like, are the Vullan. Like dark, towering gods, I see them whenever the wind blows a tent flap and reveals one of their forms.

Silent, dark shadows. I swear each time I spot one, his gaze is locked on mine.

"We've set up a bed for you in Tent B. We're busy drawing up the plans for the apartments and we'll get those built and set up soon, but the tents seem to be okay for now." She smiles at me.

I nod at her slightly. "Anywhere is fine."

"Nonsense." She grins. "You might be new here, but you get the same treatment as everyone else. A proper bed. Food. Etcetera. Though," she glances at the pack nestled between my legs, "you've probably got your own stuff, too."

I nod. I'd packed everything I'd need. More than enough to last me a few weeks on my own.

I'd thank my father for that, if he were still around.

"I know Unity might not be what you thought it was, but we're committed to making it better. To be fair," she chuckles, "it's only taking this long because we're taking input from everyone on how they want the city to be. You can leave your suggestions with Kolpak or Dri'ro. They're the main architectural geniuses."

"Dri...ro?" Definitely not a human name.

"Ah, yes." Mina grins some more. "He's Vullan. Don't worry, you'll get used to them. They're really big marshmallows if you allow them to get to know you."

There's a growl from one of the tents, almost as if in response to what she said, and if Mina didn't roll her eyes and chuckle again, I might have thought it was a coincidence.

They can hear us, even with the noise of the children and the distance of the nearest tent.

My eyebrows shoot up.

Mina's eyes crinkle as one of the children rushes into her arms, almost bowling her over.

"Where's superman?" the child asks.

Mina's gaze is warm. "Currently on timeout for almost scaring the lovely lady here." Mina grins. "Her name's Sophie."

"Hi, Sophie," the little girl says, giving me the sweetest smile. Her innocence, her happiness...it touches something deep inside me. Happy children aren't something I even thought I'd see again.

I'd expected war-torn people, tired and worn from the strain. But this child... I'd have never guessed she'd endured the last few months. There is light in her eyes.

She giggles as Mina tickles her before she dashes off again, and I watch her go, wondering if it is all really true. If the terror is really all gone?

"Who is superman?" I whisper.

Mina shrugs. "Just a name the kids have given San'ten."

"So these...Vullan. They're...friendly."

It's more of a statement than anything. A way for my mind to connect the dots. But Mina responds anyway,

"More than you know," she says.

I nod, eyes searching hers, and there's nothing within those depths that tells me this is all a trick. That these aliens are using us for some purpose I am yet to discover.

That this is all a lie.

"You're the epidemiologist, right?"

I blink at her for a moment, wondering how she knew that information.

"The drone..." she supplies.

Ah, yes. The drone that'd appeared on our way here. A human

had asked us questions through the device to "prepare" for our arrival. Like if we were carrying any weapons. If any of us was hurt, or injured. If anyone needed immediate medical attention.

"Yes, that's what I do...*did* before..."

"Good." Mina nods, lips pressing into another tight smile. "I'll tell him you're here."

"Him?"

"The medic."

The medic? "Why—"

I want to tell her I'm not ill. But she's already walking away, moving more swiftly than I expected her to.

Mina heads straight across the camp to the far end where she tilts her head back, looking at something that's descending from the sky.

At first, I think it's going to slam straight into her and I rise, hot chocolate sloshing over the edges of my mug and onto my pack, but the thing, whatever it is, slows down at the last moment.

It's a black box, like a solid cube, and I turn my eyes to the ship above, wondering if more of those things are going to fall.

But the people around me seem unbothered. It's only their lack of reaction that makes me still the sudden erratic beating of my heart.

The box settles on the dusty ground at the same time that the panel facing Mina opens to reveal...

It.

I don't know how, or why, I know it's the one she was referring to —the medic. I just do.

It's white. Different from the others I've seen so far. Completely white, not a speck of the darkness that embodies the others in its frame.

And the moment Mina gestures my way and its head tilts in my direction, my heart stops.

Even from this distance, I can feel the scrutiny of those alien eyes.

The creature steps from the box and the device closes and rises from the ground, leaving the alien behind.

It's still watching me, unnervingly so. Such intensity in that gaze that I become aware of every bit of myself. And, as Mina retreats and I'm left faced with a creature that's looking at me as if it can see inside my being, I realize something. An oversight on my part. A way of thinking clouded by the idea that we were alone in this universe.

That creature looking back at me is not a *thing*.

It...is a *he*.

Sentient. Intelligent.

And looking at me with such scrutiny that I wonder once more if it was the right decision to stay in this place.

There was no pressure to stay. No pressure to come.

It said so on the flyer; yet, here I am.

Bipedal like the others, even from the distance, I know he stands over seven feet tall. Towering over me. Towering over every human that exists here. And yet, standing so still, without threat.

Arms that seem slightly too long hang at his sides, the ridges that rise all over his body evident to me even with the distance between us. The white locs that adorn the top of his head are pulled back just like his brethren's, highlighting the sharp bone structure of his face.

Sculpted. High cheekbones. Firm jaw. Long pointed ears.

Like a work of art.

"Take your time," Mina says, somehow returning to my side without me noticing. "There's no rush."

I force an unconvincing smile. "Uh, okay, but...why do you need me to speak to him?"

"Everybody contributes here, in whatever way they can, but experts like you are hard to find. Most people..." She trails off, but she doesn't need to say more. I already get it.

Most people are dead.

Most of Earth's experts. Leading minds.

Anyone trained in anything is utterly useful as humanity tries to rebuild.

I nod at her, and she smiles at me again before patting me on the shoulder. "I'll be in Team Tent A if you need me."

My gaze remains on the alien in the distance as she steps away and all else disappears.

The wind, the laughter of the children, the people talking around me. Everything fades into nothingness as I look back at him.

And then...he disappears.

The alien turns. He walks away, and I'm left staring at the space in which he once stood.

HE'ROX

Claws and heel sinking into the ground beneath me, I sense the life source of this planet. A steady beat despite the evil it has encountered.

But there is...something else.

The thing that tethers me to the ones that came.

My focus is snagged away from something that caught my attention. I cannot remember what now, as I walk away from the camp. I'm summoned, the source of which, I am unsure.

Steady beats, ricocheting deep under the surface.

I feel it under my feet, but it is different from before. Different from all the other times I've felt this source.

Something is...*interfering*. The same thing that calls to me.

And that can only mean one thing.

I move through the camp like a wisp, few of the hyu'mans paying me attention as I walk to the boundary of their new settlement. My claws dig into the soil with each stride, and I sense the life pulsing within this planet. Faint. Almost snuffed out. But still there.

Turning slightly, I eye the trees beyond.

Water. Close by. I can scent it. It calls me as if I need it. Calls that part of me I wish to destroy, but my gaze remains on the trees.

Tall, wiry. They hardly provide shelter. But there is something there.

A distortion. A subtle *wrongness* that has been there from the moment we arrived on this world, only now, it is...

*What **is** it doing?*

Living energy, it calls to that intrusion inside me I'd rather ignore.

But I *can't* ignore it.

I am within the trees before I realize I've moved, traveled here with only a thought. My head tilts as I look around, eyes sliding over the thin trunks of the vegetation.

This is why I remain on the ship. Being out here, on the ground, I sense too much of those creatures I'd rather never see again.

But whatever I am looking for is not above.

It is below.

Falling to my knees, my claws press into the soil, the dirt coming into contact with my palm as I feel for whatever *it* is.

And I dig.

Soft earth moves underneath my digits as I push it out of the way. Unsure of what I'm searching for. Unsure of *why* I am searching.

Until...

It's her scent that reaches me first.

Hyu'man. Female. Not far behind me.

Her presence is there. And so is her fear.

If my ba'clan would react, my hackles would rise. Instead, there is only a slight shiver from them as I freeze. And even though her fear scent might not awaken my aggression, it still unlocks my baser instincts. The ones that remind me I am Vullan.

The urge, no, the *need*, to hunt.

Glancing over my shoulder, my gaze locks onto hers immediately and there is a sharp intake of air that fills her lungs. She's too slow, but she ducks behind one of the wiry trees, anyway.

It's obvious she was trying to be quiet. To remain unseen.

Yet, I can hear every breath she takes. Every beat of her life organ in her chest.

Standing several lengths away from me, she hides. *But she is upwind.*

This one is no hunter. She would be easy prey.

And...she followed me here?

Hyu'manity may be saved and we Vullan might have sacrificed much for this world, but its inhabitants still fear us. It is just the way.

We have adjusted to it, just like we adjust to everything else.

But this female...she is not like the others. That alone is clear. And she was not here before the War. I would have remembered her.

Filaments the color of Edooria's blazing moon fall down her sides like a beacon that sets her apart from the green and brown tones around us.

Now I recall.

The thing that'd snagged my attention in the camp. Here it is.

Here *she* is.

Yes, she followed me here.

Why?

I remain unmoving. I do not wish to scare her. To intensify that sweet scent of her fear that makes me want to chase and devour her. For though I know she is to be protected, that part of me does not seem to care.

In the silence, I wait. All that results is an increase of that sweet scent, anyway. I close my nostrils to the onslaught, forcing myself to remain still. Even as whatever it is below the ground that calls me renews its request for my attention.

I watch the female with filaments like Kah-deh-ya, our moon. A memory of home I didn't recall until she appeared here in this place.

And then I remember. The hyu'man they want me to meet. A scientist. It is her.

She glances my way once more, pale eyes widening when they land on me and realize my focus is still in her direction, before she hides behind the tree again.

"Fuck." A whisper.

My head tilts slightly. A mating invitation?

No.

A curse. Possibly distress. Certainly fear.

"I'm sorry, I—" A melodious voice. I hear her softly inhale as she tries to deliver an excuse. "I didn't mean to interrupt. I...I wasn't following you or anything."

I open my nostrils and sniff.

She lies.

"I'm going to go now."

She speaks. Tells me her intent. Yet, she remains behind the tree, fear scent intensifying. I inhale it this time, allowing it to fill my nostrils and energize me. There's a faint ache in my fangs. A slight priming of my muscles.

"You won't attack me if I leave now, right? Clearly, I interrupted something."

Her words swim to my ears like a song.

"Do you...can you even understand me? I don't know if you all know English. Shit, I should have asked that before coming all the way out here." Her voice lowers. "Now I'm alone in a forest with an alien who is obviously about to attack me."

Sweet, melodious song.

"What the fuck's wrong with you, Sophie." An even harsher whisper than before.

A soft rumble pulls from my chest.

It's been a while since I've felt this urge to hunt. To claim. Such urges have long withered within me.

Deep below my palms, there's a pulse in the earth, and I wonder if that's the reason. If *that* part of me is causing this development. The part I deny. The part I wish to strip from myself. One that should have never been, but is. If that part of me is taking over...

The thought is enough to make me remain still, and some other scent reaches my nostrils. The scent of my own fear.

The female curses again, and her hand forms a fist at her side. I can tell what she's about to do even before she makes a move.

"Do. Not. Run." My voice rumbles between us, my Vullan tongue shaping her hyu'man words, and she freezes. Chest heaving.

Her fear scent spikes like an intoxicating concoction of

pheromones I could feast on and another rumble goes through my chest.

This...is not me. I would never debase myself and hunt a female like this.

This is *it*.

"If you wish to leave..." I say, "...do so slowly..."

A few seconds pass where the female's back remains pressed against the tree, and I wonder, does she know how little protection it gives? If I went after her, that tree would snap like a twig beneath my claws.

"Do you not want me to leave?" she whispers.

A question that snaps my mind back to reality. To the fact I'm on my knees digging in the soil for...something. And the fact that she is here with me. That she followed me here.

"You are...curious." The words slip from my lips as realization dawns.

Her side profile is slightly visible and I see her throat move before she looks back my way, pale eyes meeting mine once more.

I see the fear there. Smell it so strongly I can taste it. And yet, she stands before me still.

She faces it.

She faces *me*.

"That is why you followed me here."

I tilt my head slightly, the only movement I've made since I noticed her presence, and her throat moves again as she watches me.

"I...don't know why I followed you here."

For the first time in a long while, humor makes me grunt.

It's such a strange sound, one I haven't heard in many revolutions, that my senses heighten at her presence.

"You followed me here because your curiosity outweighs your fear."

There is only a slight widening at the corners of her eyes that tells me I'm right. I remain motionless, claws sunk into the soil, watching her absorb whatever discovery is keeping her here, causing her to disobey even her instincts for survival.

"So...you *do* understand me," she says slowly. "Your English..."

I dip my head slowly to my chest. A gesture for the affirmative. One hyu'mans use even when verbally communicating the same. "We learned your language after arriving here."

Her throat moves again, gaze moving down my form, and like a thin veil moving over my skin, I *feel* her attention.

"You're not...going to attack me?"

I watch her, no words of comfort rising to my lips. For...I don't know if I will attack her. I do not want to. Yet, I also do. I've kept myself leashed since arriving on this world. Have not attacked any of the females we've rescued. Would never attack a female. But this one...

A plump lip disappears into her mouth as she watches me, turns toward me...and takes a step *forward*.

My gaze flies to her legs, part of me wondering if some other entity is pushing her in my direction. But no. She is moving herself.

"You approach."

She nods the affirmative.

"But you are afraid."

She nods again.

"Why?"

She pauses when she's about two lengths away from me, throat moving, fear scent still spiking before her gaze falls to my soil-covered claws.

"You said it yourself. My curiosity outweighs my fear."

CHAPTER FOUR

SOPHIE

I ask myself what the hell I'm doing even as I draw closer to the alien.

He remains motionless, only a few slight movements of the head as if he's afraid to move normally and scare me away.

And, god knows, after leaving my bunker I must have a death wish, because this should not be on my list of things to do.

Befriending an alien should not be on my list *at all*.

Yet, here I am.

I don't know why I followed the tall, pale being away from the camp. Why I trailed him into the trees. Why my feet carried me forward even though all else was saying turn back.

There's something about this one. Something that's different from the other Vullan I saw. And it has nothing to do with his pigment, or lack of it.

The way he speaks...

I can tell this is an insanely intelligent being.

But the way he looks at me, like he's looking at me now, I feel like I'm in the presence of something that's much less evolved than the being speaking to me. Something barbaric. Something carnal. Something reduced to just basic instincts, wants, and needs.

And yet still, I draw closer.

"I'm Sophie."

"Soh'fee."

Pure richness, the way he says my name. It makes me pause as I study him.

He told me not to run. There was a warning in there. One that makes awareness settle in my spine.

I can't take my eyes off him. Not for a second.

"You know, technically, you're supposed to say hello when you first meet someone. We got off on the wrong foot."

No reply.

"What are you looking for out here?"

His eyes are ice blue. So glacial, they chill the air around us.

Up close, I can see the ridges that pattern across his body even more clearly. Their purpose is unknown to me. They seem almost reptilian, and so do his eyes.

Slitted, a nictitating membrane slides over their surface as he blinks at me.

The movement is almost unnerving. *Would* be unnerving if I wasn't so transfixed. Mesmerized. Those icy eyes catch the light through the trees as he turns his gaze upon me, scrutinizing me so much I become aware of my much frailer form. And when I come to a stop just about a foot away from him, there's a slight movement that travels over his skin.

I suppress a shiver at this reminder of how inhuman he truly is. How vulnerable I am in his presence.

And yet, my curiosity still wins out. I remind myself there are humans in the camp. Happy humans. *Living* humans. And that this creature, this male, is one of many who came here and fought for my planet.

Those thoughts echo in my head like some kind of mantra as I crouch, watching for any sign of aggression, but he remains still. Waiting. Eyes tracking my every move.

"Are you digging for something?" I'm prying. I know. But I want him to speak again. I want to learn. About him. About his existence.

He's something we've hypothesized. Yet, he came to save us.

What else is out there? What else do we not know? What else can we hardly imagine?

"I am searching for...something I sensed." His words are slow, halting, as though translating his thoughts is a laborious process. "A disruption." His gaze falls back to the ground. "A *disturbance*."

With his intense gaze away from me, I can't help but stare at him.

Two small tentacles dance at the corners of his mouth, twisting as if uncontrolled and working by pure motor neurons firing independent of his input.

"A disturbance?"

I watch them flex and sway, mesmerized by their constant motion. I want to ask him if they function as sensory organs, tasting chemicals in the air to gather information, even when he remains still. But that is only one question assailing my mind.

"Affirmative." He notices my scrutiny and the tentacles pause, their incessant dance faltering under my gaze.

I pull my attention away, hoping I haven't offended him with my staring, but silence descends between us.

I clear my throat. "What is the disturbance?"

My question takes effort. Focus. When all I'd rather do is ask him about other things. Like where he came from. How he found us here.

I try not to stare as his massive shoulders lift and fall, muscles rippling under his ridged skin as he pushes his hands deeper into the Earth.

"There is something...unnatural," he says. "The frequency has been...altered by outside interference."

Frequency? Interference?

Something unnatural...

Images from before shoot through my mind of the first time I saw one of the great machines that almost ended us all. Of the sound it made. The way it chilled the air, rattling the flesh on my bones and spelling doom for us all.

"Them? Are they back?" I manage to keep my voice steady. To control the sudden spike of fear. But the hairs at the back of my neck stand on end, my intestines coiling in my gut.

Those icy eyes fall back on me as the alien lifts his head. "You are a scientist. You study the flows and pulses of existence. Do you sense it?"

My brows rise as my mouth opens for a response I don't have.

"I am—*was*—an epidemiologist. I studied patterns of disease, not this "energy" or "frequency" you refer to." I swallow hard, eyes falling back to the earth his hands are buried beneath. "You can feel something? Vibration? Frequency? *Energy?*"

Slitted eyes watch me. There is no emotion within them. And I realize at this moment that I cannot use human indicators to read him. For he has none.

He is not like us. He may be bipedal. Two arms. One head. Similar frame. But he is nothing like us at all. He is something different altogether.

But his words…they wake a deep fear within me that I've tried to bury, ever since I exited my bunker and entered the silence.

"I feel…*everything*."

Again, he has me speechless and I get the sense his words are deeper than they appear. That if he cared to explain, I might not like the answer.

And yet… "Everything?"

He studies me for a moment before his hands slip from beneath the soil and I watch, hypnotized, as the dirt falls from his skin in little particles without him shaking it off his hand.

"The greed. The pain. The yearning…" he suddenly says. My eyes snap to his and I'm once again greeted by twin glaciers.

"What about it?" I whisper.

"I feel it all."

I swallow hard. I'm not sure exactly what we're talking about here. Something tells me this is more than I currently am capable of understanding. But I want him to speak. I want him to continue.

"And?" I ask.

He pauses, staring at me for so long I squirm under his gaze.

"And their hunger," he finally says. And for the first time since I've invited myself on his journey, he moves in a way that chills me completely.

In a mere second, the alien is before me.

Face to face with this pale entity, I can't move. I am frozen, fear holding me captive.

His nostrils flare as he inhales, but he doesn't move further.

This close, I realize just how much bigger he is. How vulnerable I am. And I wonder if this conversation was the precursor to my doom.

I'd felt he was going to attack me. I'm sure of it now.

And when he bares his sharp teeth, I force myself not to tremble.

"Hunger," I whisper.

"And thirst..." he says, his gaze flicking to my neck.

I gulp again.

He's so close, I can smell him.

It is a sweet scent. Like I walked into the kitchen after my dad finished baking vanilla cake. Not the scent I expected to come from him.

His teeth bare, so sharp it's hard to stop myself from trembling. Yet, I remain unmoving as this creature leans forward, pushing me back until I'm bracing on my elbows and he's leaning over me on all fours.

There's a chittering sound that comes from his throat as he leans closer, fangs baring over my face.

I expect violence. An attack to rend flesh and shatter bone. Yet he remains motionless, scenting me as a beast might assess vulnerable prey. The strange scent of vanilla clings to him, a soft fragrance at odds with the primal fear he's stirring inside me.

A tremor seizes my limbs as moments drag endlessly by, his fangs gleaming wet and sharp mere inches away. But the strike does not come. The alien simply inhales again, slitted pupils dilating, then pulls abruptly away.

The loss of his looming presence comes as a relief, my lungs dragging in air as I scramble to my feet. He paces several steps away, then turns to face me. And in place of violence, I find intense focus. A kind of wordless knowing. As though in those endless seconds, eternity flickered past between us.

"Do not return to the camp until you have controlled your fear," he says.

I force down the lump in my throat, fist tangled in the checkered button-down shirt I'm wearing over my jeans.

"It is sweet," he says. "Tempting."

I blink at him, his words not making sense. Until they do.

"You can smell me," I whisper. "You can smell that I'm afraid."

He doesn't answer. Those intelligent eyes tell me all I need to know.

And as he turns to stalk away, I reach a hand out to him, not knowing why or what the hell I'm doing.

"Wait!"

He halts.

What now, Sophie? And what the fuck has gotten into you?

"What's your name?"

His head turns to the side, but he doesn't glance over his shoulder.

"He'rox," he says.

And then before I know it, he's gone.

CHAPTER FIVE

SOPHIE

He'rox. The strange name repeats in my mind as I stare at the space he occupied moments before.

Fingers still clenched, my knuckles go white where I grip my shirt. The sweet scent of him still haunts the air, cut only by my apprehension.

I don't know how long I stand among those trees. How long I remain rooted in the spot, trying to calm my beating heart, trying to quell the fear that only seems to rise the longer I wait here.

Taking a few steps backward, I stumble into a tree, the solid trunk pressing into my spine as I take deep, haggard breaths.

Staring into those alien eyes...

There were secrets in his eyes. Secrets so deep I know that once those truths are revealed, they can never again be forgotten.

It felt like he was going to eat me. Claw me and rip me in two. And yet, he didn't. Such control, when he most definitely could have. And I doubt I'd have been able to cry or scream for help. Doubt I could have run. Doubt I could have survived.

I grip my chest with my other hand as I take another deep breath, pulling in air as if my lungs are a bottomless pit as I lift my gaze to the canopy.

Bits of sunshine fall between the leaves, dancing over my skin to nature's melody and reminding me I haven't been transported to another world.

I'm still here. Still on Earth.

Yet, while he was with me, I forgot about everything else.

I must have lost my mind.

I'm about to pull away from the tree when my gaze lands on the ground before me, the spot where He'rox had been digging still overturned.

I should go back to camp, but I falter. Staring at the spot, I draw closer, reaching for a fallen branch nearby.

I snap the branch, making a pointed end as I crouch, knees digging into the soft earth.

I want to ask myself what I'm doing. Why I'm kneeling in the dirt, making my clothes dirty as I dig for something I have no clue about. But I continue. My limbs move with little input from me as I plow the earth and make the hole bigger, and soon I'm widening it, increasing the effort he made and overturning the earth to make a small hole.

I'm about to stop, to call in my insanity, when the stick hits something that isn't as hard as the rest of the earth around it. Softer. Smoother. The sudden change in texture enough to make me stop suddenly.

A chill goes over my spine, something sick developing in my gut as I resist the urge to shudder.

It felt like I just poked the soft body of a dead animal and as I lean to look into the hole I made, I do so hesitantly.

But what I see is not what I imagined. It's nothing I could have imagined, and I lean forward slightly, not sure that what I'm seeing is really there. Bits of sunlight dance over the spot and I stiffen.

Nestled within the earth lies a network of roots, dark tendrils pulsing and writhing as though with stolen life. But even as I look at the phenomenon, I know these aren't regular roots. They're too soft. Pulsing like channels, I realize they're *veins*. Like a web of shadow filled with dark substance, they thread through the soil burrowing even deeper than I've so far discovered.

Revulsion makes me stagger back.

This is what He'rox sensed. Why he left the camp and came to these trees. This...*thing*, whatever it is, makes my skin crawl and awareness makes me suddenly look up, gaze scanning the trees around me for anything out of place.

But there is nothing.

Whatever this is, the host is not here...or I can't identify it.

On shaky legs, I rise to my feet and stagger away from the hole and toward the tree line. Wiping my palms against my jeans, I can't get that creepy-crawly feeling off my skin.

I had questions before. But now I have even more.

The tents that mark Unity loom before me as I hurry toward them.

I need to find him.

I need to ask him what the hell that was out there.

As soon as I step into the camp, the sound of new beginnings greets me. Jarring and mismatched to the terror still running through my veins, I try to calm the erratic beating of my heart as I scan the meeting circle.

He is not there.

"Hey, Sophie!"

I jerk, Mina's sudden appearance sending a bolt of alarm through me. Her brows furrow immediately.

"You ok, dear? You can turn in early if you want to, you know. Your bed's already set up and no one will mind. We know it's a lot and this is your first day."

I'm shaking my head before she can finish speaking. "No, it's not that. I'm—I'm not tired. I'm fine."

I force a smile.

I should tell her about what happened out there. So why is my mouth not moving?

"Oh no..." Her shoulders slump. "Did He'rox say something inappropriate to you? I can assure you he meant no ill will. The Vullan can be rather straight to the point and that can be a bit for us humans to get used to."

I shake my head again, that lump that formed in my throat on the way here growing larger. "Speaking about him," I force my smile brighter, "where is he? I'd like to speak with him."

Mina studies me for a moment before her eyes crinkle.

"I...think he went back to the ship."

My neck stretches back as I tilt my head to look up at the colossal vessel floating above us.

"I...need to speak to him." My gaze flicks to the children still playing and an ache develops in my chest. This is their chance at peace. They deserve a childhood that's not filled with terror.

I can't create alarm when I don't know what I'm dealing with. But he does. I'm sure he does.

I need him.

"I don't think he'll return to the surface until tomorrow. Can it wai—?"

"No." I clear my throat. "I'd rather speak to him now, if that's okay."

Mina studies me for a moment longer before her shoulders lift in a sigh. "Well, you could go to him, if you're ready to go into the ship. It's not off limits."

I swallow hard. The thought of going up into that thing is the same as imagining myself heading into the mouth of a beast. But there's no other choice.

"It's your first day so I understand if that's too much for you right now." Mina's eyes hold curiosity but there's also warmth there. I sense no negative sentiments from this woman and I lean on that, putting my trust in a stranger I only met this day.

"How do I get inside the ship?"

HE'ROX

Soh'fee. The first human to stir something within me akin to curiosity. Frail creature though she is, her spirit burned fierce as any warrior's.

She didn't run, even when I lost control enough to approach and scare her.

In her, I already see the beginnings of what few of my brethren have found. Females for their own, their ba'clan adapting to hyu'man biology, branding them as mates. Human and Vullan. Together. A new era. Something I hypothesized when we began this journey, but a reality none of us thought truly possible.

Chances were, whatever world we found, the beings would be unlike us. Neither did not know whether this world would have females. And, if they existed, we knew not whether they would be compatible with us. So we focused on the one thing we could count on. Our revenge.

For a moment, I stare ahead, seeing nothing except memories of Edooria. My work. My experiments...

I have not thought of that place in a long time. Why now?

Pulling my attention back to the present, I know there can be only one reason.

The fire-haired female with the stark pale eyes.

One so curious, her thirst for knowledge outweighed her sense of self-preservation. Someone that reminded me so much of myself, I had to draw closer. To scent her. To determine if she is pure. Untouched. Uncorrupted.

Because I am no longer sure where my insanity stems from. The version of me from the beginning, or the one I created.

For a moment, I wondered if she might hold the answers.

But I remind myself she is a fleeting distraction. She will settle here soon at Unity and she will meld into the background like the others of her kind. And in the meantime, I will wait for my end.

Soh'fee will make another of my brothers stay. With her, he will find a home. That place reserved for only a few of us. And for some, not at all.

Like me.

It is only a matter of time before we leave this place. And I will return to my broken world with the rest of my brethren who have found no solace here.

But till then...

I stare at the creature floating in the tank before me. Hyu'man... and yet not.

Rescued from the wilds while the Gryken still roamed freely, she has been here for many cycles. And though her wounds have all healed, she remains unresponsive. Everything on her hyu'man form has healed. All the bruises. Scratches. Broken limbs and torn skin. Everything returned to perfection.

But there is something else there, something stopping her from regaining consciousness on her own accord.

Living on her, *within* her, an entity that doesn't belong.

And that thing is one I cannot remove. Not without ending her existence.

My gaze slips to the tank beside hers, to the creature within that watches my every move silently.

My nemesis.

My forever enemy.

The Gryken stares back with deep, soulless eyes. Unmoving, yet seeing everything.

We have met many times. Stared wordlessly at each other with the barrier between us. And still, even locked away, I feel the pull toward it.

The parts of me that remain intact shiver at the proximity of my foe. While that other part yearns to go closer.

It is a constant war. One I do not reveal to my brethren. It is a weakness I alone must endure.

Some sound in the lab draws my attention and I freeze.

There should be no one there. Since the War's been in effect, my brethren have left me mostly alone. And so have the hyu'mans.

There's another sound, so quiet, I shouldn't be able to hear it. A soft pitter-patter of feet coverings. Hyu'man feet coverings. And that makes me turn my head in the direction of the intruder.

Time moves without me knowing because I shift, moving from one place to another without recollection of the journey, and suddenly I am before the entrance to the lab, the hole opening within the wall to reveal the person behind it.

Her back is turned to me, but I recognize her anyway. How could I forget? Our meeting is still fresh in my mind. And as before, when she followed me into the woods, she has followed me here now.

Into the ship. Far away from the others. Where no one will hear her cries.

Before her is a small device. An icosahedron that develops a light matrix.

The moment her fingers move over the device, it activates. She springs back and freezes, but once again, her curiosity wins. She steps closer once more, so transfixed by what's before her that she doesn't hear my approach.

I am at her back, far closer than I should be, before she senses my presence.

"It is a light matrix."

"Oh shi—!" She jumps, bumping into me and then rearing forward into the counter before us, arching her body away from mine as wide eyes meet mine over her shoulder. "I was—"

"—following me again."

Her pale cheeks flush at my observation, but she holds my gaze with defiance equal parts irritation and intrigue. "You left me no choice."

I tilt my head, considering. Her boldness is...unanticipated. "It was foolish to follow me here."

Her throat moves. Such soft skin covering one of her weakest spots. The vein her people call the jugular thrums so clearly I can see it. Just one nick. An errant claw at the wrong place, the wrong time, and she would be gone.

Still, she turns to face me, not running away from the proximity, our bodies brushing, her strange garments over my ba'clan. And they shiver—a reaction I store away for later scrutiny.

"I'm beginning to believe it was foolish to do a lot of things, but I suppose, yes, I *am* a scientist, and standing by while the world erupts or is burned to ashes isn't something I could do for long. So I came here. And now, I don't know if I can leave." Her eyes dart behind me. "What is this place?"

I hesitate, torn between ire at her intrusion and strange pride in her fearlessness. "My laboratory. You should not be here."

My warning falls on air as her gaze moves over the room.

"There is nothing in here." Eyes with too much intelligence meet mine. "Where do you do your experiments? If we are to work together—"

I surprise myself for *I* am the one that moves away.

Experiments.

Working together.

Neither will occur.

"You waste your time. Your people have given you false hope. My work is finished here." And then the rest I must not say out loud. That I have given everything I can and if I continue, I might lose the last bit of myself that remains.

A slight shiver across my spine, my ba'clan moving like a wave, alerts me to the fact the female has approached my back.

Has she no sense of survival?

Prey approaching the predator from the rear, I almost expect her to wield a weapon at me, but all I'm faced with when I look over my shoulder are eyes that burn with fire as red as the filaments on her head.

Anger. She is feeling anger.

And something else.

I sniff.

Not fear, when there should be. But, instead, anxiety. She is curious. Curious to know something.

"I saw it," she says. "I saw what you were looking for."

My head tilts, ears perking off the sides of my head as I face her fully.

When I wait for her to continue, her lips press into a thin line.

"The *veins*! I saw them." Her throat moves as she turns, hands on her hips as she paces a few steps away from me before turning around to face me again. "What are they?"

My eyes narrow slightly as I take her in.

So...she dug further than I did. Found the thing that was calling me. Knows of the presence still crawling through this land like a cancer.

"Something tells me," she takes a step forward, "that the others don't know about this. I don't know what. Call it a hunch." She runs a hand through her filaments and I watch the strands fall in small clumps. "Or, or, maybe I'm crazy and all this is in my head and I'm blowing everything out of proportion. I've only just arrived. The world is frickin' saved. We're safe. I'm talking to a frickin' alien when yesterday I wasn't even sure that was possible! There are kids playing outside! People living together out in the open. Fuck, I think I even heard a bird within those trees." She laughs, but I sense no mirth. "I'm making this a big deal when it isn't. Right?" Her eyes meet mine and there is a pleading within them. One I find I cannot deny. "Tell me I'm blowing things out of proportion."

I study her and her gaze doesn't falter.

"You choose to ask me this. Your foe...instead of your kin on the ground."

Her eyebrows shoot up and I am once again caught in the vision of how malleable hyu'man skin is. It furrows, her brow curving as she stares at me.

"Foe?...You're my foe?"

"I am not. I merely repeat the sentiments on the ground. That of some of your kin."

Her throat moves again and her shoulders rise and fall as she releases a breath.

"Is this...not your sentiment?"

Again, a laugh huffs from her, coming through her nose this time. Mirthless like the first, before her gaze darts away from me, traveling over the blank walls enclosing us. "No offense to those on the ground, but it would be stupid of me to hate the very beings that freed my planet. Gave me a chance to live a few years longer." Those eyes of hers meet mine, commanding a level of respect even some males do not have. "The enemy of my enemy is my friend."

"Friend," I say, turning the word over in my mind. "You have only just encountered us."

"But I've seen what you've done." She takes a step forward and my head lowers a little to match her piercing gaze. "It doesn't take a genius to weigh the odds. You could have killed them and killed us all too. Yet, you're helping us rebuild."

I remain silent.

I was right.

Her intelligence strokes something deep within me and sets it alight. If I stayed, a partner like this would renew something within me I've long buried.

"Now," she says, "Tell me there's not more going on here."

Clicks pass between us as I study the little hyu'man standing up to me, and I do something I shouldn't.

I let her in.

"I could tell you that, hyu'man Soh'fee." She stiffens as if she knows I am about to continue. "But that would all be a lie."

CHAPTER SIX

SOPHIE

He'rox's words make a sliver of fear go down my spine and I fight to control it. To control the way my breaths want to come out in uneven gasps, and the way my belly's twisting into a knot.

He turns, leading me toward a wall that suddenly opens to an oval hole big enough for us both to walk through.

On the other side, the hole closes and we are in a room with—

I stop short, the wall at my back and two massive transparent cylinders a few feet in front of me.

Within the cylinder closest to me is a pale, slender woman, completely nude and floating motionless in translucent fluid. Her face is so calm, she looks like she's some sort of sleeping beauty caught in a forever sleep.

But my brows draw together as I step forward, that sick feeling rising in my gut as I see the dark veins underneath her pale skin. Like a writhing darkness seething in her flesh.

"What's…wrong with her?"

I don't get a response, or maybe the alien beside me answers and I don't hear it, because as my gaze lands on the next cylinder, I freeze in my bones.

There, right before me, is a creature I have never seen before. And one I wish I never saw.

It clearly isn't from here. This world. This planet.

Or, if it is, it's from the deepest, darkest part of the sea, not yet discovered by man. But even as my brain tries to understand, to make sense of what I'm looking at, I know the thing before me is from somewhere else.

It stares back at me, eyes soulless, dark and deep, completely lacking in emotion but filled with a silent intelligence that stops the breath in my lungs. It floats unmoving in the liquid before me and everything that makes me human tells me that this thing before me is evil. The hairs rising along my arms. The way adrenaline spikes deep in my veins.

Fight or flight.

My body's telling me to run.

I gulp, glancing at He'rox, and his intense gaze does not falter. He watches me though, as if he expects me to scream, to run. But even if I wanted to.

I can't.

"My father," I say, and as the words tumble from my mouth, I wonder why I'm about to tell him this. Wonder if it's probably my way of processing the creature before me. The terror just the sight of it creates in my being. "My father was convinced the world would end one day." I can't pull my eyes away from the thing. "By *disease*." I swallow hard, forcing myself to remain steady. To remain still. "Something that causes human society to collapse. An apocalypse. He built a bunker for that purpose. Stacked it with everything he'd need to last him a few months. A few years if he could go out and forage. Hunt." A breath shudders through me as the alien behind the glass keeps my gaze, unmoving, and yet so threatening even though it's locked away. "He used to make me face terrible things so I wouldn't be afraid." I swallow hard again. "Like videos of Ebola victims bleeding from their eyes, and photos of smallpox pustules erupting the skin. He'd describe how society would fall apart if disease ran rampant."

I take a step closer to the cylinder, eyes still on the thing staring back at me. "We'd go hunting together. He had me kill and gut animals when I was only six years old. Said if I could handle that, I could handle any crisis." I swallow hard again when I come to stand just about a foot away from the towering cylinder, head tilting back as I look up at the thing. "He was a popular doctor, always worried about impending doom. I grew up convinced the world would end before I reached adulthood." Above me, the thing floats so large, so unmoving, yet with my trek across the room, I know it followed me the entire way. There are no pupils, but I can feel its focus. It doesn't move, yet I know it's alive. "I became an epidemiologist because of him. Because I wanted to understand what made him so afraid." I step closer, hand against the glass. "He died working in a hastily constructed research lab, trying to contain an Ebola outbreak. Always preparing for disaster. In the end, disaster found him."

I stare at the thing before me, not sure if my story made sense. If the alien at my back will understand my unspoken words. But movement to my right, a white shadow in my periphery, tells me he comes closer.

"You are attracted to it, even though you fear it. Through your progenitor's lessons, you have learned to face your fear."

A glance at the Vullan and I realize those ice-cold eyes are scrutinizing me.

"You did the same before. With me," he says. "You did not run."

"I wanted to."

"Like you want to now."

I nod.

"Will you?"

I swallow hard, turning my gaze back to the thing before me. "No."

It's massive. Like an oversized octopus, except with fewer arms.

Thicker arms and no suction cups that I can see. Grey. Fleshy. It's about three feet long from the top of its head to where its legs begin, but the length of the legs puts it taller than seven or eight feet. An aquatic species. I can't imagine something like that walking on land and another chill runs down my spine at the thought that it possibly could. I shudder as I remove my hand from the cylinder and realize it's still watching me.

"What is it?"

"Gryken."

There's a slight rumble in his tone, as if mention of the creature before us, as if saying its name is a crime.

I swallow hard, almost afraid to ask the next question.

"They're the ones…"

"Who destroyed my world…who tried to destroy yours."

I stare at the thing, now knowing for sure that I am staring at my enemy.

I want to ask him exactly what happened on his planet. I want to know how he caught this thing. I want to know everything. But other more pressing things need to be discussed.

Like the woman floating in the cylinder next to it and the fact the veins underneath her skin look like an exact map of the ones I saw in the forest.

I turn to her now, another shiver I can't hold back going down my spine. Her body's turned slightly and more of her back is visible. Bile rises in my throat as I see the network of dark veins there, crisscrossing over and within her skin.

"She's…"

"Infested."

"Can she feel anything?"

"Her consciousness remains out of reach."

I nod slightly, taking a step toward her cylinder. "You've been trying to heal her."

No answer and I assume I'm correct. "*They* did this to her."

Again, no answer, and I'm beginning to realize these Vullan are creatures of few words.

"She has been here for many cycles, and though her wounds have all healed, she remains unresponsive."

I glance up at the tall alien behind me, gaze searching his as he continues. "Between developing the weapon we needed to win this war, she has been my other...preoccupation."

The way he says it, as if she's more of a science experiment than anything else, sends a strange chill through me.

"Utterly pale and thin...her flesh has only recently begun to hide the skeleton underneath...Humans require a variety of nutrients for survival, and this one...she had been at the brink of death."

Turning back to face the cylinder, my gaze flicks over the woman's face.

"I have looked at her many times. Watched her for countless hours." He'rox pauses. "It always remains the same."

I stand staring at her too, his words giving me more information than he's revealed. Her state confuses him and that alone is a bad thing. With all this technology, if he doesn't know why she appears to be in a coma...

As her body turns slowly, the dark veins embedded underneath her skin come back into view and I resist the urge to look away.

"Those veins are the same as the ones I saw out there." I turn to face He'rox and inhale slightly at how close he is to me. So big, yet he moves so silently. Tilting my head back, I meet the icy gaze of the alien I'm beginning to know.

"Not many of your kind know of the existence of these two specimen," he says, still not giving me answers but giving me necessary information anyway.

"But you brought me here. Showed me this when I only just arrived. Why?"

"You are like me."

I push down the lump in my throat one more time as he slides his gaze to the cylinder now at my back.

"You have discovered the cancer," he says. "An anomaly that should be dead, yet persists."

"What...what are you saying?" His gaze slides to mine, and I try to read the depth of information in those eyes. "That thing out there... it's some sort of disease?"

No response.

"You helped us drive away the Gryken, but they left that thing behind." I press. "And now you're realizing something. Aren't you?"

He nods so slightly, I almost miss it, and there in those cold eyes, something sparkles. Almost as if he is enjoying this exchange. My curiosity. My questions.

"They're not supposed to be there," I whisper, not that I needed any confirmation of the fact. What I saw was strange. Inhuman. Unearthly.

He'rox shakes his head just as slightly as his nod.

"What does it mean?"

For a moment, he stares at me but I sense he is no longer seeing me but looking past me. And then his gaze adjusts to the female floating at my back while mine shifts to the evil in the room with us.

"It means...possibly...my work here is not done."

I gulp again. "And if it's not?"

"I will have to sacrifice once again."

His words seem to have more weight, more meaning than they seem and I let them settle for a little bit before turning to face the woman living in suspended animation.

It's an easy decision. One I don't even have to consider.

"Then I will sacrifice too."

CHAPTER SEVEN

HE'ROX

Her words strike me like a blow, resonating through my soul. This fragile hyu'man, so newly come into my world, now offers a part of herself as forfeit to a battle hardly her own. A battle spanning millennia, which robbed my people of all hope and left behind but ashes.

This war is between us: Vullan and Gryken. Hyu'manity has simply been swept along—an innocent player coerced to participate, left without choice but to defend themselves.

And yet still she stands here surrounded by the shadows of that war, staring into the face of terror and does not flee. Does not falter. Only tightens her pale hands to fists and lifts her chin, eyes bright with purpose.

Purpose I had thought long lost.

"Your sacrifice will not be required." My voice is rough, unsuitable for the gentleness I intend. I slide my gaze away from the female floating at peace within her cage of glass and turn toward the exit.

That's when it happens. When the soft touch of hyu'man skin lands on my back, sending my ba'clan there rippling across my frame.

The effect is so sudden. I freeze.

She...*touched* me.

The sensation is so strange, so alien, that my life organ stops in my chest and I don't immediately notice the fact that my ba'clan responded. A growl rumbles in my chest, pleasure I never thought I'd ever feel shooting through me at the contact. But then she pulls her hand away.

Too soon.

I must have scared her with my response.

"I'm sorry, I didn't mean..." Her rushed words make something twist inside me, but I cannot look at her. Cannot face her. Because my fangs have extended, the ends aching at such a simple touch.

I will scare her more if I turn around now. And...I do not know how I will respond if I move even an inch in her direction.

She touched me. Laid her hyu'man hand upon this form as though I were not a monster, but something else. And that fleeting contact has woken sensations slumbering since my memory began.

I clench my claws, fighting for stillness though my lifeblood rages with the need to turn, to face this female who has lit a spark where only darkness has dwelt. The growl rumbles low in my chest once more, echoing the thunder of my life organ now beating in distress, or anticipation, caught in a rhythm that's new.

"Do not apologize." My voice is sand and shadows, as if I have not spoken in revolutions. I stare ahead but no longer see, lost in memory of the feel of hyu'man skin upon my own. A wonder and a terror, that simple contact.

Because she touched me...and I cannot remember the last time someone has done such. Touched me, by choice rather than misfortune, aggression, or duty.

This is...

"Still," she says, sounding so utterly small at my back, "I will keep in mind that touch isn't something you're comfortable with. I blame the hyu'man part of me for that." She releases a soft laugh. "We tend to...crave it."

Yes.

They do.

I see it all the time. My brethren with their hyu'man mates. There is constant contact. And I have observed how the others watch them, yearning for the same. I never have.

Until now.

"But," she continues, "I want to help. I don't know anything about these Gryken, I've never seen one up close until now, but if this is some sort of disease...I can help you."

I force my fangs to calm, my voice to return to its normal tone as I straighten my back, spine muscles rolling as I straighten my shoulders.

"Very well."

I hear as she releases a slow breath and then the soft steps of her feet as she follows behind me.

"I'll get my pack," she says as soon as we enter the lab and I freeze again.

This time, I turn to face her, observing rosy cheeks, determined eyes, and the way her chest heaves as she takes a breath.

"You have only just arrived."

"And if we don't get on this, I won't get to enjoy this new beginning." She meets my gaze. Gone is the frightened female who hid behind a narrow tree, scared of me. "You saved my world once before. It seems only right I help ensure it stays saved." A wry smile tugs at her lips, chasing shadows from her face. "Besides, you said it yourself—the war isn't over yet."

A growl rumbles in my chest at her stubborn will, her fearlessness. And yet, in its own way, her persistence gladdens me. That spark she's lit within me brightening at our simple exchange.

"Very well," I say again. "I will tell the others. There is more work to be done."

SOPHIE

I sit at a round table, pack braced against my chair where Mina set it down. Sitting alongside me, she braces her elbows against the dark material that makes the table, steepling her fingers as she rests her chin on them.

On my other side, my new partner sits. Back straight, eyes forward, He'rox is just as silent as the other Vullan in this room. And there are several of them. Four to be exact, and three other females not counting Mina. They may all be different, obviously not related, but all have something in common. They all wear a similar suit as Mina does. Like thick black ink, it sits on their skin and the more I look at it, at them, I swear I see it move.

"Why have you summoned us here?" The voice is so deep, almost like an animal growling, that at first, I don't recognize he's speaking words. Fierce eyes that look like fiery lava pierce across the table, directed at He'rox.

Beside him, a female leans forward, and I get the sense those two are in charge. Adira, she'd introduced herself as. And beside her sits Fer'ro. Her mate, she'd said.

And if that information was not enough to shock me, the others had arrived.

Sitting in a room that seems choked with the intensity of the Vullan, I can't help but feel small...almost useless. And the females that sit by their side are just as all-encompassing as they are—almost as if they're no longer human, carrying much greater power and strength than their forms suggest.

It doesn't take long for me to put two and two together.

They are all mated. All pairs.

That reality is staggering.

And now it all makes sense. The way San'ten had growled at those men when I arrived.

He is Mina's.

I glance at them now, noticing how Mina closes her eyes, breathing deep as if she's trying to calm herself, and how San'ten sits still, everything about him like still death except he's snarling, every second his rage becoming more evident but does not seem to be directed at anyone in particular.

The other couples, a woman named Sam and her Vullan mate Ga'Var, and another woman named Deja and her mate Fi'rox, sit calmly. Waiting.

"There is work to be done." He'rox's words seem to fall on static air. Hanging there, as everyone's focus zones in on him.

Fer'ro narrows his eyes, gaze flicking to me for a brief moment before returning to He'rox. "What work? We have purged the Gryken from this world. Wherever they are left, they are being cut down now that humanity has the weapons to defend itself. We have fulfilled our purpose."

"Not entirely." He'rox glances at me, and I offer what I hope is an encouraging smile. This is it—our chance to convince them the threat isn't over yet. "There are...concerns that require investigation."

The female—Adira—leans forward, bracing her forearms on the table. Her suit ripples over her skin, shadows chasing shadows. "Explain."

He'rox inclines his head. "The veins."

Silence falls on the group, and I glance from one to the other. It's clear they already knew about these veins. Their reaction says it all. But then, Mina shatters.

"I knew it," she says. She grips her head, digging her fingers so hard through her hair as she grips her skull that my eyes widen in alarm.

San'ten growls, reaching for her, but she shakes her head, even while accepting his embrace.

I blink several times, struggling to follow the rapid exchange of information. Questions race through my mind as I try in vain to piece together meaning from the fragments of unspoken conversation around me.

"I felt it. Even though they were dying I could still feel them. *I can still feel them.*" Mina's voice trembles and there is a haunted look in her eyes as she stares at the table, not seeing it before her, but seeing something else entirely behind those eyes.

I frown at her words, glancing at He'rox for some understanding. His gaze is unreadable as he looks down at me.

"Mina and I..." he says after a few moments. "We have something in common."

I don't imagine it. A chill goes through the room at his utterance and no one speaks. I try to smile, to soften the mood, whatever this is.

"Intuition? You went to the spot where the veins were, almost like you could sense them."

He simply stares at me and I force away the shiver wanting to go down my spine.

There's more to this. More I don't know.

"You hypothesized the veins would disappear once the last of the Gryken dies," Fer'ro says.

"Aye," He'rox responds.

"But?"

There is tension in the room, so much that I could probably cut it with a knife.

"It has changed. *Is* changing." He'rox's voice is so calm, so reflective. If I didn't understand his words, I would think he wasn't talking about something so potentially dangerous.

Adira inhales deeply before resting her back against her chair. She places a hand on Fer'ro's arm. "Let him go investigate. What harm could it do? Best-case scenario, it's nothing to worry about."

"And if it is?" San'ten growls. He looks like he's ready to fight and again the tension intensifies.

Fer'ro leans forward, eyes on He'rox. "You go investigate. You go alone."

My brows dive immediately. "I'm going with him."

All attention turns to me.

Fer'ro's eyes seem to blaze before that fire turns on He'rox. *"You've convinced her?* She's only just arrived. Our responsibility is to keep her safe."

"He didn't." My voice is steady despite the erratic beating of my heart. I move my gaze to the other women before me. "That's what I'm here for, right? To help? I'm here to help. Let me help."

Adira's throat moves. "We may have liberated most of this area, but it's still dangerous out there, and I'm not talking about the Gryken."

I know exactly what she's talking about. She's talking about other humans. Wild animals that survived. Even just the fact that there is no shelter and out there is like an uninhabitable wasteland.

"There are gangs," Deja says.

"Cults..." Sam adds, and they glance at each other.

"I know," I reply. My father's lessons were like little apocalypse packs, filled with information about what he thought would happen. How society would devolve. Growing up, those lessons felt like nightmares. But now, I'm glad he raised me that way. Prepared me, even for this worst-case scenario.

Maybe that's why when the first alarm sounded and I saw one of those machines heading my way, I knew exactly what to do. It hadn't been panic or terror, but practiced movements, my brain kicking into gear with everything that had been drilled into me for as long as I could remember.

My only regret as I climbed into that bunker was that I was doing so alone.

It had only been me and my father, and after he passed, that left me only me. I lived alone. And I was going to die alone.

"I know what's out there," I repeat, leveling the women and the Vullan before me with a steady gaze.

"And you still want to go with him." Fer'ro speaks directly to me, and I have to remind myself that this is real. That I'm in a room with aliens and this isn't some ultra-realistic dream.

"I do."

I force down a lump in my throat and shoot He'rox another smile. I don't expect him to respond, and his stoic calmness is almost comforting. Steady. Something I can trust in this world filled with uncertainty.

"We should tell her." It's a whisper, Adira to Fer'ro and then Sam to Adira. "Do we really? It's more alien than the Vullan themselves. I don't think she's ready..."

Deja barks a laugh. "I don't think any of us were."

All eyes are on me again and I suddenly feel under the spotlight. "What?" I whisper. "What is it?"

Adira locks eyes with her mate before he nods slightly and she stands.

I stare at her, wondering what she's doing or about to do. Moments pass and nothing happens.

"What is it?" I laugh, but I hate how nervous and unsure it sounds. And then time stops for a moment. Because Adira's body shifts.

No. Not her body. Her *suit*.

It stretches from her hand like dark ink curving up from her palm in a small whirlwind. My eyes widen as the ink rises. So much of it, yet her body remains covered. The small whirlwind spins before settling and taking form. A black rose.

I...don't know what to say.

"How...did you do that?"

She doesn't answer, simply looks at Deja, who stands, eyes locked with mine before she stretches her hand in my direction. Something forms in her fist. A spike and she pulls her arm back before throwing it forward.

I react, jerking back, but if she meant to hurt me, I would've been too slow. Beside me He'rox growls, as if in some warning, his gaze locked with hers at the same time that her mate, Fi'rox, growls back at him. I don't even have the mind space to contemplate the fact that some male aggression is taking place. All I can focus on is the spike that's embedded in the table before me. It's sharp. Sharp enough to pierce the hard material and I'm sure if she wanted it to, it would have gone right through me.

My wide eyes fly to her. "You made that out of thin air. Your suit...the technology..."

"They...are more than a suit," Fer'ro says.

My gaze falls back to the spike in the table, my breath hitching as it slowly...disintegrates. It turns almost fluid once more before shooting through the air and right back to Deja.

Looking back at her, the spike or whatever is nowhere to be found. Her suit is intact. Smooth.

"They?" I ask.

"Our ba'clan," Fer'ro responds and Adira releases a sigh, pressing her hands down on the table.

"I know this is a lot to take in. Think of it as a crash course about the Vullan. Just so you know who they are before you get any deeper into this. They are much more powerful than they appear."

My eyebrows shoot up. Clearly, she isn't seeing the same males that I'm seeing here. They already look more powerful than any walking being I've ever seen.

"And the ba'clan, they are also an entity," she continues. "They live alongside us...alongside *them*."

My throat feels dry as my gaze moves from one Vullan to the other, trying to reconcile this new information with my preconceived notions about this species.

But now it all makes sense. The slight ripples I've seen going over their skin. It's been the ba'clan all along.

When my gaze lands on He'rox, it almost appears as if he stiffens.

He's different from the others, but I already knew that. His ba'clan are white and they're not as obvious as the others.

"You cannot take her with you." Fer'ro's words sound so final they snap me back to the task at hand.

"Fer'ro..." Adira begins.

"He is not equipped..." Fer'ro stops, eyes boring into He'rox and when my gaze lands on him too, I wonder why he doesn't defend himself. "He is our best warrior. Even better than I. Completely committed to whatever cause he fights for."

I blink at him, brows furrowing. He's not making sense. "Would that not be a *good* thing?"

They're all looking at me now, the humans with a note of withdrawal and sadness in their eyes.

"No," Fer'ro almost growls.

"I might not protect you if we go out there together. My ba'clan... are no longer operational. And..." He'rox pauses, eyes unreadable.

"And?"

"He'rox is committed to his cause...and nothing else. To have a female..." Fer'ro pauses. "If you go out there, find something...if you fall in danger, we do not trust his instincts to protect you first above all else."

I scoff, my brows diving deeper. They're joking, right?

Reaching into my pack, I bring out another little gift my father left me. Flipping off the safety on the semi-automatic pistol, the metal cold against my skin, I point it in Fer'ro's direction.

Fer'ro doesn't move, but his ba'clan do, rising behind him in a series of sharp blades that make me want to lower the weapon. But I don't.

"I think you'll find I'm not entirely helpless." I keep my voice steady as I meet Fer'ro's gaze. I've been on my own for a long time. Fighting for myself is only natural.

For a moment all is silent, before Fer'ro's ba'clan slowly settle.

"So be it," he says, and through the corner of my eyes, I see He'rox's attention. All enveloping and completely focused on me.

There's a twinkle in those cold eyes. *Pride.* And something deep within me reacts in response.

CHAPTER EIGHT

SOPHIE

Preparations begin immediately.

The meeting ends and the Vullan file from the room, leaving only the humans behind.

In the corner, Mina paces as Adira speaks to me. Letting me know for the tenth time that it's no requirement for me to go out there. To risk myself.

I could stay at the camp and wait like the other civilians on the ground.

And despite how good that may sound, it doesn't sit well in my soul. I need to go out there. I need to figure out what's happening for myself.

Maybe it's just experiences of the past fueling my decision. Of governments that hide the truth from the populace. But I want to see everything first-hand. This isn't a time to sit back and let others decide my fate.

"I've made my decision," I say to her. "I'll accompany him out there."

The alien I just met and yet feel more affinity to than the very humans before me. It's something I don't understand, but I do not question it.

Understanding settles in Adira's eyes as she leans back in the chair and releases a slow breath, jerking her chin at Sam in some silent message.

"Okay, we understand." She levels her gaze with mine one more time. "We were the same. We know exactly how you feel. We won't stop you."

I nod. "Thank you."

Rising, she pushes away from the table. "You should take this time to rest. You two leave at first light. Sam will show you to your room."

I nod again, rising as I stash my gun back into my pack and throw it over my shoulder.

Following Sam through the ship, I hardly notice the interior, as my mind is filled with only one thing. When morning breaks, I'm going on a journey that I know will change my life.

It's a deep knowing that hits me with such surety, I have to force myself to breathe through the unsteady feelings swirling in my gut.

Given a room, I sit on the strange bed, just staring at the wall for far too long.

Was I making the right decision?

At some point, I must have fallen asleep because a sound wakes me up.

It's already morning, and Sam is back to take me to the ground.

"He'rox?" I ask.

"He's already on the ground," she says, "waiting for you."

She looks back at me, studying me for a moment as I grab my pack and we walk through the corridors. "You can still change your mind, you know."

I shake my head and she nods.

"Well, there's breakfast being served down there. Canned

chicken soup. You can also wash up down there if you haven't done so already."

I give her a small smile and nod again.

Everything moves quickly, but not quickly enough.

I wash my hands, my face, I get a bowl of soup and I drink, all the while my gaze on the white shadow standing at the edge of the camp, waiting for me.

He'rox doesn't move, and the longer he stands there, the more those butterflies rise and fly in the pit of my belly.

Setting the bowl down, I jerk my chin at Adira and the other women still serving the others, and they do the same. Behind them, their Vullan mates stand watching as I head toward my shadow.

He'rox turns as he sees me approaching, and I glance back at the camp as we head toward the trees. I've only just arrived, and I'm already leaving.

There's a slight part of me, the little girl who didn't ask for any of this—not a father who spent more time harkening the end of the world than appreciating the present, and not an alien invasion that's ripped her world in two. But I keep walking, footsteps falling within the larger ones of my guide.

I expect him to stop at the spot we found before, to dig the hole deeper so we can get samples and run some tests, but he keeps walking, forcing me to pick up my pace to keep up with his long strides.

"Where are we going?" I ask, glancing around at the thick foliage surrounding us. Everything looks the same. If I got separated from him, I'd be lost in seconds.

He doesn't answer, just keeps walking with purpose, navigating the wild terrain as if he knows exactly where he's headed. A white shadow moving silently through a world not of his own.

And so we walk.

For minutes, hours...he does not seem to tire, and soon my mind shifts from the anxiety of our mission to other things.

I can't help but notice the way his body moves. I follow behind him, distracted by his fluid grace. Like water flowing on air.

For such a large male, he navigates the dense forest with uncanny stealth and efficiency. He's silent. Not even a twig snapping underneath his foot, while I can hear every step I make echoing all around us.

He'rox's body shifts and glides with a dangerous beauty, every muscle working in perfect unison. I find myself staring at the flex of his broad shoulders beneath his strange armor, the way his ba'clan cling to powerful thighs and calves.

A flush spreads over my cheeks as I realize the direction of my thoughts. I tear my gaze away, heart pounding for reasons that have nothing to do with our hike. What is wrong with me? He isn't even human. I know nothing about the Vullan or their mating practices. For all I know, the women back at the camp—Adira, Sam, Deja, and Mina—all had to do something, give up something, to be mates with beings so different from us.

He completely ignores me, and I wonder if he even remembers that I am here.

And yet, as we continue trekking through the wild terrain, I struggle to ignore the effect his commanding presence has on me. The confidence in his stride, the air of focus and control that surrounds him.

I keep my eyes on him, watching the way he moves undirected. There is no pause, no moment of contemplation as he heads through the thick. And I realize that maybe he *does* know where he's going. I don't know the extent of his senses or abilities. I only know what I've been told, and clearly, there's more to them than meets the eye.

The farther we go, the denser the forest becomes. Vines and thorns tug at my clothes and hair, scratching at my skin. The air grows heavy and damp, filled with the smells of moss and rotting leaves.

An uneasy feeling washes over me. We're now far from the camp, from any kind of help. If something were to happen out here, no one would know. I grip the gun I'd moved from my pack to tuck into the waist of my jeans, taking comfort from its solid weight.

And before me, the alien goes on. He doesn't stop.

In silence, we trek, the sun already moving past its halfway mark on its way to the horizon.

It's so silent out here, but for once, I welcome the silence.

Before, when the machines came, the noise they made right before they attacked vibrated the air, beating against your eardrum and sending chills straight through your bones.

I don't know if I'll ever forget that sound. Even now, my heart thumps unsteady, the chance of hearing that sound again not completely gone. And as He'rox continues on, I realize Fer'ro's words were true.

I am with him, but I am alone. I'm the only one here who is influenced by being in the presence of something so different from myself. Something so utterly captivating.

For I can't take my eyes off him, even though I tell myself I'm staring at his back because I don't want to lose sight of him.

But he is so focused on something, as if led by a force outside of ourselves that's drawing him to a particular spot, that he's forgotten all about me.

"He'rox is committed to his cause, and nothing else."

I remind myself I'm used to this. Used to being alone. This is fine. When we finish this mission and head back to camp, I can always get to know the other Vullan. Learn about their planet, their species. Find out about what brought them here...and if they're going to stay.

After hours of difficult hiking, we emerge into a small clearing, moss-covered rocks leading up to the entrance of what looks like a cave. Everything is deathly still and quiet. The trees loom over us, branches intertwining to give us shade.

He'rox stands like a statue, completely focused on the cave entrance, ice-cold eyes reflecting nothing as if seeing something I cannot. His stillness is unnerving, reminding me of the fact he is very different from me.

I step up beside him, determined to appear as unaffected as he is. "What is this place? Why did you bring us here?"

His gaze remains fixed on the cave. "This place may hold answers. Or more questions. It is...difficult to say."

Cryptic as ever. I release a slow breath, thankful for the moment's relief on my muscles as I kick my legs before running a hand through my hair, pushing back tangled strands. "Well, do you want to go inside and investigate?"

When he finally looks at me, pale eyes peering into mine, my breath catches for a heartbeat.

"Yes," he says, voice rough and low. "But be on your guard. There are things in the dark that even my kind fear."

A chill dances down my spine at his warning. I grip my gun and nod, preparing to follow him into the depths of that opening even with the light dying around us.

I've never been afraid of the dark...well...not until those things came. With them, the darkness moved, vibrated. It became alive with monsters and filled with terror.

I gulp as He'rox moves from the edge of the tree line, climbing over the rocks as he heads to the cave entrance and I watch him go, my eyes on his back for a few seconds before I follow behind him toward that cave and whatever dangers may lie within.

It's quiet in here, even quieter than it was outside. And dark.

I reach into the pack on my back and grab my flashlight. A flick of the switch illuminates the tunnel and He'rox stops to glance back at me.

The light illuminates him, the ridges across his body hiding shadows and waves, and his eyes glowing with the light put upon them. My breath hitches as I stare at him and the utter magnificence that he is before he turns back around.

Forcing that breath through my nostrils, I berate myself. *Yes, he's alien, but so am I to him*. I don't see him gawking at me every second he gets. I'm supposed to be a scientist. I'm supposed to be better at this.

As we begin walking, the beam of light swaying and bouncing with each step, I turn my attention to our surroundings.

The walls of the cave are damp and rough, jagged rock formations rising on either side of us. This is definitely a natural formation. So why is my heart racing as we descend deeper into the twisting tunnel?

The air grows thick and heavy, filled with the scents of stone and water and earth. We descend for a while, some passes far narrower than I'd like, but He'rox squeezes through them and I follow him, trusting he knows where he's going.

I doubt he found this cave by accident. Of all the directions in which we could have gone, this is where he came.

Flicking my wrist, I shed light on the walls and floor, scanning for any sign of life. Snakes, bats, spiders...anything could lurk in a cave system this expansive. But so far, all seems quiet. The only movement comes from rivulets of water trickling down the stone and gathering in shallow pools.

After a winding trek that leaves me thoroughly disoriented, the narrow tunnel opens abruptly into a massive chamber. I stagger forward, my breath hitching in my nose automatically as some kind of scent fills my nostrils. *Something* in the air. Something...*wrong*. My heart beats so hard in my ears, I can hear it.

Only it's not my heart. And the sound isn't coming from me or anything inside of me.

I sweep my light upward, unable to see the ceiling high above, and slowly pan it over the expansive space surrounding us.

The sight steals my breath away. Sends a chill down my spine. Definitely makes it hard to breathe apart from the scent choking the air around us.

The chamber is filled with thick veins. Pulsating cords of deep red winding through the rock and emitting a deep vibration, almost like a heartbeat in its rhythmic thumps. The veins branch into a tangled web covering every surface of the cavern, looking like the circulatory system of some unfathomable being.

I step forward in wonder and apprehension, my light flickering over He'rox's pale form as he strides ahead without hesitation. The red veins thrum with power and strange energy prickles across my skin. This technology...or whatever it is, was left by *them*. And even though they're no longer here, it lives on. Thriving. Surviving.

How?

Somehow I know, whatever answer we find won't be one I like, but probably the one I anticipate the most. My father's warnings ring in the back of my mind while the promise of discovering what this is wars with a knot of fear in my gut.

He'rox stops right at the edge of the veins that crawl along the floor, eyes glowing with the light from my beam. "This place holds power," he says.

Yep. Exactly what I want to hear.

I step up beside him, fighting a shiver.

"We need to take some samples." I'm already reaching into my backpack, eyes surveying the walls around us as I take out a test kit filled with a sterilized scalpel, syringe, collection tubes, pH strips, and other basic equipment for field sampling. If I can collect tissue, liquid, and samples from these strange veins and the surroundings, it may provide clues about their composition and purpose.

I move slowly toward the nearest vein, hypnotized by the pulsing liquid flowing through its alien circulatory system. The vein is as thick as my arm, its surface smoother than glass.

"Do you think it's safe?"

A long silence. "Safe is...relative."

I want to tell him he's freaking me out more than helping but then I remember he can smell my fear. He already knows.

He crouches and I follow him, swallowing a lump in my throat at the unnerving beat of the "heart" around us.

Reaching forward, I almost jump out of my skin and stab him with the scalpel as his hand suddenly closes around my wrist.

I swallow hard again. "What is it?"

The feel of his skin on mine sends a rush of warmth through me, despite the chill of our surroundings, and I struggle to understand my response. To reconcile it with the person I know I am.

I meet his icy gaze, struck again by his unearthly beauty and the strangeness of this moment. Those two tentacles at the sides of his mouth curl with my attention and I forget I need to breathe.

"What is it?" I repeat, whispering this time.

He'rox releases my wrist slowly and I hate that I am aware of the fact he's letting me go.

"This technology...senses beyond the physical. Your presence may have unforeseen effects."

"What?" I blink at him. He's saying... "You're saying this...thing... has some form of consciousness?"

More silence. And then... "We seek to understand it...but it may end up understanding us, instead."

His warning echoes through me as I turn my gaze back to the structure surrounding us. Because it is a structure. Pulsing. Expansive.

I realize at this moment that things will never be the same. The world I knew is changing. *Has* changed. I can only hope humanity will change with it...and survive.

Swallowing hard, I meet He'rox's icy gaze. My voice emerges in a hoarse whisper. "Where do we even start?"

The veins pulse around us, hinting at something I, *humanity*, was never meant to grasp. I can't escape the feeling this place is just the tip of the iceberg. That there is more to come. That this is nothing compared to what we'll soon discover.

Even with my father's teachings, the future has never felt so frightening.

"Here," He'rox says, long thick fingers closing over mine as he takes my test kit from my hands.

With smooth dexterity, he takes a sample off the top of one vein, scraping it so lightly and with such care, he doesn't break the surface.

"You must not touch it," he says.

I nod. I don't want to touch it. But the question tumbles from my lips anyway. "Why?"

He'rox pauses slightly, before continuing. The only way I know he heard my question being the slight twitch of his ears.

"Because," he says, "this place holds the remnants of the last of our power here on this world."

I swallow hard. Our power? But that's a good thing, right?

Why does it feel like he's saying it *isn't* a good thing? And if it's a source of our power, why does this place make my skin crawl so much?

"This place gives the Vullan power?" I ask. He'rox stops moving.

Curiosity—no, a *need* to know pushes me forward. "You said 'our power.' Humans too then?"

He'rox turns to me so slowly that I force myself to remain where I crouch.

"Not the Vullan. Not huu-man," he says, eyes sliding to me in a way that makes my breath hitch in my throat.

I swallow hard. "Then we *who*?"

I almost don't want him to answer because I think I know what he's going to say and I don't want to hear it. I don't want the terror those words will incite. But He'rox's gaze bores into me as he opens his mouth and says...

"We...the Gryken."

CHAPTER NINE

HE'ROX

My secret is out.

If this hyu'man is as smart as I perceive her to be, then she will understand the words I have not said.

Fear scents her again, spiking sharp and acrid, and around us, the veins thrum harder.

Her hearing is not as acute as mine, and it seems she does not notice the change. Neither does she sense the network's yearning for her.

But *I* sense it. Sensed it even before we entered this chamber. The network's awareness of our presence. Of *hers*.

It wants her. Wants to feed on her. Wants me to bring her closer.

A sacrifice.

I stare at her, warring with both sides of myself, yet knowing I could never submit. Will never submit to that side of myself. And not only because it is monstrous, but because this female...is...

I can't pull my gaze from her, watching how she closes her mouth, eyes leveled with mine though slightly widened as her chest heaves with breaths that take an effort to calm.

Throughout our trek to this place, I kept her at my back, because if she were anywhere else, I would be tempted to gaze upon her. I could scent her all the way...and she smells delicious. When her fear wanes, it's replaced by another sweet perfume that's even more intoxicating than her fear. That intoxicating sweet pull that makes me want to run my nose against her skin, ba'clan and ridges over sweet smoothness, as I pull her in.

I remained downwind of her, keeping her at my back, just to soak it in. Pathetic for a male of my station. But I cannot deny that her sweet scent left me wanting.

Wanting something a Vullan like me will never have, because my bloodline must die.

I have cursed it.

Soh'fee stares at me in a heavy silence that weighs between us.

My secret is one I have carried for so long. Just the potential of revealing it to this small creature before me is having a surprising effect. That weight that has settled on my shoulders, the one I chose to bear...feels lighter.

This little female...

I have never revealed my secret to others. If the other hyu'mans know, it is because their Vullan mates have told them. So it is strange this little one before me now is causing me to lose my reservations.

She is something I didn't know I needed until now. She...*calls* to me.

And as unaware as she is of the veins around us and their heightened attention to her, so she is unaware of my growing obsession.

It must be her curiosity. For though the other hyu'mans are tenacious and fight for their own, I have never met one quite like this.

Soh'fee is different. But I remind myself she is different for the same reason I was different before I changed. Her thirst for knowledge overrides all else.

I can only hope it brings her favor, rather than ruin. As it has done me.

Before we arrived on this world, our ship woke us from stasis as soon as we entered this planet's star system. At our first glimpse of this world, we knew I could not reveal myself to the inhabitants of this little blue rock. The potential species of this new world would not understand what I now am. And, after we arrived here, we knew our decision was the right one.

Hyu'manity barely understands my brothers who are pure Vullan. The Gryken invasion. Our arrival. We are their first contact.

Why would they understand something such as myself?

An anomaly. Unnatural.

Something that should not exist.

In the damning silence between us, Soh'fee's gaze burns into mine, silently demanding answers I have kept locked away for lifetimes.

"Y—" she begins, words failing as her eyes hold on to me with a tight grip. "You're—"

I remain unmoving. Allowing her to take me in. Waiting for that horror to seep into her gaze.

But Soh'fee simply stares at me, her strange hyu'man eyes growing wider and wider, the white parts bigger and bigger as if the whole ocular structure will pop out of her head if she continues. It is unnerving to see...and yet, I cannot pull my eyes away from her.

The thrumming in the background, the call of the network around us beats at the back of my mind as the seconds tick by.

If I must find out why this thing led me here, if I am to discover its purpose, I must do so now. While she stares at me in shock, whatever preconceptions she had regarding me stripping away one by one.

"Go, Soh'fee. Leave." I pull my gaze from hers and to the vein before us.

"L-leave? Why?"

I stiffen.

Did she not hear what I told her? Did she misunderstand?

"I—"

"—am my enemy."

I stiffen even more, not even breaths moving in my chest.

"You are my enemy." I hear when she swallows, forcing her spittle down her throat as she repeats the words. "Is that what you're saying? That you're one of them. That you and this thing..."

She trails off, gaze shifting to the structure around us. All along her arms, thin filaments almost invisible to the naked eye rise. A bit like how my ba'clan used to rise along my form when they sensed danger. It is a warning response. One that is telling her she should find safety.

Why does she not run?

Pale eyes land on me again. "You're saying you're my enemy."

I...cannot answer her. I started this. Revealed this fact. Yet, I cannot respond. To say it out loud even when it screams at the back of my mind will call it into physical existence. So far, that part of me has only taken form in my mind. In the dark of night where it is cold and I am alone.

"Affirmative."

She is silent. Silent enough that I brace for the disgust, hatred and horror that will shine through in those expressive eyes.

All that I witness is...nothing.

Nothing.

"You are my enemy..." she whispers again, gaze leveled with mine. "Fine. I can work with that."

My nictitating membrane slides over my eyes as I hold her in my focus. I do not know what she means.

Sniffing I lean toward her. She does not budge and...I do not smell her fear.

This is...impossible.

"You are mentally compromised." My voice is low, my words rumbling across the short space between us.

"Is that your way of saying I'm crazy? Mad? Insane?"

"You are," I whisper, forcing myself not to draw closer to her as her sweet scent fills my nose.

"A little," she whispers.

I have only been in this female's presence for one cycle...and she puzzles me. Her reactions are uncharacteristic of her kind...and because of that, I deviate from my norm. Around her, I am as unlike myself as she is unlike any I have known of her species. She is a variable I did not expect to encounter.

And as if that was all I needed, I decide to let her see *me*.

Rising, I stride away from her to the nearest vein conduit large enough for me to interact with. Claws sliding over its smooth outer edge, I can feel it calling to me, wanting to connect.

Off to the side, Soh'fee remains in the same spot, eyes glued to me, and for a moment, I wonder if this is the right thing to do.

"Do it." Her voice whispers across the space between us, stroking over my ridges like a silky caress.

Eyes on her, I rest my palm on top of the vein and I see when she inhales, chest rising as her lungs fill with air.

At my touch, the vein thrums with interest, recognizing our affinity, while, at the same time, recognizing the threat. For like with Soh'fee, I am its ally and its enemy. I can sense when it pulls back, its intelligence not as great as those that created it, yet enough to know its survival hangs in the balance.

"I am not here to destroy you," I whisper, eyes still on Soh'fee as I speak to both her and the network itself and I see when her throat moves. She gives me a slight nod, chin moving toward chest, and I turn my attention to the Gryken structure underneath my claw.

It is true. I am not here to destroy it either. *Not yet, at least.*

For it all must die. Every last bit of it. Even if I have to go along with it.

"Soh'fee," her name comes out with a growl, "you should leave."

"Why?"

"Go through the tunnels far away from here."

"Not a fat chance. Whatever you're about to do, I need to see it too. I need to know what the fuck is happening here. Your people...*my people* need to know what we're dealing with."

I keep my hold on the conduit, sensing the life force thumping through the vein. I don't know what I'm about to do. I just know that I must try to connect. Try to let go. To open the vacuum in which I have situated myself all this time.

"So be it," I say.

Shadows crawl at the edges of my vision as I unfocus my eyes. And for the first time since my greatest sacrifice, I let go. Instead of fighting the connection as before, I open my mind to it fully. The vein feeds me knowledge in a rush, the connection shooting through me, filling my mind with information that comes all at once.

I jerk, the barrage almost too much to handle, but I do not let go.

"He'rox?"

There. Right there. Sweet, soft voice. I hold on to it, to the grounding that Soh'fee provides here in the present.

"What's happening?" Her voice sounds closer and adrenaline mixes with my own fear coursing along my spine. I am not yet in full control. I expected her to stay away, *not come closer to me*.

My body jerks again and I fight to keep my hold on the vein, to not let go and give up the growing connection between myself and it.

I can sense its grandeur. Its reach.

"This network spreads far beyond this chamber." The words grind from my lips. "Far beyond anything we, hyu'man and Vullankin, have realized."

It touches areas of this planet we have not yet visited. Collecting information. Feeding.

Feeling.

But I cannot tell her this. Not yet. Not until I have understood this better.

"It is..."

The pull of the connection threatens to take me away until something else snags my senses. Something that pulls me the other way. Sweet scent of the female Soh'fee.

I growl as it fills my nostrils.

She *is* insane. She has come even closer still.

"Go on," she whispers.

I open myself some more, breaking down barriers I've built to separate this side of myself. But the more I open my mind, the more I can feel it taking control.

"The veins are changing. Adapting."

My head tilts, teeth clenched as I search through the barrage of information coming my way. Yet, their new purpose is one I cannot grasp.

I can sense it, almost see it, but the image is cloudy, fading in and out the harder I try to hold on to it.

It will not tell me its secrets...because it knows I am not pure. But one thing is certain, it is not attracted to the Vullan in me. What it wants is something else.

Filled with the lifeblood of Soh'fee's people, this structure yearns for only one thing. *Control.*

Hyu'man blood.

My Soh'fee.

This...thing wants to connect with her in a way I cannot allow.

The tentacles at the side of my face curl and writhe incessantly as the structure's demand rises.

"He'rox?"

I must return Soh'fee to camp, and I must find a way to protect her, her people, from a force that threatens to destroy them for good.

For this war is not over yet. That is certain. I have one more purpose.

There is still more to be done.

"He'rox?!"

Something touches me and I suddenly arrive back in the present. With a roar, I pull my hand away from the conduit as I step backward, gaze moving over the web of the structure before me and only realizing at that moment that the thing that touched me was...*her.*

But as I turn fully toward her, the network pulses, flooding my senses with its demands. Its wants.

Its needs.

And it wants her.

The feeling is overpowering.

I opened myself too much.

A growl vibrates in my chest as my gaze meets hers and I sense the moment she realizes something has changed within me.

Her throat moves, hand going to the weapon I know she carries at her waist even though she does not draw it.

"He'rox? Can you see me?" She takes a step backward. "Are you in there?"

My head tilts slightly. My vision has changed.

I can see everything. The fine hairs on her smooth skin. The golden ring around her pupil. And I can hear her heart beating. Erratic, it thumps against the bone structure beneath which it is caged. And there it is. The sound of the smooth rush of her lifeblood through her veins.

Soh'fee takes another step back, hand tightening on her weapon. "He'rox? Can you understand me?"

I stare at her, senses flooded by the network's clamor. Its hunger beats at me, raging to be fed, urging me to give it what it craves. *Her.* The sweet blood within her fragile form.

No.

I clench my fists, fighting back the urge. But it is in my head.

Soh'fee's eyes widen as she raises her weapon. Her hand shakes but her gaze does not waver from my own. "He'rox. I don't want to hurt you. Fight this—whatever it's doing to you. Come back to me."

Her words pierce the fog shrouding my mind. Come back...*to her?* I grasp at her voice, her scent, using them as a lifeline to claw my way back to clarity.

"Come on..."

That slight tremble in her voice appeals to that other part of me I want to kill, the war between me and it only making me snarl harder, for that part of me can only die if I decide to let myself be erased with it.

Taking a few more steps backward, she stumbles, falling on her behind. But that does not stop her from scrambling farther away on the back of her arms, fear scent spiking.

I don't know if she can hear it now. The incessant beating of the network around us. How it rises and falls. How it calls to me. Calls for her.

She is running away. *The one thing I do not want her to do.*

And the scent of her fear...

The Vullan part of me rises alongside that other part I'd wished to keep hidden, and I growl low, fangs lengthening. With a roar I lunge forward, my muscles like a well-oiled machine I haven't used in a long time. On all fours, I launch myself after the female running away from me.

I cannot stop and her eyes widen as I approach.

"He'rox!" She screams my name, sound bouncing off the network around us before being lost in space as her back hits the wall near the entrance to this chamber.

Trembling hands lift her weapon, but she is too slow. Or maybe she waited too long. *On purpose.* Giving me a chance to prove myself.

In another time, at another place, her hesitation would have meant the death of her.

Not this time, though. I do not wish to see her blood spilled.

Instead...I want to taste it.

The image of sinking my fangs into her neck while my stiff shaft pierces her, filling her to the brim all the while enveloped in this sweet scent of hers almost makes me thrum with need. My pupils dilate, fangs dripping with a desire I never knew I could still feel as I close the distance between us. I pause only when I'm braced over her, the cool metal tip of her weapon pressed into my chest.

She has good aim. It is pointed right at my life organ.

If she fires, it will slow me down for a few minutes, and she might get out of this chamber. My ba'clan won't block the attack. They have no power to do so.

I wait for her to fire, to sink several projectiles within me. I wait for the pain. Crave it.

Expect it.

But it doesn't come.

Instead, watery eyes watch me with too much intelligence. Her chest heaves as I press into her, press into her weapon, but she allows me to. Her finger not finding that trigger she obviously needs.

"Do it," I growl.

She stares at me, lips trembling even as those eyes search mine.

"No."

I stare down at her.

She is so close to me now, her body presses against mine and I can feel every inch of her. Every curve, every valley. She is soft, sweet, *perfection*.

Now I understand what keeps my brethren here. Now I see why the others yearn so much to remain. Here lies a promise of home.

A place to stay in a female's arms.

Chest heaving, I freeze as her free hand rises, gently coming to my jaw. Her eyes widen slightly as the tentacle closest to her fingers wraps around the nearest one. But...when I expect her to startle, to pull away, she doesn't.

She accepts as that monstrous part of me touches her flesh, and she touches me back. *Touches* me, even though I am braced above her in the exact stance of attack.

Behind and around us, the network pulses, wanting its prey.

But I resist.

She is *mine*.

The thought hits me with enough shock to clear some of my bloodlust, and I have a moment of clarity.

I have underestimated my control. Fer'ro was right. I should never have been allowed to exit the safety of that camp and with a female on my watch.

"Shoot me," I growl.

The pain will help. The pain always helps to ground me. Remind me the monstrous parts are not all of who I am. Remind me that somewhere in there, my pure bloodline still exists.

"No," she says again, voice shaking slightly.

"Do it." My command chills the air, but the female beneath me doesn't budge.

"You're not going to attack me."

I stare at her. Her words sound so sure. As if she believes in me more than I believe in myself.

"I *want* to," I growl. I don't know why I say it. The Vullan aren't known for their ability to tell lies, but this goes beyond that. I watch for her reaction. Wait for the fear to overtake her. The disgust.

But still, it doesn't take root.

"You won't." Her whispered challenge holds me still, and as I look down at this soft little thing pressed against me, I wonder if she realizes just what she really asks.

I lift a claw and her breath quickens. "I could rip you in two."

"I know you can."

My gaze narrows as I watch her. "Are you not afraid?"

She swallows, throat moving as she pulls those plump rosy lips into her mouth, causing wetness to make them shine.

Her light beam's been abandoned somewhere behind us, the illumination shining off to the side and I wonder if she can see me well.

Is that what's causing her to act like this? Is the darkness giving her courage?

You can speak with a monster if you don't have to lay eyes on him.

"Can't you tell?"

For a moment, I wonder what she's talking about and then it comes back to me. Around this female, my mind goes into a tangle.

I inhale, the sweet scent of her fear overpowering the even sweeter scent of her being. It is like a drug that I take in, filling my lungs, and a growl rumbles in my chest until I catch the scent of something else.

Pure sugar mixed in with spice.

Her throat moves again as I stiffen even further, not willing to believe what I scent. Her fingers curl around my jaw, tugging me closer even as my tentacle writhes along her digit, taking every inch of skin she's willing to let me touch.

And then, her chin tilts up, those plump little lips closing over mine as her eyes flutter closed.

My world stops. Time ceases. Existence ends.

With Soh'fee's lips against mine, the incessant chatter in my brain suddenly stops. For a moment in space and time, I am at peace. And I can only feel.

Emotions long ago lost come crashing through me all at once, and I am relieved her eyes are closed because she cannot see me. Cannot see how, for the first time in what feels like eons, my ba'clan...*react*.

They stand up against my back, facing the threat all around us, protecting the female at my front. To feel them alive again sends a new wave of emotion through me.

Soh'fee is touching a dark cold place within me that I thought died a long time ago.

Deep within me, a thrum develops as I press into her kiss. Into *her*. This fragile creature who dares defy death to embrace a monster. Her soft body yields to mine and I groan, shoulders hunching as her limbs come around me. Hold me to her even as I try to pull back in shock of what's happening between us, caught in a war of wanting more and fearing that want.

In all the years I've lived, none have brought me this sudden peace and desire. None have stilled the screaming voices and calmed the raging beast. How can this be?

When I manage to lift my head, to stare down at her in wonder and dismay, she gazes up with half-lidded eyes. Dazed, yet aware.

Accepting.

It is inconceivable!

My body trembles against her smaller one and a growl rises in my throat. The urge to flee wars with the need to stay, to claim, to cherish.

Mine, my blood roars, ba'clan activating further at my back. Sharp spikes lengthening even as they move against my fingers, itching to go to her.

The ba'clan always know. The ba'clan are never wrong. Their whole existence relies on us finding suitable mates they can populate with. Our young carrying more potential for even greater survival of their species.

But Soh'fee can never be mine. I have damned myself, and will not do the same to her.

With a snarl I tear free of her embrace, scrambling upright on legs gone weak with hunger I dare not name. She props herself on her elbows, watching me step farther away with eyes too accepting for her own good.

"Get out." The rasp leaves my throat before I think better of it. But it is already done. "Leave."

Shock and pain cross her expression, followed swiftly by defiance. She pushes to her feet in a single graceful move, gaze locked with mine. I expect arguments, questions—for her to assault me for reasons I cannot give.

But she turns on her heel without a word and strides for the exit, snatching up her abandoned light source and gear on the way. Each determined step takes her farther from me, but I remain frozen in place, fighting for control as the veins pulse and churn around us. Their call beats at the walls of my mind, but for the first time since arriving, I ignore them.

When she squeezes through the chamber entrance and disappears, I stagger back against the nearest wall. The veins fall eerily silent without her presence to sustain their interest. For they do not want me. I am too much like them already.

Or perhaps I have simply gone deaf in the aftermath of what just occurred, senses overwhelmed.

I shared touch with a hyu'man...and if I died now, in all my years of existence, nothing would have ever come close to the feel of Soh'fee's lips against mine.

Minutes or days may pass; I lose track of all but the memory of her lips on mine. The feel of her body yielding, accepting, setting me aflame. Part of me shrivels at the loss already while the rest hungers to hunt her down, to finish what her challenge set in motion.

I have lived over a hundred years by hyu'man count, and I have never come so close to losing myself. All my training, discipline and denial shattered with a single brush of soft skin. I thought myself long past such base needs and reactions.

I was wrong.

I sink to the floor, unable to move. Unable to go to her.

For if I do, I know I will claim her.

And she may be confused right now...but I am positive that's the last thing she wants.

Or needs.

CHAPTER TEN

SOPHIE

I don't know what the hell I was thinking. I have no clue why I did what I did. And even then, why my heart's beating so hard in the center of my chest even as I storm away. Not from fear. Not from shock. But from the fact that the simple contact of my lips on his sent shockwaves through me that shouldn't exist.

Fuck.

Gripping the straps of my pack, I breathe hard as I make my way back through the winding tunnel. My heart pounds so hard I almost mistake it for that incessant thrum of the network of veins that had surrounded us.

Just thinking about those sends a chill through me that provides some grounding, some clarity, in what is quickly becoming possibly some fraying of my consciousness.

I *kissed* him.

In the middle of him chasing me, I kissed him. I... fuck! *Why did I do that?*

Seeing him come after me like that, my fear overrode everything else. His eyes changed. Bled to black. I've never seen anything like it. Just like the eyes of that thing floating in the back of his lab, his eyes were a deep, empty void. And yet, I still knew he was in there.

For unlike when I looked into the eyes of that beast and felt nothing but evil, here I felt hope. And in the middle of that chaos, something else woke up inside me. Something that defied all logic and reason. At that moment, I hadn't seen a dangerous alien chasing me. I'd seen a powerful male driven by raw need—a need I realized was completely primal. Completely pure. Completely...unsullied. Perfect. And I remembered where I was. At the end of the world. The loss of everything. The finality that is there when faced with my mortality.

So I kissed him. And for a few seconds, it was bliss. His lips were surprisingly soft, his skin like smooth leather, and his embrace almost tender despite the fact he could rip me in two. And that fact, the thrill of the chase and the 'forbiddenness' of it all only heightened the contact between us.

But then he pushed me away. Ordered me to leave. And the rejection stung.

Even though this whole thing is madness, his rejection hit me like a brick that's left me reeling.

I don't even know He'rox. Not really. I know nothing about his kind, his past...who he is...*what* he is. Yet I gave myself to him. If only for a moment, I...*opened* myself. And that moment has ruined me.

I know it.

We're at the cusp of something here. Something bigger than it seems.

Maybe I should have stayed in my bunker after all. But I know that isn't true. I stayed hiding long enough.

"Shit!" A breath shudders from my throat as I continue on, fighting my heart to calm down, my breaths to even.

I'm muttering to myself, arguing with no one but my stupidity for the entire time I trek my way back through the cave. I don't know how I do it, moving through this winding cavern without stumbling or feeling afraid. Without He'rox as my guide, this place is terrifying. But my whole focus is no longer on the journey, or where the hell I'll end up.

By the time I emerge from the tunnel, the sun's gone down so much, night's crawling in. I stand paralyzed at the entrance, afraid to face what might come next. Afraid He'rox will avoid me now, and I will never have the chance to solve this mystery I've stumbled into.

For although he just revealed to me something that sends fear to the base of my cells...I am still not afraid of *him*. He isn't what I thought he was, and yet, despite it all, I still yearn to be in his presence.

Maybe he was right about me being insane. This is a lapse in judgment.

Releasing a heavy breath, my fingers turn into fists at my sides as I remain outside the tunnel entrance, pacing back and forth as the sun sinks lower in the sky. Anger and confusion war within me. I don't know how long I stay pacing there, caught up in a war of emotions that fight with my ego and my heart.

Until I suddenly stop. Eyes focused on the darkening forest beyond, I stop pacing and face the encroaching night.

As darkness falls, the anger fades, leaving only confusion and hurt in its place. I wrap my arms around myself against the chill of the night, but it's not enough. I still feel the ghost of He'rox's embrace, the heat of his body, and the tender brush of his alien lips.

None of it makes any sense. But it doesn't have to.

I've always prided myself on two things: remaining objective and rational. I'm logical to a fault. Growing up with a father like mine, there was no other choice. I had to always have a level head. Be ready for whatever the world threw at me. Yet one encounter with this alien, and all my reason has gone out the window.

Either this is some kind of psychological effect—maybe he manipulated my emotional state somehow. Caused me to elicit that response. Unlikely, but not impossible. I know nothing about his physiology or abilities.

I run a hand through my hair, the silence of the world around me only making my thoughts louder.

Or, maybe there's something primal and visceral occurring here beyond my control. Some kind of biological imperative or attraction that defies the science I know.

A breath shudders through me as I stare out into the quiet night.

Both options scare me. But as much as I wish, nothing about that kiss or its aftermath felt manufactured. The heat, the thrill, the unexpected tenderness—it felt real. Beyond my ability to rationalize away or resist.

Fuck. There are too many unknowns here.

What he is. What he wants. What he will do. What will happen to us now.

What will happen to the world.

Standing right here, I wonder what I should do.

I can't return to camp. I wouldn't be able to find my way back on my own, especially in the night. So I do the next best thing. I settle at the cave entrance and get the stuff I'll need from my pack. There's no sound behind me, no sound on the outside either.

Whatever He'rox is doing down there, it doesn't look like he's going to come after me. I have no choice but to wait. So I will.

I'll wait for this alien to return to my side.

And in the meantime, I'll take care of myself.

HE'ROX

Silence envelops me, but my thoughts are consumed by the hyu'man female, Soh'fee. Her name whispers through my mind on a loop, one I cannot banish from my consciousness like everything else.

On Edooria, I disciplined myself to ignore such base needs as intimacy or touch. It wasn't a choice. It was a *necessity*. A sacrifice for my people. And after the Gryken came to our world, that sacrifice took even more and more of me.

I thought myself stronger than this.

While my brethren were swayed by the beauty of hyu'mankin, the presence of females, I remained unmoved. Yet with one intimate contact, Soh'fee has shattered all my defenses, leaving me raw and aching.

It cannot be.

I am never to have a female. My duty to my people surpasses any personal desires.

Yet still, I crave the feel of her against me. Still, I taste her lips, soft and pliant, branded into my memory.

A growl rumbles in my chest, claws flexing against the stone floor. I must purge this weakness from my system. I cannot allow it to grow. To continue.

But I still have a duty to protect her.

I will just have to do so from a distance.

I turn to the exit, life organ thumping in my chest as I head in Soh'fee's direction.

I should not have sent her away.

This part of her world might have no Gryken, but it is not without danger. For it is clear now the threat is no longer above.

We walk above it. Unaware of its growing presence.

Moving through the tunnel, heading to the surface is much faster solo. And yet, while descending, I'd not realized I'd slowed down so Soh'fee could keep up with me. That her constant little grunts and sighs as we descended had kept me company.

Now, the silence threatens to eat me whole and as I near the entrance of the cave, I wonder where she is. I'd expected to find her resting somewhere along the tunnel.

Did she leave for Unity?

She might be surprising, but she is no fool. We are far from the camp. Doing the journey alone would be a bad decision.

But the farther I go through the tunnel and do not come upon her, the more I increase my speed.

A feeling I have not felt since I watched my people being ripped apart on Edooria surges through me so hard that my ba'clan react, rising all around me in a display of aggression I long since thought dead.

And then, I see her.

Halting, I stop mid-haste.

Remaining in the shadows, I watch her pace until the light of her star is snuffed out over the horizon. Er'th's blue sky darkens, worlds far beyond twinkling in its expanse.

One of them is mine. My home...or, at least, the place where I belonged. But now I stand in the dark watching the only other thing that has caught my full attention since then.

Soh'fee paces. Grumbling to herself, her words too muffled for me to hear.

For what feels like hours, she continues, and I wonder if I should approach.

Negative. I remain hidden.

Distance. For her sake.

Finally, she stops and faces the forest beyond before crouching down, a heavy breath leaving her shoulders. She fights with her gear for something within before pulling it out and setting it along the hard rock floor.

She settles on it before reaching into her gear for something else.

Sustenance.

I can scent it from here. Whatever it is. She chews slowly, eyes focused on the exterior of this hollow system before she turns her attention inward.

She looks directly at the spot in which I stand, but there is no recognition on her smooth features. Her light beam is off, possibly to conserve power. She cannot see me.

I lower into a crouch as I watch her, a skitter going through my ba'clan as my muscles flex and prime.

It is yet another movement from them. Several now, when they have been silent for so long. I should be rejoicing. Eager to return to my lab so I can run some tests. But...I cannot. A part of me already knows what I will find.

They have found their mate. They want her.

I push the thoughts away as Soh'fee licks her lips, cleaning away small particles of whatever sustenance she consumes.

Another skitter goes through me. Partially from the fact I am crouching here, watching her like the predator *killishis* would watch young Vullan as they played in the dark sands. And partially from the fact that seeing her tongue move over her lips ignites a hunger in me that wells deep.

Swiping my own tongue over my lips, I taste the ghost of her kiss.

And now I want.

The urge to go to her is so strong, I force myself to step backward. Farther into the darkness. Farther into oblivion.

I cannot go to her like this.

I cannot go to her at all.

And most of all...I cannot be near her.

Because the part that calls her might not be the He'rox she's safe with but the one that wants to consume her whole.

CHAPTER ELEVEN

SOPHIE

I wake with a start.

Surrounded by darkness, it takes me a moment to remember where I am.

A smooth breath releases from my lungs as I ease up on my elbows just as fear shoots through me so quickly, my heart stops.

Right in front of me, a flash of white in the shadows, is He'rox.

He leans closer and I *hear* him inhale, nostrils filling as he leans closer. There's a deep rattle in his throat, so distinctly inhuman that just hearing it stops me from moving.

Panic fills my veins as I freeze, eyes wide, sleep forgotten as I try to make out his face from the darkness that swallows us.

I don't move. I don't breathe. I search the darkness, trying to make out his eyes. And by some light of the stars, I see them as he leans closer.

Blue. Ice-cold blue and not the cavernous black orbs that they'd bled to earlier.

My heart thumps so hard, I cannot breathe.

"He'ro—?"

A claw closes over my mouth, smooth velvety skin sliding against mine and my words die against the contact. My eyes widen as I stare at him, heart slamming into my chest as I remain frozen.

And just like before in the cave, I rely on the one thing my father had taught me to always rely on. My instincts. That part of me that never leads me astray. That gut feeling that always gets things right.

And right now, it's telling me I shouldn't move. That I shouldn't scream or try to run. That I should remain as I am.

So I hold my breath, even though my heart's beating so hard it may crash through my ribs to fall on the cave floor as it tries to escape this body that remains still and is doing the exact thing my brain's telling me not to do.

Because my brain's telling me this is dangerous. Insane. *Stupid*.

But then, that's when I hear it.

At first, I can't make out what it is and I frown, head turning toward the sound. For it isn't coming from He'rox, and it isn't coming from me. It's coming from out there. In the darkness, the forest beyond.

Something is approaching.

The sound comes again, faint but growing louder. A clicking, crackling sound, like twigs snapping underfoot. And it's getting closer.

People?

My heart thumps hard in my chest.

No. If it were people, why would He'rox be reacting this way? This is something else.

He'rox looks up, gaze fastening on something in the darkness, and his tenseness only makes more fear pool in my gut. His claw lifts from my mouth, but I don't move. I fight to breathe evenly, even as my blood freezes in my veins.

The clicking speeds up, coming nearer. My heart pounds so hard I feel dizzy, but I keep still. Trusting my instincts. Trusting He'rox.

A shape emerges from the black, shambling and erratic. Only the dim starlight gives it form, but it's enough for me to see the twisting antlers and recognize what it is. A deer.

Except no deer moves like this. I've hunted them before. I know how graceful they can be. This...*thing* before us is nothing like that.

The deer jerks and twitches unnaturally with every step, antlers gnarled and deformed, clicking with every swing of its head.

This isn't right.

As sure as I was before, trusting in my gut instincts, so I am sure again. For now, they tell me to run. To get the hell out of here before this thing comes any closer. Because there is something very wrong here.

I open my mouth to whisper this to He'rox when he suddenly stiffens as if the air itself has gone dead.

It is only a moment. There is no time to react. Because the deer, a peaceful, graceful prey animal that it should be, suddenly snaps its head in our direction. I don't know how I know—possibly a gift from a sixth sense—but I know the creature is focused not on He'rox, but on me. I can feel its attention like a dark sickly shadow crawling over me.

And just like that, it charges.

Its rattling shriek cuts through the silence of the night as it lunges forward, antlers aimed straight at me. The darkness is no ally, for the speed at which this thing moves, I get a moment's clarity that I'm about to be impaled. He'rox roars, pushing me back against the sleeping bag as he leaps to meet the deer's attack.

I scramble back, gun in hand almost automatically as I lift it and aim. But even if the night wasn't hindering my vision, it wouldn't matter. I can only track them because I can barely make out He'rox moving, and for a moment, I can only stare, stunned.

He moves so smoothly, it is like a dance instead of a fight between life and death.

With silent surety, he grabs hold of the creature even as the animal bends and bucks, snapping at him and trying to pierce him with its antlers. He'rox grabs on to one and with a vicious wrench, he pulls, snapping the antler in two.

The deer screams and another chill goes through me. For the first time since brandishing my gun, it trembles in my fingers as the sound hits me. It is chillingly unnatural. Not any sound I've ever heard a deer make before.

As it rears up, He'rox brandishes its broken antler like a spear and lunges forward, driving the antler straight into its chest. The creature's shriek cuts off, legs spasming out from under it. It collapses to the ground in a tangled heap and silence suddenly returns.

My breaths are uneven as I engage the safety on the gun, a lump in my throat that I force down as I lower the weapon and He'rox turns to face me.

I can't make out his expression from the distance between us, but I don't need to.

He just saved my life. Despite what happened between us down in that cave, it's obvious he's still on my side, and that's all I need to know for now. Because it's clear we need to work together. Something's gone wrong. The natural order of things has shifted.

Before I open my mouth to speak, I look out over the forest beyond, eyes narrowing as I try to make out any shapes along the tree line. I can't see anything, but even then, I hold my breath.

"It was traveling alone." He'rox's voice reaches me and I nod slightly. Still, I keep my gaze on the forest beyond.

"Something was wrong with it," I whisper.

He doesn't respond, and I don't expect him to. I stated the obvious and yet, I needed to say it out loud.

When I pull my gaze from the forest, I realize he is still standing by the slain creature, unmoving. Watching me with the darkness enveloping him on all sides. Standing there, he looks everything as threatening as the deer that just tried to attack me.

I should be afraid. I know I should be. But of all the emotions that linger at the base of my spine, when I look at him, fear isn't one of them.

Pushing the gun into its spot at my waist, I grip my flashlight and turn the beam on. Flashing it in He'rox's direction, he stands against the night like a white sentinel. Still unmoving, his eyes reflecting the glare of the flashlight like a cat's would do, and a shiver goes through me that still has nothing to do with fear.

So tall and strong. The only thing that mars his perfection is the splash of blood that's smeared across his chest. Evidence of the battle he just won.

He'rox doesn't move as I direct the beam to the creature lying dead at his feet and as the light settles on the animal, my breath stops in my lungs.

I can feel him watching me, waiting for my reaction, and I fight to keep my features schooled. Because nothing should surprise me anymore. I've seen the effects of the worst diseases. How they can deform and destroy. Nothing should make my stomach turn.

But this does.

I turn away to compose myself, pretending I'm only searching for another field test kit in my bag, and even when my fingers close around the smooth plastic, I take a moment before turning around again.

With legs that feel like jelly, I close the distance between me and the creature dead on the ground, my mind circling all the information it's received in this short time. Even before I close the distance and shine the light on the creature, I know everything's connected.

Those veins, how they've networked in the cave, how they were pulsing in the forest...and now this.

A slight gust of cold air circles around us as I point my flashlight at the deer at our feet.

"Deer can get this thing," I swallow hard as I crouch over the carcass, "um, this thing called chronic wasting disease."

He'rox is silent. I don't expect him to respond. I don't even know why I'm talking, saying this out loud. Maybe because my thoughts are too loud, the potential implication of what's before my eyes too great to ignore.

"It's...degenerative. Always fatal." I gulp again as I get gloves from the test kit and slip them over my hands. Easing forward slightly, I grab a stick off the ground and push the carcass. It flips to the side, the extent of the horror is revealed even more.

Dark, thick veins run along every inch of the carcass before us. The creature's eyes remain open even in death, bloodshot and bulging, its mouth dripping saliva that's drained unto the cut at its throat, thickening and hardening it.

"This...isn't CWD."

I knew it wasn't. From the way the creature reacted when it came upon us, became aware of our presence and decided to attack, I knew this was something different. But seeing it up close...

Forcing a steady breath through my nose, I use the scalpel to remove part of the infected flesh, stomach turning as I bag it and remove some other samples from the carcass. Fur, bits of the antler, blood samples, the lot.

"This isn't CWD," I whisper to myself again, rising on unsteady feet as I look out into the darkness beyond. "It wanted to kill me."

"Incorrect." He'rox's deep voice makes me turn to face him. He's been silent at my back the entire time. Watching me take the samples, his constant presence at the edges of my awareness. "It did not want to kill you."

I swallow hard, forcing another breath through my lungs as I wait for him to continue.

"What did it want then?"

"It wanted...to control you."

I stare at him, only the breath swelling and releasing from my chest. "Control me." I push down the lump forming in my throat. "The deer?"

It's a deliberate question. One I know isn't the right one, because the implications are already clear. It isn't the fucking deer. Of course, it isn't the deer.

He'rox's head tilts slightly as he studies me and my throat and lips go dry.

"The veins," I whisper. "You know what they're doing."

No answer. Instead, those too-intelligent eyes bore into mine. Waiting for me to put the puzzle together. Except, I don't have all the pieces.

Taking a step away from the carcass, I shine my light on it, watching in horror as the veins still embedded under the deer's skin writhe as if with new life.

"You know what it's doing," I whisper again. "Some kind of neurodegenerative disease?"

"I must return to my lab," he says. "I cannot know for sure otherwise."

Swallowing hard, I give him a sharp nod. "Let me get my pack. But first..." I take a few steps before turning back to face him, "I don't think we should return yet. We need to know more." He'rox watches me, not saying a word and I can't believe I'm about to say this. "We need to go further."

CHAPTER TWELVE

SOPHIE

He'rox stands unmoving, still by the carcass where I left him, like a silent guard in the cold night. He doesn't budge, doesn't come closer, and even as I get my pack ready, rolling and stuffing my sleeping bag inside it and carefully stashing away the sample I just took, he remains in the same spot.

More than once, I glance over my shoulder to see him still standing there. He doesn't move. Doesn't even look like he's breathing.

Far across the sky, the sun is starting its journey once again and dim light chases away some of the darkness. The early morning dew settles over the ground and the freshness of the morning fills my lungs as I zip up my pack and hoist it onto my shoulders.

When I turn around, He'rox is still standing there. I gulp, looking at him, beats of silence passing between us that make me aware of nothing else around us. Just me and him.

"Which way?" I whisper.

He doesn't answer, simply turns his head in a direction off to my left and I jerk my chin in a nod. Adjusting my pack, I take one last look at the carcass at his feet before heading off.

I'm down the little rock incline that led up to the cave in just a minute before I reach the tree line. Only then do I glance behind me. My breath stutters in my chest as our gazes lock and I force another lump down my throat.

This whole trip is giving me more questions than answers. Everything I thought I knew about, well, everything seems inconsequential and useless.

I pause at the tree line and He'rox stops walking at the same time.

He's perfect again. The blood I was sure stained his chest has disappeared.

He doesn't move to catch up with me and I frown slightly before turning and pushing into the tree line. Leaves and twigs crunch underfoot as I walk, the only sound in this silent expanse. Glancing behind me once more, those ice-cold eyes meet mine as if he hasn't taken his gaze from me the entire time, and a delicious shiver moves like a lance through me.

I grab hold of it and snap it in two immediately at the same time that I notice He'rox slows his pace slightly, keeping the distance between us.

I frown again but say nothing as I turn and continue making my way through the forest. Here in the middle of the thick, the little light of morning that had begun to lighten the darkness seems lost. I stumble for a few hundred meters, hoping I'm going the right way until I give up and get my flashlight from my pack. Powering it on, I keep going, the cloying vines and low-hanging branches brushing against my skin like ghostly fingers. Any sense of comfort I'd felt on my journey here is gone.

There's been the thrill and anticipation, anxiety and a bit of dread, around what we'd discover. Now all that's been replaced by a lingering sense of unease.

But I keep moving forward, flashlight beam dancing ahead of us. Every time I stop and glance behind me, He'rox stays a few paces at my back. The entire time he remains there, never walking at my side or even before me as he had before.

It's obvious it's on purpose.

Every time I look back, shining the light his way, just to ensure he's there, those predatory eyes are locked on to me like I'm a target. He's staying away from me, yet close enough to ensure I know he's still there.

I don't dare break the silence to ask why.

But even though I know he's behind me, his presence greeting me every time I glance over my shoulder, once I face forward again, the darkness and stillness around me swallow me whole. He'rox makes no sound. Almost as if he isn't there, and I'm slowly beginning to wonder if he's part of my imagination.

Am I still in my bunker, slowly going insane? Is this all really happening? The mass of pulsing veins embedding themselves in the earth beneath my feet? The zombified deer that tried to kill me. And him. The alien that I was mad enough to kiss.

I don't fucking know anymore.

The morning light is slowly creeping in, lightening underneath the canopy, but I keep my flashlight on, deciding to let it guide me for a few more minutes. And with good reason too. Without it, I might have missed the massive log that was in my way.

Head down, I clamber over it and just on the other side, as soon as I lift my head and my light, I'm faced with two sets of eyes as wide as my own.

The man squints, raising his hand against the light and I'm knocked back into my senses.

People.

I never expected to meet anyone out here.

Scrambling with my flashlight, it almost slips from my fingers as I flip the switch and the light dies.

"Sorry," I start. "I didn't see you there."

It's a man and a woman. A couple, it seems, based on the way she quickly grabs on to his arm. There's hesitancy in her gaze. Suspicion in her narrowed eyes.

They're wearing packs like I am. The only difference is that theirs seems overburdened, as if they're carrying their entire lives on their backs. And probably they are.

"You shouldn't walk around with a light like that." The man jerks his chin at my flashlight. "May draw the wrong attention."

I flash him a small smile and nod.

His gaze jerks behind me and I stiffen. Shit. He'rox.

"You alone?"

His question makes my eyebrows want to shoot upward, but I manage to keep my face schooled. Years of having to control my reaction at stomach churning events have finally come in handy.

I smile again, glancing over my shoulder to see...*no-one there*. My eyebrows furrow slightly before I turn to face the people again, the corners of my eyes crinkling with friendliness I don't feel.

And shouldn't I feel friendliness?

I force a smile at the couple in front of me, hoping it hides the unease settling in my gut. "Yes, I'm traveling alone."

"Looks like you're heading away from that place," he says.

I tilt my head slightly, gaze sliding to the female at his side who hasn't said a word yet, before moving back to him.

"Place?"

"Haven't you heard of it?" He tilts his chin, looking down the line of his nose.

I'm not imagining the tension. Or maybe, it's just a result of everything I've encountered since I left my bunker. Maybe I'm imagining what's not there because the reality of everything I've seen is too hard to believe.

"Heard of what?" My gaze slides to the woman again and lingers. She doesn't even blink.

They're both dressed in worn clothing. Brown from days of use, tattered in some places. But they both look fed, and most of all, they're alive. Which means they've been surviving fine.

They exchange a glance, suspicion lingering in their eyes. They don't trust me. Heck, I don't trust them either. But, I can't really blame them. I'm in relatively clean clothes. I don't look haggard or drawn. I'm traveling "alone", and my pack is small and light compared to theirs. I don't look like I've been living it too rough.

"That place," the man continues, gaze piercing me, noticing my every movement. "Unity. The new city."

The only thing I reveal is my eyebrows rising. Should I say yes or no?

"A city?" I say instead.

The man makes a sound in his throat as to the affirmative.

"Which way is it?" My gaze bounces between man and woman once more. She's still staring at me as if I'm not human like she is, and the man's eyes narrow slowly.

"You don't want to go there," he says. "It's not what it seems." He jerks his chin at the woman at his side and I see her jaws clench before she reaches into the pocket of her overalls and pulls out a crumpled piece of paper. She throws it at me and it lands about a foot away from my feet.

I know what it is even before crouching to pick it up, eyes on both of them as I do. It's a flyer for Unity. One just like the one I found a few miles away from my bunker.

I open the crumpled piece of paper anyway, schooling my features as I do, and watching the area through my peripheral vision.

Where the hell did He'rox go? He clearly saw these people leagues before I even became aware of their presence.

"This is..." I begin.

"Some advertisement. They fly over us, dropping them from their ships," he says.

I glance at him. "They?"

"The *aliens*."

I don't let any emotion on my face. But I don't need to, because he continues all on his own.

"Humans are working with them," he says. "Turn it around."

I force a lump down my throat as I turn the paper around and sure enough, there's the image of a Vullan on the back.

The man spits and it hits the ground with such force that my gaze flies back to him. His suspicion of me seems gone now, only to be replaced with derision.

"Only a fool would go to a place like that," he says. For the first time since this whole conversation began, the woman at his side smirks a little.

"You should come with us," he continues. "We've got a camp not too far from here. Many of us there. *Humans.* We're gonna rebuild this world."

I blink at him. "There's a camp?" All I can see is a replay of that deer that came after me. The veins embedded underneath its skin. The network in the cave. The unknown danger lurking all around us. "How many of you?"

"About fifty, last I checked," he replies with a shrug. "Families mostly. We get new folks from time to time. Some are running from Unity, some just trying to survive, like us."

"Fifty," I repeat, my mind racing. That's a small community, enough to share tasks, provide security, a measure of companionship and solace. But it's also enough to draw attention from hostile humans...or worse.

If that unknown danger out there gets to a group of humans so large, it will be disaster. I swallow hard, thoughts racing in my head that I hide from my face, my father's teachings repeating in my head over and over again, the image of that deer overlaying all of it.

"Yeah, and we could always use another set of hands. We've been scavenging for food and supplies but it's not easy out here," he continues. His gaze is calculating, sizing me up. I feel a wave of discomfort under his stare, and I silently wish He'rox were still by my side. Not that he'd even wanted to stand close to me after what happened between us.

I resist the urge to groan.

Fuck. This is all messed up.

"Why are you so far from your camp?" I ask, changing the subject. It strikes me as odd that they'd be out here, alone, without any visible means of self-defense.

The woman's piercing eyes never leave me and the man's brow furrows at the question. "We were headed to Unity, hoping to find someone," he admits. "A family member who went there. Haven't heard from them since."

"And you found...?"

He shakes his head. "Nothing. Even if we get there, there's no telling they'll let us in. The city is a fortress. They don't let anyone in, or out, unless you're part of them." The bitterness in his voice is unmistakable as he shakes his head, chin gesturing to the flyer still in my hand. "And I'm never going to be a part of them. Not when they're working with those things right there."

"Aliens," I say, my gaze falling to the crumpled paper in my hand. The Vullan depicted there stares back at me, looking everything like my companion but not at the same time.

Staring at the picture, I realize now that He'rox's limbs are a little longer than the others. There's the fact that he's white too. His ba'clan having lost their color as if they've been bleached, or maybe not. Maybe they were like that from the start. But then there are also the tentacles that hang at the corners of his mouth.

Thinking about them now, I can almost feel them brushing against me at that moment I'd kissed him.

"Yeah," the man says, a dark laugh in his voice. "Isn't that a kick in the head? After everything, we end up in bed with the very things that ruined our world. But Unity doesn't care about that. They're all about power, control. They'd sell us out to those things if it suited them."

My gaze flicks to his as I swallow back the first words that come to my mouth. That he's mistaken and he's got it all wrong. Still, I can't help but frown at his words.

The world I'd known was already gone when I emerged from my bunker, but when I arrived at Unity and saw the Vullan in person, even I knew they weren't the same beings that came to destroy us. They were different. Apparently, not all of us think so.

"Come with us," the man suddenly says, his gaze intense. "It's not safe out here. Not for someone alone."

I swallow again and glance back over my shoulder, half-expecting to see He'rox hiding behind a tree or something. But there's nothing. Just the forest, the underbrush, the silence.

I force a smile on my face, my decision made. "I appreciate the offer, but I can handle myself. I've got someplace I need to be. I'm also looking for someone."

Understanding dawns in his eyes even though he looks like he wants to argue, but instead, he just nods.

"Come on, Maisie," he says to the woman at his side. "Gotta get these herbs we found to Bert. Kara's probably gotten worse off."

Something tugs inside me and I bite the inside of my lip.

Don't do it, Sophie, you have other things to take care of. The fate of the world hangs in the balance.

But my tongue doesn't always listen to my brain.

"Someone's sick?"

They pause and look back at me, suspicion still in their eyes. "Why do you wanna know?"

Fuck me. "I'm a doctor." The words tumble from my mouth before I can stop them.

Well, I did go to med school. Passed all the tests. Didn't need it for epidemiology but tell that to a father who spent his life trying to cure the world's most dangerous diseases.

They glance at each other and it's clear the woman, Maisie, doesn't want me to come along with them. They share a look, a battle of wills, a silent argument before the man gestures with his head. "Come on, we might need your help."

Maisie narrows her eyes, a clear sign of disapproval. But she doesn't contradict him. Instead, she merely turns and begins to walk away, the clear expectation being that I'll follow.

And, after a moment's hesitation, I do, only a glance at my back and the nothingness still there.

As if I'd been walking all this time on my own.

CHAPTER THIRTEEN

SOPHIE

The walk to their camp is quiet and tense. I try to make small talk, but Maisie's icy demeanor discourages me, and the man, though not unkind, seems preoccupied with his thoughts. He keeps watch as we move through the undergrowth and more than once I see his arm move to something at his waist, hiding underneath his loose flannel.

A weapon. Gun most likely.

I keep watch too. Every little sound making me turn my head, hoping to see He'rox still trailing us, scared to see another one of those deer. But no matter how many times I turn, eyes searching through the bushes behind us, I never see him.

He...left me?

I don't know why I can't believe it. After everything that's transpired between us. Everything he told me.

Was this why he was lagging behind? Did he take the first chance he could get to ditch me?

I swallow hard as we walk, unable to shake the feeling of being utterly alone. Even with two strangers as company as they lead me to their camp, without He'rox's presence, I feel exposed. Vulnerable.

This is unlike me, and I realize now how I'd leaned on the fact that he was so utterly otherworldly, so strong, that I'd allowed myself to relax as we'd made our way out here. Not even the gun tucked tightly against my skin gives me the same assurance.

He'rox was the one constant in all of this. My guide in this strange new world I've found myself in since leaving my bunker. And now he's gone. Vanished without a word or warning.

And just like his rejection, it sends an ache that shoots deep, landing like a stone in my gut. I don't know where he's gone or why he left. And I have little time to ponder it as we push through a final line of bushes and their camp comes into view.

By the time we reach the camp, it's mid-morning. The sun is high in the sky, its light shining down through the canopy. The camp is in the center of the forest, melding in among the trees. It's larger than I expected. A mix of makeshift tents and semi-permanent structures, all arranged in a loose circle. The center is dominated by a small fire pit, currently lit and providing a warm glow.

People mill about, going through the motions of daily life. But there is one stark difference here than when I stepped on the grounds of Unity.

A few heads turn as we approach, expressions ranging from curiosity to wariness. A few people greet the man and Maisie, their voices just above a whisper. The atmosphere is tense, like a string pulled taut, ready to snap.

No children play here. No people laugh as they make jokes. There's a somberness that weighs heavily on the air like an anvil about to drop.

"Who's she?" a woman asks as we pass her.

"She says she's a doctor," the man replies. "She might be able to help Kara."

A few other people glance up as we enter the camp, suspicion and curiosity in their gazes. Clearly, strangers are not frequent visitors here. But the man leads me through without pause, heading for one of the larger tents near the center of camp.

"Bert!" he calls out as we approach. "Bert, get out here. I brought help."

An older man emerges from the tent, worn ball cap shielding his eyes. His gaze passes over me with a frown before settling on my companions. "Where'd she come from?"

"Ran into her in the forest," the man says. "Says she's a doctor."

Bert's gaze swings back to me, narrowing. "A doctor?"

I offer him a small smile. "Medically trained, yes."

"I'm Bert," the man gestures to himself. "Me, Nathan, and Maisie here, we run this place." His tone makes it clear I'm being assessed. Judged on whether I can be trusted.

"Sophie," I say, extending a hand.

Bert eyes it for a moment before grasping it in a firm shake. His palm is rough and calloused. A working man's hand.

"So Nathan says Kara's taken ill?" I glance behind him but I can't see inside the tent.

Bert nods glancing at Nathan before reaching to his back, scratching an itch he doesn't quite seem to be able to reach. "Been sick for days. Fever, chills. Thought we had her on the mend but she's gotten worse."

He tries to scratch that itch again and I notice the beads of sweat on his brow.

It isn't hot out here. As a matter of fact, the morning is cool. Under the canopy, the sun's rays don't penetrate the camp.

"Anybody else sick?" I ask, turning my gaze to the rest of the camp. Almost all their eyes are on me and someone coughs.

Not creepy. Not creepy at all.

It's mostly women, a few older men. Maybe about ten people.

I glance at Nathan but his attention's on Bert. I thought he'd said they had about fifty people...

"A few people have got the flu. Nothing to worry about. No one's as bad as Kara," he says.

The three precede me inside the tent and I take one more look behind me, eyes scanning the group of people watching us before I follow them inside. There's hardly anything inside the tent, not that I expected much. There's a small bowl of water that sits beside the mass of blankets on the floor.

I don't immediately see the woman, not until I step farther into the tent and pause next to Nathan and the other two who have stopped, somber gazes fixated on the blankets.

And then I see it. Peeking out from under the blankets, there's an arm so skinny it's almost completely skeletal.

My brow dives as I move into action without thinking. My hand's on my pack as I swing it across my shoulder. I'm about to open the zip when a heavy hand stops my own.

Ice prickles up my arm and my gaze darts to the hand, Bert's hand, the air stopping in my lungs. His hand is freezing, even though he's sweating like he has a fever. But that's not what's caused me to pause. What's set my heart into a staggering pace is what I see on his hand, peeking just underneath the cuff of his shirt.

Bert pulls his arm back and I pretend I didn't just see the dark network of veins spreading along his arm. Pretend I don't see a thing as I give him a stiff smile.

"Just getting my tools," I say to him and he glances at Nathan, who gives him a curt nod.

A lump forms in my throat as I take out a fresh pair of gloves and slip them over my fingers, all the while aware of the three people whose attention has switched solely to me.

"How long has she been sick?"

The woman, Kara, hasn't moved since we entered the room, and judging by the health of her arm, I don't have much hope that when I pull back the covers she'll even be there. Alive.

"F-few weeks," Bert answers, reaching back once again to scratch that itch that he isn't able to reach.

I nod, jaw clenching as I crouch. The other three step back and the hairs along the back of my neck stand on end.

Whatever's going on here, it's clear it's no simple flu.

And I think they already know that.

But like with everything in my life, I face this with the same blind bravery my father instilled in me. James Jericho Seltzer would turn in his grave if he saw me bending to fear. So I reach forward, and I pull the covers away.

CHAPTER FOURTEEN

SOPHIE

The first thing I hear is a screech before there's a flurry of movement.

I stagger back, hand on my gun and eyes wide as the creature before me snaps and snarls, bloodshot eyes locked on to me and mouth snapping like a dog gone mad with rabies.

This...is no woman. Not anymore. Whatever happened to the Kara they knew is gone. Stripped of everything, including her humanity.

Her eyes are wild as she snaps and tries to come after me once more, only the rope binding her other arm and tied to something that keeps her in that spot stops her from fulfilling her sole purpose—which is to sink her teeth into my skin.

She's emaciated. Far thinner than I've ever seen a human being go to and still survive. I've seen malnutrition, when resources are scarce and people are left with skin hugging their bones too tightly, eyes too large in gaunt faces. I've seen cholera, where healthy people turn into hollow shells in a matter of days. I've seen what things like cancer and autoimmune diseases can do and through my training,

I've been taught to approach each case with a level of detachment, to see the disease and not the person it was killing. But it isn't always easy.

For although Kara is far gone...I can still see the person she once was.

Her clothes hang off her emaciated frame, torn and filthy. Bones protrude sharply where once there was softness. Deep scratches mar what little skin remains uncovered, proof of her struggle to escape this cage.

But it is her eyes that strike me most forcibly. Dull and lifeless. Though her body jerks and twitches, there is no thought or recognition behind that vacant, bloodshot stare. Once they would have held life, emotion, thought. Now they are dim, hollow sockets.

And I've seen those same eyes before.

Just last night.

In that deer.

I kneel in front of her, voice measured and even, hoping beyond hope that there's a light in the darkness here. "Kara..."

On every spot of her skin I can see, thick dark veins run deep like a network of tattoos embedded underneath her skin.

Like the deer. Like the woman floating in that cylinder on He'rox's ship. Like that chamber in the cave. That hole in the forest.

It's all connected.

"Kara," I say again. For despite my father's morose warnings, I've never actually given up hope. My whole point of becoming an epidemiologist was so I could prove him wrong.

If we can understand the disease, then we can beat it. And if we can beat it, then we win.

For a moment I imagine I see a spark of awareness in the woman's eyes, but just as quickly it fades.

With a snarl, she lunges forward, jaws snapping inches from my face. I fall back with a start, heart pounding.

"How long has she had these symptoms?" My gaze snaps to Bert, noting the increased sweat on his brow. He's infected too. Whether the others realize, that's unclear, but all I know is I have to be careful.

Whatever this is, it's transmissible to humans. And if it's transmissible to humans, that means the longer I take to figure out what it is, I'm in danger. If it's airborne, I'm already fucked.

"Started with the fever 'bout a week ago," he says. "Thought it was just a bug at first. But she got worse each day. The snarling. The shakes. We've been trying to break her fever but nothing's worked."

I stare at him before my gaze shifts to Nathan and Maisie. They can't really think this is just a fever. They see the dark veins all across her body, don't they? They see the fact that she's obviously gone out of her mind.

I nod before turning my attention back to Bert, keeping my voice low. "This looks like Rahzer's fever. Has anyone else been showing symptoms?"

His eyes widen. "No, just her. You sure? Never heard of that one before."

I nod, standing and putting some distance between me and the still-snarling woman. Despite being emaciated, she moves as if she has the strength of a well-fed male. When Bert talks, her attention turns to the other three in the room and she snarls at them too.

So it's not because I'm a stranger.

I make note of that before meeting the other's gazes, building on this fake disease I've just made up. I nod. "The rash, fever, swollen tonsils. It's textbook. How long since the outbreak?"

"There hasn't been an outbreak," Bert says, shaking his head. "How soon until she gets better?"

My gaze slides back to Kara. "That depends," I say.

"On what?" It's Nathan that speaks this time and I glance at Maisie before answering. Can she even speak? She hasn't said a word since I've met her.

"You said there were about fifty people here." I meet Nathan's gaze. "If there are others with the flu, it will just keep reinfecting the whole group. But I don't see fifty people outside."

Nathan stiffens slightly, jaw ticking slightly as Maisie sends her gaze to him.

"We're fighting a war, love," Bert says.

"A war?" My gaze bounces between the three. "The war has ended. We've been saved."

Bert scoffs. "You've been listening to those brutes' propaganda, have you?" He takes a few steps toward me, sidestepping the snarling woman reaching for his legs as he passes her, and levels me with his gaze. "Let me tell you something. There's things out there you couldn't even imagine. Horrible things. And they're here to take everything we have and kill us all. You better wise up and join the resistance while you've still got blood running in those veins."

My gaze darts back at the couple standing on the other side of the tent. "Resistance?"

"Around thirty-five of our strongest have gone to defend what's ours," Nathan says. "We aren't letting 'em win."

I shake my head, closing my eyes briefly as I try to understand just what the hell they're saying. "Gone? Gone where?"

Nathan grins at me, but his smile is filled with worms and spiders that skitter down my spine, telling me I shouldn't trust him or this place. As if the snarling woman on the floor wasn't warning enough.

"Don't tell me you've forgotten already, sweetheart," he says. "They've gone to Unity. They've gone to kill those fuckers."

A chill goes down my spine.

Over thirty most-likely infested individuals are headed to the one place on this planet where I know there's some hope.

I have to return to Unity.

I have to warn them.

Turning, Bert hazards lifting a blanket and throwing it over Kara, who settles down and stops snarling as if we're no longer in the room.

"She doesn't attack if she can't see you..."

"The darkness calms her," he says.

I nod, flashing a smile I hope is genuine in Nathan and Maisie's direction. "I'm glad I found you all," I say. And I mean it. Because now I understand what's happening here. It's all coming together now.

Nathan smiles, eyes skating down my frame. "Likewise."

I resist the urge to barf.

Well, look at you now, Sophie. The alien turns you on more than the human male who's obviously checking you out.

Adjusting my pack on my back, I head toward the exit. "You need to quarantine this tent. No one in or out. Rahzer's is highly contagious. It may already be spreading through the camp."

Bert reaches for me, hand closing around my arm in a way that makes me cringe, jaw clenching. "What do we need to get rid of it?"

"It will take a while for me to figure out the dosage of…" I begin, but his smile stops the words on my lips.

"Well, good thing Nathan found you, huh? You'll have all the time in the world while you stay here. With us."

My gaze flies to Nathan who is looking at me with an air of possession that I don't miss, even as his arms encircle Maisie and she melts against him.

They're not going to let me just walk away from here.

I have to be smart.

I nod at Bert. "Sure thing."

CHAPTER FIFTEEN

HE'ROX

Soh'fee has disappeared from view and my ba'clan *hate* it.

Getting used to *feeling* them again has come as a surprise. And I know it's all because of her.

Keeping to the tops of the trees, I scan the small settlement below.

Hyu'mans are so easily tracked. Hunted. I have been within their presence for so long, watching their every move, and none have become wiser.

But it is not only these hyu'mans' lack of awareness that works in my favor.

I move from my perch in the tree high above the center of the camp, climbing higher to improve my vantage point.

The place reeks of death and illness.

These hyu'mans will all die soon. They are rotting from within.

And Soh'fee is in the midst of them.

The moment before she met the male and female in the woods, I camouflaged. I saw the uncertainty, the confusion in her eyes when she turned and looked right at me, but couldn't see me standing right there, looking back at her.

That male and female mean to use her. This camp reeks of more than just disease and death. There is an underlying current of malice here. Selfishness. They will try to keep Soh'fee here. Use her for some purpose.

I will not allow that.

Dropping silently to the ground, I move through the camp unseen. The stench this low is overpowering. Deep-seated fear mixed in with decay.

This entity that plagues my being is corroding theirs. Tainting them. Putrefying them from the inside out.

It is difficult to maintain my camouflage. All I want to do is cleanse the area of the necrosis. But the ailment affecting these hyu'mans is not like the one affecting the female who floats in silence in my lab. It has evolved.

But I knew that already.

I saw the effect right before my eyes in the hooved creature that tried to sink its teeth into Soh'fee.

I cannot stop the growl that goes through me, and a female sitting close by turns, widened eyes pointed in my direction. She stares right at me, hand moving to a weapon by her side, before she returns her attention somewhere else.

I can already see the corrosion spreading in the veins along her collarbone, rising up her throat to reach her ears. Not enough for Soh'fee to notice. Not yet.

But Soh'fee is smart. If she hasn't yet realized something is wrong in this place, she will do so soon.

Tilting my head, I catch her scent. I'd decided on distance. I must break that vow now. They've taken her to one of the large tents at the center of the camp. The flaps are closed, but that poses no obstacle. I move across the damp ground, wind barely catching my scent before I slip inside, claws emerging as my ba'clan rise at my back.

Soh'fee stands with her back to the entrance, shoulders tense.

"Sure thing," she says in response to something I already missed.

The scent in here is worse than that on the outside. Something has been festering in here. Something that needs purging. And I see what it is just a moment later.

There in the center of the floor. The source of the spoil.

Hyu'man judging by the visible limb. Skeletal. Near death.

And the male before Soh'fee. My gaze snaps to him. He is standing too close. Instilling fear and exerting control. The male's hand rests on Soh'fee's arm, his grip too tight.

A low growl rumbles in my throat and Soh'fee's head jerks up. She stares right at me, pale eyes widening slightly, the intelligence behind them moving like clockwork. And though she cannot see me, I can tell the moment she realizes the sound must have come from me. Her free arm reaches back, covertly reaching out to me, and that soft palm presses against the ridges leading down to my pelvis.

My sazi pulses in its sack and I almost reveal myself.

Another reason to keep distance from this female.

She touches me...and I had not known her touch would be my weakness.

Soh'fee's pulse quickens, the sweet scent of her fear flooding through me mixed in with her relief. She does not pull away from the male's grasp. To do so now would rouse suspicion. But she lifts her chin, squaring her shoulders, showing me she still has fight left.

Brave Soh'fee.

"Of course, I'll stay," she says, eyes meeting the male's. He bares his teeth, hand loosening from her arm as he reaches back to scratch some itch.

There is a mass of nerves at his back. Populating, the veins digging deeper. He is a live rotting carcass. A paradox. Something that should not be.

All of these hyu'mans are.

We must leave at once.

"I have some tests I need to perform so I can help, um, Kara."

Soh'fee's throat moves as she swallows hard. "You won't mind if I mingle with some of the others out there, will you?"

The male looks back at the other two hyu'mans standing in the tent before jerking his shoulders. "Sure, whatever you need, doc."

His toothy grin makes me clench my claws. Otherwise, I would have closed them around his neck and ended his existence right here.

He intends to take my Soh'fee. I can scent his arousal. It is enough to make me move closer to her, pressing my frame into her back.

She inhales deeply, chest rising and falling with the contact. But she does well to not reveal my presence. Not yet.

There is something she needs to do. I can tell.

Soh'fee pastes a smile on her face before turning and exiting the tent. I don't immediately follow. Instead, my gaze falls on the males in my presence, lingering for a moment.

When this ends, they will be the first I kill. My decision is made as the one that had held on to Soh'fee runs a blackened tongue over his lips.

Especially this one. I will make him bleed.

Outside the tent, I spot Soh'fee heading to one side of the camp, far from the others. She glances behind her, eyes on the tent before she looks around.

Searching for me?

As I move closer, I hear her hushed whisper. "He'rox?"

My name. She has always called me by my name. Not the other designations I've been awarded, but the name my mor gave me. To her, I am not her medic. I am simply He'rox.

"Did I imagine it?" she whispers, gaze darting to the camp and the group of hyu'mans watching her there.

They do not know it yet. Don't understand it. And Soh'fee does not yet realize. That their gazes are not just of interest and suspicion. Caution and fear. But there is something primal there. Slowly overrunning their basic functions.

They are looking at her because she is the only one here whose blood is still pure.

And they want to taste it.

I will rend their flesh from bone before I let that happen.

"Fuck. I'm lost in the middle of nowhere and, to make things worse, I'm hallucinating." Her voice takes me back to the present. I stand beside her, watching as she paces before pretending to crouch and search through the bushes for herbs. She's pretending to work. "Should have stayed in my fucking bunker. Then the world could end and I could die alone, but in peace." She gulps as she rips a weed from the ground, turning to glance over her shoulder. I can see the shiver that goes through her shoulders as her gaze catches on the hyu'mans watching her. Salivating over her and not aware of it. Yet. "Who the fuck am I kidding? Given the chance, I'd do this again. Because I don't know when to fucking stop. *Shit*."

I crouch by her side, camouflage still intact. "Because you are curious," I saw low. "And brave."

Soh'fee rears back, falling on her ass as her eyes widen.

She recovers quickly, glancing behind her and forcing a laugh. "Ha, thought I saw a mouse."

The people don't respond and Soh'fee's lips tighten before she rights herself and crouches again.

"How the fuck are you doing that?" she whispers.

I lean closer to her. I can't help it.

Her scent is the only thing keeping me from turning and eradicating the ill behind us.

"Do what?" I ask, mouth brushing against her neck.

She stiffens but does not pull away. Little hairs rise along her nape as her breath quickens.

I am taking liberties here when I'd decided on distance. When being so close to her makes me behave so unexpectedly. She is a part of the equation I have not yet solved and for that reason, I should be more vigilant.

And yet…

Her skin is so sweet, I am tempted to taste it. Will it taste as good as her lips?

"He'rox," she breathes.

Wrong word to say. Not my name. Not when I am in this state. I growl against her neck and her breath hitches.

I want to hunt. I want to kill.

And I want to claim. Her.

Right now.

"Y-you're invisible."

"I am cloaked."

She releases a slow breath. "You're…incredible."

"Mmm," I growl. Something about being here like this. Concealed and at her back is making…things occur inside me. "Compliments."

Soh'fee giggles before stopping herself. She squeezes her eyes tight before schooling her features. "I thought you left me."

"I would do no such thing."

"You've been walking far behind me the entire time."

"For your own safety. I am—"

She nods. "Right. Because you're my enemy." She turns her head slightly, gaze focused on where I crouch. "Then why don't I feel threatened when you're so close? Like now."

My ba'clan wave and a thrill goes through me.

"This is no experiment, Soh'fee." She blinks my way, taking my words in. "There are no defined parameters."

"I could get hurt," she whispers.

She has answered correctly. I am not to be trusted. I do not trust myself. And when I don't reply she nods and a small, sad smile graces her beautiful face.

"Sometimes, to achieve anything, you have to sacrifice."

I fall into myself.

There is no way she knows.

No way she can understand.

"Hey, who're you talking to?"

I turn, a growl rising in my chest immediately, as the corroded male appears at our back.

CHAPTER SIXTEEN

HE'ROX

Soh'fee stiffens, pulse quickening as she slowly turns to face the male.

"Oh, Bert!" she says.

His gaze skates over her, lingering on her throat, and the soft flesh there. When his tongue darts out to wet his lips, I rise.

He cannot see me. Cannot sense me. But he wants what is mine.

I have no claim over Soh'fee. This is madness.

But I have never been quite sane.

She is mine. Whatever the rek that means. My ba'clan know it. I am not a fool to not comprehend why they have woken up after so long of being silent. Using their last energy reserves to reach out. To survive.

Soh'fee is *mine*.

The word echoes in my mind, ba'clan raging. I clench my claws to keep from attacking the male before us. From tearing into his flesh and spilling his tainted blood.

Soh'fee blinks up at the male. Bert, his name is, and I detest that he is causing her eyes to go wide with uncertainty. Her knuckles are white where they grip the plants in her hands. "I—I was just talking to myself. I do that while working."

The male grins, taking a step closer. "All alone out here. That's not safe." Another step. "You should come back to camp. We'll keep you protected."

Soh'fee shakes her head. "I'm fine. Just collecting some herbs for—"

"You've collected enough." His smile slips, impatience clear. He reaches for her arm. "Come."

A snarl rumbles in my chest as I move to stand between them. Though he cannot see me, the male pauses. His dull eyes narrow as his head tilts, like an animal trying to catch an elusive scent.

Soh'fee's breath catches and I urge her back with a brush of my claw against her chest. My ba'clan react at the contact. Wanting to go to her yet not having the power or energy to do so. We both know why I have been able to camouflage for this long. Why I've been able to power such an energy-sucking part of myself, and they are not happy.

They wish to survive against the part of me that is slowly growing stronger.

But even as they roil at my back, stretching to get to Soh'fee, in its pouch my sazi grows impatient. It swells and bunches, fighting to extrude. To take her. To claim her. Even in the midst of this danger before us.

Because my senses are clouded.

Opening myself to that conduit...I am no longer sure what is Vullan instinct and what is simply a need to control. To compromise. To take.

At my back, Soh'fee takes a hesitant step away from the male, then another. She is smarter than I think. She may not have instincts to scent the heightened danger here, but she somehow feels it. She watches me though she cannot see me. Trusting that I am here. Protecting her.

The male's jaw clenches. "What's wrong? Why are you moving

away?" He takes another step, hand outstretched, and slams into an invisible barrier. Me.

A growl slips past his lips at the contact.

Hello. Catalyst.

The evil that lurks within him has made contact with its natural enemy. The part of me that is still pure. My Vullan blood. And it will know now it is not safe here.

As I expect, right before us, the male begins to change. The process within him catalyzed. Accelerated. He is morphing.

The veins along his neck pulse, dark threads spreading into his face. His pupils dilate until his eyes are nearly black, fixated on Soh'fee. The desire to feed, to corrupt, grows stronger within him with each passing second.

"Bert?" The other two hyu'mans that had been inside the tent step out. One female, one male. The male calls out to his friend, eyes widening when Bert turns and snarls his way.

"Fuck," he curses.

"Stay back!" Soh'fee says. She pulls her weapon from where she'd had it hidden.

No need. I am here. I will take care of this for her.

"Bert?" she calls.

And this is why she is special.

Despite the odds before her, the male slowly morphing into a nightmare, Sophie stands and calls in hope.

Surely, everything within her being is telling her she should run. Abandon him. Save herself.

"Bert, can you hear me?"

"What the fuck have you done to him? He was fine just a second ago!" The male by the tent releases the female he was holding. But his gaze isn't on Soh'fee, even though his words are directed at her. His gaze is on his counterpart.

There is no hope in his eyes. Only fear.

Fear for himself.

And that makes him...*despicable*.

"Nathan, tell me the truth." Soh'fee's voice is steady as she lifts her weapon and levels it at Bert. "What's really going on here?"

The brute takes a step back, thrusting away the female who reaches for him. For a moment, pain shoots through her gaze before she stiffens. And all around the camp, one by one, the remaining humans stand, all focused on the man backing away. He reaches back, trying to scratch some itch he cannot reach as he continues to retreat.

My senses twinge, but I can't take my gaze from the more pressing threat. The male before us, who is now snarling so much, he froths at the lips.

"Nathan!" Soh'fee calls. "Where the hell do you think you're going?!" Fire shoots in those pale eyes and pride fills me. This is the female my ba'clan have chosen. And they chose well. "What the fuck is happening here?!"

But her attention too is pulled from the events unfolding in the background as the male before us lunges for her.

He slams into me again, confusion spreading across his face for but a second. Because he has gone mindless. Only one thing on his focus. Capture Soh'fee. Submit her.

He will die before he does.

I have seen something like this before. In my experiments. Way back on Edooria. Though, they did not produce the same results. There are different variables here. Possibly a similar outcome.

This male's mind has been altered. His physiology too.

The darkened veins have overtaken his own, pumping the corrosion deep into his tissues. His skin no longer has that rosy color of human blood, but is now pale and dead. Before our eyes, he completed the change.

He slams into my barrier again, claws emerging from his fingernails. "Give her to me!"

Soh'fee cocks her weapon. "Fat chance." Her brow furrows. "He'rox, move. I don't want to shoot you."

Something rumbles in my chest.

She cares for me.

The male screeches, throwing himself at me again and again, mad in his quest to get to her. To taste her untainted blood. His hunger will never be sated. There is only one way to end this.

I drop my camouflage.

For a moment, some of his humanity returns. Black eyes widen at the sight of me. But it is only a moment.

"Hello," I say, remembering one of Soh'fee's first lessons to me.

A low groan escapes him. Not fear, but darker want. He recognizes me as a threat to his purpose, an obstacle in his way. With a snarling hiss, he rushes at me.

His claws scrape against my armor and my ba'clan rear up. He is no match for me.

With a roar, I grasp him by the neck, lifting him from the ground. He still tries to get at me and, through the corner of my eye, I see Soh'fee.

I can sense the tension in the camp. Something is changing that I have not the resources to investigate. I only see the male named Nathan running away and the female he left behind standing there as if caught in a decision and she doesn't know what to choose.

Palms fist at her side as she watches her mate run away, leaving her there defenseless.

Dishonorable male.

"I must kill this one," I say, pulling my attention back to the infested male in my grip. That part of him that relates to me calls out, seeking survival.

But something greater calls me. And she is standing by my side.

"He must die," I repeat. Maybe for those cells warring within me. Maybe so Soh'fee can understand I will slay one of her kind right before her eyes.

Soh'fee shakes her head even as she agrees with me. "I agree, but we shouldn't. We need to test this...whatever it is."

At the sound of her voice, the male's gaze snaps to her. Both of his hands grip on to my arm, claws trying to dig deep to no avail as his legs flail. But even as my wrist tightens at his throat, cutting off his air supply, he does not pull his focus back to me.

And then. The unexpected.

They rip from his back. Veiny black tentacles that tear his garments apart as they shoot through the air and curve, heading straight for Soh'fee.

"What the—" Her weapon fires—a deafening sound that sends my ba'clan awry—and I feel the heat of the bullet as it skims past me, but I'm already moving.

Launching myself away from us, I slam the male into a nearby tree. His head lolls back for a moment before his consciousness returns and one of those veins shoots straight at my head. I grab it, claw sinking into its fleshy exterior as I snap it in two. Blood sprays all around us, the stench of it filling my nostrils.

But this isn't like Soh'fee's pure blood. This is different.

Wrong.

It sends my ba'clan into a frenzy and they fight to gather enough strength to form into blades so I can cut this abomination down.

They cannot.

And so I pull my fist back, prepared to pummel this male into nothingness when the deafening boom of Soh'fee's weapon sounds again, this time, far too close.

Bert's head blows up in an explosion of blood and matter.

I turn, Soh'fee's wide eyes on the space where the male's head once was, as I release the body and it falls to the ground.

A shudder goes through her and I move toward her, the urge to comfort her rising strongly within me, even as the sounds within the camp finally pierce my consciousness.

Groaning and echoes of pain.

Something makes us both pause.

Gazes locked, the unsaid passes between us.

This is just the start.

Turning together, Soh'fee takes a step back, shoulder brushing against my chest as we face the scene evolving before us.

CHAPTER SEVENTEEN

SOPHIE

I don't know what to say. I don't know what to think. All I know is that I clutch my gun between my fingers, holding on to it as if it will give me life. Because in the next few moments, that might just be the case. Life or death may come right down to how good of a shot I am, because the scene in front of me...

I take a step back, He'rox like a rock when I bump into him.

Before us, the people who'd been sitting in the camp, watching me with eyes that were too cold, too unfriendly for me to ever feel comfortable, have now turned to face us.

They must have seen what evolved. They must have seen Bert transform into something dark. Insipid. Not entirely of this world.

But they aren't running, screaming for their lives.

Instead, they're standing one by one, all watching us, unmoving in a way that is so completely inhuman that I take another step back, pressing into He'rox as I swallow a lump that's risen in my throat. The pistol trembles in my hand and I hate the fact that fear's shooting so strongly through me, it's making it hard to breathe.

Because right before me, I see the people watching us changing.

Those veins that seemed to pulse and grow, completely overtaking Bert, seem to be growing underneath their skin, too.

"They're all infected," I whisper, eyes flicking from one to another. "Bert said it's been a few weeks."

My heart hammers as there's movement in my peripheral vision. Two or three of the camp people walk slowly toward us from far to my right.

"What do you hypothesize, scientist?" my companion says.

I glance up at He'rox. He seems more focused on me than anything else around us, despite that my heart's hammering in my chest, anxiety curling my gut, as everything within me screams that we're in danger.

He's plastered with Bert's blood, but it doesn't even look like human blood anymore. Too black. Too thick.

But despite all that, I'm frickin' happy to see him here. I thought he'd really gone. Hearing that growl, knowing it was him, had sent something warm and sure right through me.

I gulp, turning my attention back to the slowly advancing people. "Whatever this is, it doesn't appear to be airborne." I'd take another step back, but He'rox is rigid, facing the danger before us. "No coughing, sneezing or other airborne transmission modes that would spread an infection."

"And..." He'rox presses. Something tells me he's already figured this out but wants me to do so myself.

"And..." I continue, back pressing into his chest. "Not bacterial or viral. Bert's transformation was too quick."

He'rox makes a sound in his throat as if he agrees.

"Not fungal," I continue, watching as two more people appear to our far left. "Fungal infections don't usually cause such severe symptoms."

He'rox makes that same sound in his chest and it vibrates against my back. He feels so strong behind me. Unmoving.

I take a deep breath.

"Could be prions..."

"Hmm," He'rox says, his nonchalance the only thing that's keeping me calm.

"They're, um, misfolded versions of normal cellular proteins. But..."

"But what, little light?"

"That's not what this is." I'm not supposed to make declarations such as that without proper evidence. But this has nothing to do with my study of science or past lab work I've done. This is just my gut.

"Humans don't act like this." Even as I say the words, the change continues in the people before me. I can see the veins crawling up their necks, getting darker the paler their skin gets, as if they're being sucked dry from the inside out. And their eyes...the hollow darkness of their eyes.

"It's parasitic," I say, back pressing even harder into He'rox. "Those veins...they're parasitic. Just like that woman back in your ship. She's infected. You've healed her but she doesn't wake because you haven't removed those veins from her back."

"If I do—"

"She will die."

I sense he tilts his head. "Affirmative."

I take another deep breath, leveling my gun at a male who is at the front of the group. He looks right past the weapon, almost as if it isn't there.

"These people," I say, forcing my breaths to steady. "They aren't human anymore, are they."

Not a question, a statement, and for a moment, I don't expect He'rox to respond.

"Their humanity," he finally says, "has been destroyed from within." Hearing him say it, the finality of it, sends a wave of hopelessness through me. "They are simply vessels now."

I nod, looking down the barrel of my gun straight at the male in front. If I fire, it will go right through the center of his head.

He doesn't seem to care. Advancing anyway.

"Stop," I warn him. "Don't come any closer."

He opens his mouth to snarl at me, eyes wide with something wild and dangerous, mouth filled with thick black fluid that covers his teeth.

"Stop right there!" I shout as he advances still.

He's not going to stop.

He's not going to.

In one sudden movement, he lunges my way and my fingers move automatically. The trigger depresses and his entire body is thrown backward, head first.

Fuck.

My hand trembles as my eyes widen.

That's the second person I've killed in a matter of minutes and my heart hates it. My whole being hates it. Hunting deer is one thing. Cutting down people is another.

But I have to remind myself these aren't people anymore. They've been taken over by another entity much more powerful than themselves. More powerful than any of us.

And I'm given an exact picture of just how much that's true when the man I just shot in the head staggers to his feet. Blood runs down his face from the hole in his head as his gaze locks on me again.

I pull the trigger. No thinking.

Once. Twice. Three times I shoot. The bullets hit him in the chest, throwing him backward, yet he continues as if pushed forward by something bigger than himself. Something that doesn't care about his survival but only what it wants.

"What do they want? I don't know what they want!"

He'rox's steady voice manages to cut through the chaos rising in my mind.

"I do," he says, moving to stand before me. "They want your essence," he says. "Your lifeblood."

My world stops at his words at the same time that he launches himself into the air, taking the approaching male with him.

Something seems to snap then. As if a cord's been broken, the marionettes suddenly given another assignment. As He'rox slams the male into the ground and twists his neck, every single person advancing on us screeches.

The sound is enough to make me slam my hands over my ears at the same time that they charge all at once.

"He'rox! Look out!"

I fire, hitting more than one of them while very aware that I'll be out of bullets soon.

They're going to kill us. But as I use one hand to shoot, running as I reach into my pack, hand digging into the side pocket for a fresh set of bullets, I realize one thing. They're *Corrupted* and they aren't trying to kill *us*.

They're trying to kill *me*.

As they all charge, dark veins making them look like things possessed, the fact hits me like a speeding train. They're after me. And in the background of the fray, as I run and scream He'rox's name as he grabs one of them chasing after me and snaps them in two in a way that should send a shiver down my spine at the fact he can do that, I see something else.

Far in the background, the woman who was traveling with Nathan stands. Watching us.

Unmoving.

CHAPTER EIGHTEEN

SOPHIE

"Aah fuck! Fuck! Shit! FUCK!" A frustrated scream leaves my lips as my gun clicks. Empty. "He'rox! Run!"

I dart through the trees, tempted to drop my pack so I can go faster, as too many footfalls sound behind me. The sounds of their snarling, the bushes being cut down as they run through them, and the terror at my back sends me into survival mode.

My heart's in my throat as I run, praying I don't fall because my life depends on me keeping ahead. Depends on me putting distance between myself and these possessed creatures until I can find a weapon to defend myself.

"Fuck!" I almost fall over a root and I stumble but manage to keep on my feet. "He'rox!" I glance behind me, but I don't see him. I left him behind. I had no choice. If he's hurt...

I'll have to find a way back and find him. I'll have to—

Another glance behind me and terror shoots through me as I see the horde at my back. But something else catches my eyes through the trees. A flash of white. He'rox?

I almost stumble again.

When my father used to tell me about the end of the world, he didn't mention any of this. I don't think he could have imagined it. I don't think he could have actually lived it.

Shit. I'm barely surviving.

The more I run, the more my lungs burn, and the more it feels like my heart is about to spill from my mouth.

I glance behind me again and there it is. That flash of white. Except, it's moving toward me with incredible speed and…

I skid to a halt, heart in my throat as I fish blindly in the pocket at the front of my pack to find a few bullets. My fingers close around three and I take them out, eyes wide, panting as I reload the gun. My hands shake as the final bullet slips in just as one of the Corrupted dashes through the bushes right at me.

Boom!

The gun goes off by mere instinct, but it only slows the woman down. I aim, ready to fire again, when something flashes before me.

A scream pierces from my lips as all I see is white and my world suddenly goes topsy-turvy.

I struggle, fear causing me to fight against whatever's lifting me, for my feet leave the ground as something twists around my midsection, carrying me high above the forest floor.

Another scream leaves my lips as my pack falls and all I have is the gun in my hands. I lift it, ready to shoot whatever it is, when I'm finally steadied enough I can see.

And I freeze.

He'rox holds me tight in his grip…

Only, it's not He'rox anymore. At least, not the He'rox I know.

A long thick tentacle holds me in a firm grip, wrapped around my midsection and lifting me high into the canopy, away from the snarling, hungry Corrupted intent on getting to me.

But even with the danger heading my way, I can't pull my gaze away from the alien who has me in his grasp.

The tentacle holding me feels soft and fleshy, yet, I can't understand how. Because three more tentacles come from that same spot in his back. He stands using two, hardening them enough that they pierce the ground below, while the other free tentacle swerves in the air.

A gasp lodges in my airway as that same tentacle swoops down on an approaching Corrupted, the end piercing right through the male, slicing him in two. I'm frozen, unable to understand what I'm seeing as my gaze flicks back to He'rox's face.

An inhuman, fanged snarl is on his lips and the familiar stoic features gone, replaced by complete fury. Darkened eyes shine with what can only be hatred as he spins, taking out another of the Corrupted heading our way, the tentacle wrapped around me writhing and pulsing as he holds me steadily out of harm's way.

He lifts me higher as one of the Corrupted tried to climb a tree, desperate to reach me. Their mindless focus should send a chill through me, but all I can focus on is him.

Something is telling me this...*change* has nothing to do with his Vullan physiology but everything to do with what I saw back in that cave.

He's a hybrid. Gryken and Vullan? How? When?

Were all the Vullan like this or only him?

Was this what he meant when he said he's my enemy?

A low, guttural noise comes from He'rox as he takes out two of the Corrupted with a single slice of his tentacle and I stare, awed at the fact that it's such an effective weapon. With a flick of the tentacle, he tosses another of the Corrupted back. When another charges through the bushes, he grips them in a vice-like grasp as he is holding me now, the tentacle softening to twist around the female's body before crushing it easily and tossing the shattered remains to the forest floor.

"He'rox..." I whisper.

I don't think he'll hear me. Not from the desperate, bloodcurdling screams of the people attacking us or the sound of his own snarling, but by some miracle, He'rox turns his gaze on me and I see the terror on my face reflected in those dark pits.

I flinch and I swear I hear the rumble of a purr in his chest.

He'rox holds my gaze, and for a moment the fury and violence seem to drain from his features. I see a flicker of the familiar stoicism…and something else I haven't seen in those cold eyes before.

Sorrow.

He turns away, focusing again on the threats around us. The Corrupted seem endless, pouring from the trees with their pale, veiny skin and hungry snarls. I'd thought there were around ten, but some must have been hidden in the tents surrounding the camp.

The thought sends another shudder through me as I grip the tentacle around my waist, leaning into it for support as I stare at the carnage happening around me with eyes filled with disbelief.

He'rox spins, slicing through two more of them with a flick of his tentacle. Black blood sprays, covering the ground and speckling the trees.

A scream bubbles in my throat as one launches himself at the tentacle holding me. He'rox snarls, the sound feral and inhuman, as he swats the Corrupted from the air. The body slams into a tree, the sickening crunch echoing. Yet still, the Corrupted staggers to its feet, bones protruding from its skin, and charges again.

He'rox growls, the rumble vibrating through me, as he lowers himself to his feet, snapping the tentacles he'd been using to stand from the ground. A white blade erupts from his heel, and with a swift kick, he impales the Corrupted through the chest. He tosses the body aside, turning to block two more Corrupted climbing a tree.

I whimper as his grip tightens around me, my ribs creaking under the pressure at the same time that all three remaining tentacles begin to swing, cutting the damned down one by one.

Bile rises in my throat as a Corrupted drags itself forward, intestines spilling from its abdomen, still snarling and grasping upward for me. He'rox crushes its skull under his foot with a sickening squelch.

I squeeze my eyes shut, unable to watch any longer. The sounds are enough, screams and tearing flesh and the thud of bodies hitting the ground. My body trembles in He'rox's grip, breath coming in frantic gasps.

This can't be real. This has to be a nightmare. I'll wake in my bed, locked up safe in my bunker, and this will all have been some terrible dream. But I can't keep my eyes closed for long.

He'rox fights, vicious in his intent, cutting them down with swipes of sharpened tentacles, crushing them underfoot and tearing them apart with his bare hands.

Out of fucking nowhere, one of them launches at him with inhuman speed, bypassing the tentacles to grip He'rox around the neck.

"He'rox!" I scream, struggling against his unwavering grip. He looks up at me at the same time that Corrupted sinks its teeth in his shoulder. With an angry snarl, he swats the Corrupted away.

But something is different now. He'rox sways, unsteady on his feet, and I can only watch in horror as he takes awkward swings at the Corrupted, each hit less powerful than the last. They begin clinging to him like leeches, dragging him down with their mindless persistence.

"He'rox!"

Lifting my gun, I aim and fire. Only two bullets left, but I take one of the fuckers down with the first shot. Aiming again, I'm about to fire when something catches my gaze through the trees.

Her.

That woman. Maisie.

She stands there, eyes focused on me with what can only be cruel intent. But she doesn't come forward. And I can't deal with whatever's happening with her right now. Because He'rox is in trouble.

With a strangled noise, He'rox drops to his knees. The tentacle holding me swings and dips, lowering before going slack, and I tumble to the short distance to the ground, rolling a few feet away. I scramble upright, adrenaline thrumming in my veins as I watch the few remaining Corrupted descend upon He'rox, clawing at him.

"No!" I shriek, stumbling forward a step.

Aiming, I release my last remaining bullet, hitting one of them in the head.

A tentacle bursts free, swinging and slicing the remaining two Corrupted that had been clawing at him.

For a moment, I can only stop and stare. Is it over?

The forest descends into eerie silence.

And then a figure staggers from the mass of bodies. He'rox emerges, flesh soaked in blood. My heart leaps in hope for one brief second before he turns to face me.

His eyes are dark and empty. Not ice-cold like before. No longer unfeeling, because they hold...nothing.

Without a word, he turns and disappears into the forest too quickly for me to even react.

My eyes widen, my heart thumps hard in my chest as I sink to my knees. My mind still reeling from what's happened here.

"He'rox?"

I whisper his name even though I know he's gone.

Except, this time feels different from the last.

Why does it feel like I've lost something before it even began?

And then...her.

Movement catches my eyes once more and I spot Maisie turning and running back through the forest.

Inexplicable anger rushes through me like a tsunami through a tunnel as I rise, gun in hand as I step across the battlefield and unmoving bodies. Grabbing my pack, I set off in her direction.

CHAPTER NINETEEN

SOPHIE

Walking at first, then breaking into a run, I chase after Maisie as she flees into the forest. Twigs snap under my feet and leaves crunch, but I pay them no mind. My sole focus is on the woman in front of me.

Because He'rox is gone, and even if I could track him down, I doubt he wants me to. Why else would he leave me alone after just fighting so hard to protect me?

Something happened near the end there, and sooner or later I'll get answers.

After I find him.

Or when he eventually comes back to me.

"Maisie!" I shout, my voice cracking. "Stop!"

She ignores me, darting between the trees with purpose. More anger rises within me, and I push my legs to move faster. After everything that's just happened, after He'rox revealing that side of himself to protect me, I refuse to let this woman just run away because something tells me she's a key in all of this. Something to make this shitshow make sense.

I cut through the bushes like I'm made for the terrain. No longer running terrified, scared for my life, I remember those times I used to run barefoot through the forest near where I grew up. Running with my dad. Practicing for this very moment.

I grit my teeth, resisting the urge to fucking scream her name as I spot her not far ahead of me. Forcing air through my lungs, I gain on her quickly.

"Stop!"

Of course, she doesn't. One glance behind her and she pushes forward even harder.

"Fuck this." I lunge forward, grabbing her by the shoulders as I tackle her to the ground. We hit the ground hard, her taking the brunt of the fall as we roll through the leaves, and I pin her beneath me.

"What the *fuck* is going on?!" I can't mask the fury dripping from my voice, and I don't try to.

Maisie just smiles up at me coolly, and for the first time since I've met her, she speaks. "I have no idea what you mean."

"Cut the bullshit!" I shout. "Those...things, the people who attacked us..." My eyes widen as I glare down at her, eyes roving over her uncorrupted skin. "You're the only one not infected..."

Maisie shrugs nonchalantly, a response that only serves to piss me the fuck off.

I grab her by the front of her dress and slam her against the ground again.

She smiles at me, eyes widening with madness I've only seen when people go mental. Just that look alone in her eyes has my awareness heightening.

"What does it matter?" She shrugs, completely unfazed.

"It *matters*," I seethe, "because innocent people died. Because my friend turned into...*something* to protect me. All because of whatever sick game you're playing!"

Because I know she has something to do with this. I can feel it.

Her reaction alone is proof.

"You're delusional," she replies, that stupid fucking smile still on her face as if she has all the winning cards in her hand and I'm about to lose everything.

Over my dead body.

I tighten my grip on her dress. "Don't play dumb with me. Those people...the way they attacked...What they turned into...What Bert turned into. You have something to do with this!"

Maisie laughs. "You have no proof."

Rage swells within me and the cool metal of my gun presses into her temple in a movement that's so deadly I almost momentarily pause. "Tell me the truth. *Now*."

She looks up at me, eyes suddenly cold. "Or what? You'll shoot me? Go ahead then."

"Don't test me."

Maisie smiles. "I didn't infect those people. I am no monster...not like your *friend*." Her eyes go cold again as she pins them on me and I stiffen at her reference to He'rox.

"You don't get to talk about him." I press the gun harder against her temple as I lean in closer. "And I don't believe you."

Keeping her gaze locked on mine, Maisie slowly raises one hand. I watch her warily, ready to pull back at any moment. But she simply pulls up her sleeve to reveal intact, unmarked skin.

"See? No signs of infection." Maisie lowers her hand calmly. "Now, if you'll kindly release me—"

I stare at her, moments ticking by between us as our gazes remain locked. Staring at her like this, it's like I can see into her soul. And all I can see is black. A soulless black pit.

Her eyes are human, yet, there is something else there.

Brows furrowing I ease up a little only to flip her onto her back. She lets out a surprised yelp as I grip the neck of her dress and rip it across her back.

My eyes widen, a lump swelling in my throat as I'm faced with something I've seen before.

Back in He'rox's lab. Except now, right here, it's a bit different.

A singular thick black vein pulses from her tailbone right up her spinal column, disappearing into the nape of her neck.

Rising, I stare at her.

"You...infected yourself," I whisper.

Maisie freezes. Then she smiles sweetly. "Now why would I do that?"

"To control the others." I release her and step back, a chill going through me. "You did this. You made them attack us."

Maisie rises to her feet, brushing dirt from her clothes. "It was necessary for the greater good. A small sacrifice."

"The greater good?" I raise my gun, aiming it at her heart. "You're *sick*."

She turns on me, eyes suddenly spitting venom and I realize something else. Her moods are ill-placed. Almost as if she's not in complete control of herself.

"The world has ended, if you haven't noticed," she spits. "Maybe because you're one of those bitches fucking the enemy."

I can only stare at her, my neurons working overtime as I try to make sense of all this.

"How did you know that?" I whisper. "How do you know about the others mating with the Vullan?"

It wasn't on the flyers. There's no way she'd know unless she's been to Unity or...

I gulp, eyes dropping to the earth beneath my feet.

The network of veins...

For a moment, just a flash of fear shows in Maisie's eyes before it disappears and she's soulless again.

"None of your business. The world needs leaders again and you've come and ruined it all." She glares at me, face contorting with rage and once again, I note her sudden change in emotion. "*You ruined everything!*"

I tighten my grip on the gun even though I know I'm out of bullets. "What are you talking about?"

Maisie snarls. "My whole life, I've been an outcast. Poor,

unwanted Maisie with nothing and no one. Until it told me it didn't have to be that way."

"It? What are you talking about?" She ignores me, but I'm pretty sure I know what *it* is. I met it. Saw what it did to that deer. Those people who were part of this camp. That woman floating in He'rox's lab.

Maisie's eyes glow with victory at some memory replaying in her mind. "It felt so good to have power over someone, make them do whatever I wanted."

Realization washes over me. "Those people...they were your servants."

"Slaves!" Maisie spits. "Doing my bidding, getting me food, gifts, anything I desired. I was omnipotent! They did whatever I wanted. I only had to think it."

"At the cost of their lives," I whisper. "They were people, with families, hopes, and dreams. They survived a fucking apocalypse! And you turned them into your puppets to feed your ego."

Maisie shrugs. "Whatever."

I stare at her, struggling to comprehend how she could be so callous. So cruel. "You don't even care that you killed innocent people. Their lives mean nothing to you?"

"Not nothing," Maisie replies. "But sacrifices have to be made." She smiles at me, sending a chill down my spine. "This is a new world," she whispers, voice going so low, it's almost hard to hear her. "Those aliens came here to make this world anew. They left us a *gift*, Sophie."

My whole being stiffens. "You're a monster."

The smile slips from Maisie's face as she lunges for me. But she's too slow. The whole time I stood there, I waited for her to move. For her to run. Grabbing her hands, I spin and slam her into the nearest tree.

She lets out a soft sound of pain before she slams her knee upward into my belly. I grit my teeth, biting so hard that I draw blood.

"Fuck you!" I spit on the ground and spin with her, slamming her into the forest floor. She chokes on what I hope is blood.

Pressing down into her, I hold the gun at her temple again.

"Tell me how you did it. Tell me how you infected those people or I will fucking kill you right now, right here, I swear it."

Maisie chokes again and laughs but I see the fear in her eyes.

It's enough for me to press the gun harder.

"I've only got one bullet, Maisie," I lie, "and it has your name on it. You think I'll spare your life? You're fucking mistaken. You mean nothing to me. I'm giving you until three. One..."

All mirth leaves her face as she stares up at me, throat moving as she gulps.

"Two—"

Still nothing and I let all emotion drain from my face, putting on that mask I've been taught to wear when looking at nasty, disgusting things.

"Thr—"

"Fine! I'll tell you. It's—"

But she doesn't get to finish.

The world erupts around me in a boom as I'm splattered with liquid and my ears ring.

Eyes wide, I stare down at Maisie's lifeless body, blown apart by what could only be some powerful weapon.

Turning, eyes wide and heart hammering into my throat, I look up to see the wide dark eyes of Nathan and the barrel of the gun he'd just used to kill his woman pointed straight at me.

"Get up," he says.

CHAPTER TWENTY

SOPHIE

I stand on shaky legs, raising my hands slowly. "Nathan, I-"

"Quiet," he growls, eyes still wild. "That bitch must have infected me. Made me do things..." He shudders. "She had to die."

I gulp as I spot a tentacle swirling at his back. Just like the ones that had sprung from Bert's.

This parasite. Those veins. The effect isn't uniform.

That sends a chill through me more than the Corrupted male talking to me now. And I notice one thing: he isn't mindless like Bert was. Another different effect.

I glance at Maisie's mangled body, bile rising in my throat. "She infected you? How?"

Nathan's eyes harden as he focuses on me. "How *the fuck* am I supposed to know?" He takes a step closer and behind him, the single tentacle snapping in the air like a whip. "You know how to heal people. How to stop this."

I shake my head, heart pounding. "I don't—"

He cocks the gun, aiming it at my leg. "Don't lie to me! Fix this or I'll shoot!"

Seeing the desperation and rage in his eyes, I realize he's beyond reason. "Okay, okay!" I raise my hands higher. "But I need to go back to the camp. There are tools there I can use."

More like the weapons the others had left behind. I'm banking those guns aren't dead like mine. A live bullet is all I need. His forehead the target I'll be aiming for.

Nathan hesitates, eyeing me warily. "You're lying. Trying to trick me."

"I'm not." I put a whimper in my voice that almost makes me shrivel inside. "I think I can help you. But not out here."

He considers for a moment, then jerks his head towards the woods. "Move. And no tricks or I'll shoot you in the back."

I start walking slowly, keeping my movements calm and predictable. "When we get to camp, I might be able to create an antidote. To flush the infection from your system," I say, keeping up the ruse.

"And that freak?" Nathan sneers. "How do I kill it?"

"Freak?"

Nathan growls. "You know what the fuck I'm talking about. That thing! The alien. The one that was with you."

My lips press into a line as I try to come up with a quick response.

"Don't even think of lying to me." His voice holds a deathly warning that I would be a fool to miss.

I hesitate. "He'rox doesn't want to hurt people. He was trying to help."

The gun presses into my back. "Tell me how to kill him."

I stiffen some more. "There may be a way," I lie. "But first you need to be cured. Otherwise, he'll kill you easily in your state."

Nathan hesitates. "I swear, if you try to trick me..." He leaves the rest unsaid. "You're friends with that monster. Why would you help me kill it?"

"He's my enemy."

I start walking again, formulating a plan as I move through the bushes.

Gain access to a gun without alerting Nathan. Then blast him into nothingness. The tentacle suggests he may already be partly influenced by the parasite, not fully himself. Reasoning with him is impossible now.

As we walk, I glance over my shoulder and see two writhing tentacles now bursting from Nathan's back. The infection is progressing rapidly. I have to act quickly before he's totally lost.

When we reach the campsite, Nathan keeps the gun trained on me while I move about, gathering supplies. I notice three pistols lying on the ground near one of the tents, likely abandoned when the whole camp took off after me.

If I can distract Nathan even for a second, I might be able to grab one.

I turn to him, rambling about needing more medical equipment as I subtly edge closer to the tent.

"The infection is advanced," I say. "We need a serum, anti-inflammatories..."

Nathan waves the gun impatiently. "Just do something!"

I keep talking, inching closer. When I'm within reach of the guns, I make my move, diving for the ground, fingers closing around a pistol. I hear the gunshot right before there's a searing pain in my shoulder as I crash into the ground.

But before I can turn and fire to defend myself, there's a sickening squelch.

I turn wide eyes to the man as I watch a white, clawed hand materialize, protruding from his chest.

He'rox comes into form behind Nathan as Nathan turns wide eyes over his shoulder. He tries to turn his gun, but it's too late. He'rox tugs, dragging Nathan as he pulls his hand out Nathan's back and I glimpse a bloody organ in his grasp, right before the world goes dim.

The pain in my shoulder fades in and out as darkness pulls at the edges of my vision. I'm vaguely aware of being lifted, strong arms cradling me gently.

"Sophie, can you hear me?" He'rox's voice echoes from far away.

"You...came back," I whisper, head lolling only to be supported by a large claw.

"I was always close by..."

I close my eyes, letting the rocking motion of He'rox carrying me lull the nausea.

After a while, I crack my eyes open again. We're moving through the forest at a trot. He'rox's eyes shine with concern as he glances down at me and I would smile if pain wasn't shooting through my arm like a bitch on steroids.

"Where are we going?" I whisper.

"Somewhere safe," he says.

Darkness clouds my vision again. "Unity?"

"Too far," he says. "Somewhere where I cannot sense them."

I don't ask who or what he's referring to, because I know. Instead, I grip his forearm, a bit concerned with how weak my grip is. "The others from this camp. They're gone to Unity. We have to warn the people there."

He'rox jerks his chin toward his chest in a nod and I notice those tentacles he'd walked on, the same tentacles that had kept me safe, are nowhere to be seen.

Darkness threatens to pull me under again, but I force myself to stay conscious. "We...stick together," I whisper. "Figure this out. Stop...the parasite."

A flicker of something crosses He'rox's eyes and his ears flick at the sides of his head. Those tentacles that hang near his mouth twitch and writhe as if reaching out to me and for a moment, I'm caught in the beauty that's him.

"Don't leave me again," I whisper. "It..." I don't know what I'm saying. Something screams deep within me that I should shut the hell up. And yet... "I don't like when you do."

He glances down at me, something passing through those eyes again that I can't quite place. Maybe because they're always so ice-cold. Seeing any form of emotion within them now is almost unnerving.

"We're...in this together now." My eyes start to drift closed again. "Just get...us somewhere safe. Rest. Then we fight back."

"You extend an alliance to a monster..."

For a moment, I don't realize he's referring to himself.

"You're not a monster," I whisper. "You're not my enemy either. You're my...friend."

"Friend," he replies.

He'rox's grip on me tightens softly, his voice a whisper. "If you only knew how much more than that I'd like to be."

His words soothe me as darkness claims my vision. I let my weary mind and body surrender to oblivion, trusting that He'rox will keep us both safe for now. When I wake, we'll begin figuring out how to fight back against this insidious parasite infecting our world.

And maybe I'll have someone fighting by my side.

CHAPTER TWENTY-ONE

HE'ROX

I hold Sophie gently as I maneuver through the forest underbrush. She's so soft, I worry I might crush her in my monstrous claws.

Because that is what I am.

A monster.

The shame that came over me once I exterminated the threat that sought her blood was one I could not run away from. For the first time since Edooria, I became that version of myself. One my own people were afraid of. Shunned.

I could expect no less from the little hyu'man in my arms.

I glance down at her now, eyes moving over her smooth face. She is...beauty. So different from myself, yet I yearn to keep her in my sight even when I risk her turning me away.

Her steady breathing indicates she has finally lost consciousness to her wounds. Now that she is unable to object, we must move faster to find sanctuary. For holding her to me like this is quickly affecting my thirst more than it should.

Her shoulder wound still seeps blood, the red a stark contrast against her pale skin, and just the sight of it makes my fangs ache.

The monster within me sees a part of her that it wants. But I will resist.

I must.

For rather than harm this little fighter, I will eliminate myself.

I am a blur as I move through the underbrush, following an unknown thread, the steady beats of the source of this planet. Instinct guides me to a secluded cave, but I hesitate.

She will not wish to wake up in a place like this.

Turning, I scan the area around us.

I must find somewhere else.

As I continue moving, Soh'fee's steady breathing is the only sound that penetrates the uneasy silence. Above us, the sky darkens and I have no choice but to stop in the center of the forest.

Sniffing, I don't catch any scents. It's a guarded section of the thick, easily defendable. I can make a shelter here. Keep her safe. Heal her.

Setting her down on a bed of soft moss and vines, I get to work.

A structure is easily made, thick branches broken to make walls and a roof, thrust into the earth below for support. I cover the top with large leaves from a nearby bush and secure it with vines.

By the time the showers begin, Soh'fee is well protected underneath the shelter.

I stand outside, watching her as the waters fall in a torrent over me.

The water helps. Her scent is lessened now. The scent of the rain washing it away, along with the temptation of her blood. So I stand outside. And I wait.

Wait for my life organ to stop thumping the unsteady beat. For my fangs to stop aching. For my ba'clan to give up the fight to get to her and go back into hibernation.

For I cannot have her.

The moment I decided to become what I am, I gave up the chance, the desire, to have any female.

And yet...

My ears twitch the longer I watch her, small pulses going through my ba'clan like an itch.

I must tend to her. She needs medical assistance, and I am a medic.

Yet, I stand here, frozen in fear.

This female...of all the things in the universe, this female scares me the most.

Rek.

I cannot let her bleed. I will just have to exert maximum control. Refrain from scenting her too long. Bandage her wound and stay away.

An unbidden growl slips past my lips—a part of me rejecting that idea.

But I must.

I should not even be in her presence now.

Decision made, I move forward, water sliding over my ba'clan to drip into a small pool as I enter the small structure.

Another growl slips past my lips.

Her scent is so strong in here I am not sure I can withstand it for long.

That only means I must make haste.

Blocking my airway, I rummage in her pack for medical supplies and set about cleaning and bandaging the injury. My claws move with a surprising delicacy, my sole focus on ensuring she recovers.

As I work, my eyes stray to her face. So fragile, this hyu'man female, and yet possessing an inner strength and fire that ignites something within me. A fierce desire to protect her rises in my chest, though I know I should keep my distance. I am tainted, a monster unworthy of her light. She has seen what I have become, witnessed the horror of this new threat facing her world, and yet she faced both. When she wakes, surely she will cast me away in fear and disgust.

And yet...she called me "friend" before darkness claimed her. An offer of alliance in this fight against a shared enemy. I cling to the hope that perhaps, for reasons I cannot fathom, she will look past the beast and see the soul still trapped inside. The part of me that grows desperate to have her, but never will.

Maybe we might stand together. Two unlikely allies joined against the coming storm.

Shaking my head, I block my nostrils even harder as I try to focus.

For now, I will watch over her as she heals and rests. Guard her against the dangers prowling this forest, both hyu'man and otherwise. Be here when she wakes with frightened eyes and a thousand questions, offering what comfort my tainted form allows.

It is clear we have a long and perilous road ahead, but at this moment, all that matters is that she lives. My Soh'fcc. The female who looked into the eyes of a monster and called him 'friend'.

Wound bandaged, for a moment I test my limits as I settle beside Sophie as she rests, watching the steady rise and fall of her chest. For now, she seems stable, her body working to replenish the blood she's lost.

She is so peaceful now. Eyes closed, no longer defiant. No longer curious. Like this, she is almost like every other hyu'man female I have met so far. And yet...

I've moved closer without even realizing, the fact only hitting me with full force when my nose brushes against her soft skin.

I freeze, fighting the sudden urges threatening to make me go even closer. To brush my nose into the softness of her neck. To run my tongue there. To lick her skin. Taste her.

My thoughts churn as I remind myself I must keep vigil.

But the fates are playing a game with me. The gods of Edooria looking at my soul even though I am far from home.

With a low growl, I rake my claws across the soft dirt beside me. I should not have these feelings. But my ba'clan disagree, stretching from the tips of my claws, trying to get to her.

No.

I pull them back even as I fight to pull myself away. For she is intoxicating. Making me consider things I should not.

I have no place courting a female, let alone binding her to me. She deserves a mate of her own kind, untainted and whole. Not some shadow creature torn between two worlds.

And yet, when she looks at me, I do not see fear or revulsion in her eyes. She alone sees beyond this corrupted flesh to the soul still caught within. And for a moment, I can recall who I was before. The Vullan I might have been, had I not—

A soft moan draws my attention. Sophie stirs, her eyelids fluttering as she regains consciousness. I lean over her, claws tingling with the urge to touch yet staying a respectful distance away. Her eyes open and meet mine, a flicker of relief passing through them.

"You stayed," she whispers. Her uninjured arm rises as though to reach for me but then falls away, fingers curling into a fist.

That alone fuels the war within me.

I bow my head. "I will remain by your side."

"The others..." She tries to sit up but winces, her shoulder protesting the movement. "Unity. The others are in danger."

That foolish thing growing deep inside me warms and thrills and a wave goes through my ba'clan. I watch as her gaze snaps to the movement, waiting for her to withdraw from me.

But she doesn't.

"We should go warn them."

Again, she tries to rise. This time, I place a claw against her chest and force her to remain still.

"Your people have the best protection this planet can offer."

A small smile graces her features, her flat white teeth peeking between her lips. Lips that had pressed against my own.

The memory resurfaces and I cannot pull my gaze away.

"The Vullan?"

I nod slowly, forcing my gaze back to her eyes. "If those Corrupted attack, the camp will be safe."

She nods, her shoulder relaxing somewhat. "We still don't know how Maisie was able to control them. Or what happens to them now that she's dead. That fucking idiot shot her right as she was about to tell me."

There is nothing for me to say.

No comfort to give.

No insight.

The network refused to reveal its plans to me before and even now that its intentions are clearer, I am still as lost as Soh'fee is. I watch her keenly, waiting for her questions. Her demands.

To her, I have revealed more than even some of my brothers have seen. And yet still, no questions come.

She...confuses me.

No. She *intrigues* me.

Soh'fee shivers, though whether from cold or the memory of what we witnessed at the camp, I cannot tell. I long to wrap my arms around her and ward off her fears, but I do not dare. I can never be what she needs.

"We have to stop this, He'rox."

"Yes. We must." Because I am going down a path, the end of which not even I can predict. It is not the way of a scientist. The variables here are not ones I can control. But as she continues speaking, I realize my own thoughts are clouding my senses.

Soh'fee isn't considering what is happening between us, because to her, *nothing* is happening between us. Because I have forgotten one important thing.

Soh'fee has no ba'clan. And even though mine are almost dead, their base instinct to find a mate is still there. They have told me she is mine.

But to Soh'fee, I am nothing to her.

Her eyes blaze with determination, reminding me once more of why I find myself drawn to this small yet fierce female. "This threat, whatever it is...we have to contain it before it destroys everything."

I make a sound in my throat for I cannot speak.

It appears it is enough, for Sophie smiles then as she turns her gaze to me. "Partners, then. In this crazy, impossible fight." She extends her uninjured hand toward me.

I stare at it for a long moment, hardly daring to believe she means what I think. Slowly, gently, I extend my own claw and clasp her hand with the utmost care. Her warmth seeps into me, chasing back the dark voices whispering of my unworthiness. For this moment, I allow myself to hope.

"Partners," I say, and her fingers tighten around mine.

But her touch is too much.

I release her hand as gently as I can before I am overpowered by it and exit into the darkening forest.

She is safe now.

She will be fine.

CHAPTER TWENTY-TWO

SOPHIE

As He'rox shakes my hand, he abruptly releases me as if my skin were a poison that burns and I watch open-mouthed as he stumbles from the shelter.

Directly outside, he stands in the rain. The raindrops hitting his ridges run down his frame like water moving over a terraced landscape. I stare at him for a few moments, unable to pull my gaze away.

We still haven't spoken about what happened out there. How he changed. Why he disappeared and left me alone right after—though now, I realize he mightn't have gone anywhere at all, but simply camouflaged. But that only increases my confusion.

I gulp, forcing myself up on my good arm as I watch him.

Having him carry me, feeling his warmth as I waned in and out of consciousness, was the only thing that kept me comforted. He was here, and he was taking care of me. This alien creature I've already gone through hell with and survived it.

When I came to feel so much for this strange being, I don't know.

And just a moment before, when he'd been leaning over me... Waking up to see him there, my heart leaped for a reason that wasn't fear.

I don't know what's wrong with me, but I'm pretty sure it's not something normal. Or regular.

But I've never been regular.

Where little girls used to dress up as princesses for Halloween in my little town in the middle of nowhere, I used to dress up as a zombie, Frankenstein, or my favorite one—various afflictions I'd been reading about. I'd made my father proud. And in high school when teens my age used to obsess over the latest music or dance moves, my obsessions had been something else completely.

Death. Disease.

Again, my father had been proud.

Would he be proud now? If he saw me here, shamelessly watching streams of water run down the body of an alien and wishing it was my fingers instead? Or would he be horrified?

Swallowing hard, I try to clear my thoughts.

I'm way off the mark here.

Nothing He'rox has said or done has communicated he finds me even mildly interesting beyond the fact that I'm a scientist like he is and a creature not of his kind.

Yet...

I swallow hard once more, running my tongue over my lips as I pull them into my mouth and bite down hard.

Just a moment ago, I came back to consciousness to smell the sweetest vanilla hovering over me. It reminded me of home. A place where I felt safe.

He'rox reminded me of something I'd lost...and maybe...maybe this whole confusion that's happening deep inside me is just my brain trying to latch on to the one thing I'd lost because of this apocalypse.

Home.

Forcing an even breath from my nose, I reach for my pack, wincing only slightly as my shoulder protests. Pulling out my sleeping bag, I spread it on the floor to ward off the cold and wet before turning my gaze back to the outside of the shelter.

He'd found the first aid kit and patched me up well. Even that is surprising, given that he doesn't—or at least, he *shouldn't*—know how to use my stuff. But if one thing is clear, humanity isn't the smartest thing out there.

On the grand scale of things, we're just reaching levels of intelligence other lifeforms in the galaxy have already surpassed.

We were lucky they came here. The Vullan. We were lucky they came to save us.

The rain picks up, coming down harder, and He'rox remains unmoving outside. His shoulders are hunched, his arms hanging stiffly at his sides. He makes no move to get out of the onslaught, yet does not seem bothered by it either.

After a long moment, he finally crouches, gaze finding mine through the entrance of the shelter. His eyes pierce through the encroaching darkness with an intensity that leaves me nervous and unsettled, given the thoughts swirling in my head.

I want to say something, yet I fear breaking this strange silence that has descended over us. But finally, I can't take it anymore.

"He'rox," I whisper, sure he can hear me. "Please, come back inside."

He doesn't respond for several beats, those eyes colder than the falling rain, before he finally says, "No."

His voice is flat, devoid of emotion and I remind myself he is not a human. I can't judge him based on how I would relate to another being like myself.

"Why not? You'll catch a chill out there."

"I do not catch what you hyu'mankin call colds," he replies, though still he does not move.

My confusion grows. But so does a bubble of humor in my gut. Is he throwing some kind of tantrum? Did I do something I shouldn't have? Did I say something?

I'm not sure I should, but I risk asking him anyway. "Why are you out in the rain?"

He doesn't answer immediately. Instead, he watches me with that same intensity that makes a thrill skitter across my skin.

"You are in danger," he finally says.

"Danger?" Any humor that had been starting to seed in my gut is killed as I glance behind me, eyes scanning through the gaps in the shelter as my heart lurches against my ribs.

"From me."

His words make me freeze and turn to stare at him.

Moments pass as his gaze remains locked with mine, the silence between us only punctuated by the constant hum of the rain.

"What are you talking about?" I finally whisper.

His body tenses and I half expect him to get up and walk away. But he remains still. "I must keep my distance."

The meaning behind his words slowly dawns on me and I glance down at myself. He's saying he'll hurt me? But...

My brows furrow as I meet his gaze once more.

It doesn't make sense.

All this time, he's been warning me he'll harm me, that he's my enemy, basically telling me he's not to be trusted, and yet, not once has he harmed me. Instead, he's protected me. He fought to keep me alive. If it wasn't for him...

"He'rox," I whisper, unable to find words to explain to him I'm not scared of him. Not anymore. Not like I was the first time I met him and followed him into the bushes. Fuck, that feels like so long ago now. But even then, something beyond my fear had pushed me to trail behind him without protection.

And now, here we are.

"I'm not afraid of you," I finally say.

He'rox's ears flick off the sides of his head, pointing outward like an elf's and completely contrasting with his expressionless face.

"I'm not afraid of you," I say it again, this time with more surety, as if just realizing the fact myself.

"You should be," he says, head tilting slightly as he gazes at me.

"Why are you not afraid?"

For the first time since exiting the shelter, he moves forward a little, peering at me through the entrance as if I am some strange thing. Lifting a claw, he doesn't take his eyes off me and I watch as his claws extend to sharp points that I have no doubt could rend me if he wanted to. I've seen him do it.

"Why do I not scare you?" The low timbre of his voice makes a delightful shiver go through me that I'm not able to hide. Even then, he tilts his head the other way as he notices.

"I...I don't know." Stupid answer to a good question. One I wish I had better words for. But there are none. "I trust you."

He'rox's ears flatten against his head suddenly as he backs away once more.

"Come inside," I whisper.

He's not getting wet. The water seems to roll off his skin almost as if he's hydrophobic. So why am I inviting him in?

"Your blood," he says. "Your scent."

My brows furrow again, trying to understand what he's trying to say.

"Your skin..." His gaze skirts down my body and I try not to squirm. *"You."*

Swallowing the lump that's risen in my throat, I dare to ask, "What about me?"

He turns away from me then, eyes focused far beyond into the forest and silence descends between us once more.

"This...sensation," he suddenly says. "I have never felt it before. I do not know what will happen if I allow it to grow." He turns his gaze back to me and I'm arrested by the intensity of it. "I want you, Sophie. All of you. Every inch. Every drop. And I fear it will destroy you."

"What feeling?" I ask, though my heart's now thumping against my chest so hard, excitement and anticipation flooding through my veins, that I fear I already know the answer. I can hardly breathe as I wait for He'rox to respond.

He stares at me for a long moment before speaking. "My ba'clan urges me to claim you. To mark you as mine." He looks away. "I have never experienced such an impulse before. But your scent, your touch...they stir something primal within me. And...there's a part of me...a part..."

He trails off and I wait for fear to rise within me, but instead, I only feel curiosity and something else that calls to that part deep within me that I've ignored all these years. Longing. Curiosity to know this strange being more fully, and longing for whatever we could share.

Because I noticed something while on that ship with the others. Those females with their Vullan mates... There was something different about them. A surety they shouldn't have in a world such as this. They were no longer alone.

"Then claim me," I say, the words escaping before I can stop them.

He'rox's head snaps up, his ears sticking off the sides of his head once more. "You...do not know what you offer. My nature is not like yours. I could harm you."

I rise shakily to my feet and step towards the shelter entrance. The rain soaks into my clothes but I ignore it.

My voice is but a gentle whisper as I move closer. "You have not harmed me yet. Even when you say your instincts drive you to. That tells me there is more to you than primal urges. There is kindness... and care."

He'rox stands now as well, towering over me with an unreadable expression on his face. I continue. "I trust you, He'rox. And I..." I falter, then summon my courage and continue, "I care for you too. More than makes sense or I can explain."

For a moment he is still, then in two large strides he is in front of me, his hands hovering inches from my face. "You are in danger."

I meet his gaze. "Perhaps I am."

He lets out a deep shuddering breath and slowly, hesitantly, presses his fingers to my cheeks. His skin is cool and pleasant and even though his touch is feather-light, it sends shivers down my spine.

He leans closer, his breath fanning my face. "You honor me by trusting me. It is foolish, for I am not worthy of it…and yet…"

"And yet what?" The rain pours down on us and I couldn't care less, my voice a breathy gasp as it leaves my lips.

He'rox lets out a soft growl and suddenly he is wrapping his arms tightly around me, lifting me off my feet. I'm dimly aware that he's crouching down with me in hand, causing me to straddle him as he goes to his knees. His skin grows warmer and I nestle closer, breathing in his scent, no longer caring about logic or instincts. There is only this moment. And him.

He finally pulls away enough to look at me, and at that moment, I realize I really do want this. Wherever this is going, I want it. I want it more than anything.

He'rox stares into my eyes, his face only inches from mine. The intensity in his gaze makes my heart race, and I can feel my body responding to the electricity between us. It's a constant thrill that makes anticipation flutter in my belly and heat warm my veins.

A rumble emits from his throat as he watches me, and without a word, he leans in and captures my lips between his. It's a hot searing kiss, completely unlike the first time our lips met. This time, his tongue presses against my mouth, demanding entrance and when I open up to him, a deep growl rumbles through his frame as his tongue slips into my mouth.

It's unlike any kiss I've ever had before.

His tongue is huge. Thick. Thicker than I imagined, and it searches my mouth brushing over my own tongue in languid strokes before reaching the back of my throat.

"Sophie…" He calls my name in a way that makes me shiver with need. "I have waited a long time for the end," he says. "But now that it is here…I am not sure I wish to embrace it."

I have no clue what he means, but he continues.

"For now, you're here…and all I want to do is consume you."

CHAPTER TWENTY-THREE

HE'ROX

I've scented female arousal before from the hyu'mans...but it has new meaning when that arousal is meant for *me*.

Soh'fee wants me.

It's a shock and a delight.

My ba'clan pulse, eager for me to mate with her and I'm glad the showers from above rain down on us, for it dampens her scent, and that's possibly the only thing keeping me sane enough. Holding me back from pinning her into the wet earth beneath us and tasting her, taking her to the oblivion that just the thought of her is sending me to.

But even with the rain, her faint scent still makes my sazi throb in its pouch. It presses upward, eager to extrude, and I wonder if she can feel it pressing into the soft flesh of her behind.

I've never felt it this hard before. This insistent.

This hyu'man...what is she doing to me?

Reactions I've never had before, occurring even while my ba'clan fight to survive.

It shouldn't be possible... But I want nothing more than to enter that shelter and investigate the source of this sweet, sweet scent that makes me want to press my nose between her legs.

I have never seen Soh'fee's suu'ci, but I can imagine exactly what it's like. Soft and warm, like the rest of her. Just the thought makes a rumble go through me, my sazi hardening so much in its pouch it almost extrudes, and I know I should move away from her. Know I should do what's right by her and extract myself from her presence. For she is too good for me.

Pure...perfect...Soh'fee.

She shivers against me, possibly from the chill, and her fists tighten against my chest, sending warmth straight through my ba'clan at the spots she touches.

I fear to even move.

If I have misinterpreted this...

If I harm her...

Soh'fee shudders and she holds my gaze as she takes her bottom lip into her mouth.

I'm transfixed.

Every movement...every sound that she makes...I'm recording this in my mind for later playback. It might be one of my last good memories, seeing Soh'fee like this, and I relish the feelings it creates in me.

Tilting her chin back, small breaths pant from her lips as the torrent rains down on us. It creates a beautiful spectacle across her skin as her gaze slips back to my mouth.

I can still taste her, and when she leans in, I am lost in the sensation of her lips on mine once more, the softness of her skin against my claws. I hold her as gently as I can muster, afraid to harm her. Afraid she will pull away like she should. And as the rain continues to pour down around us, creating a symphony of sound that fades away, I am lost as I focus only on Soh'fee.

With a groan that rumbles against my tongue, her hand slips down my torso. It sends a flurry of shivers through my ba'clan as they reach for her, snapping to her fingers like glue, and in horror, I stiffen.

She has seen the monster in me, but this is all new to her. *I am new to her.* But Soh'fee simply moans and presses her lips against mine even more. I dare to touch her. To allow myself to take a bit of what she is offering, and my claw skates down her back.

She shivers at my touch and when I pause, a soft whimper leaves her lips to die in my mouth.

Rek me. She is the strangest, most addictive thing in the universe.

For a moment, I do not know what to do. I can only stare at the female in my arms.

Perhaps, I am still in the regen tank...back on Edooria. After the experiment. After *it* occurred. The change. Or perhaps, I am in some state of psychosis... Perhaps I never recovered and all this is a dream. Maybe I am stuck in my underground lab back on my planet, the war having ravaged my world and the Gryken having moved on. Maybe I'm stuck there. Alone. And this is all a dream.

But as Soh'fee whimpers against me again, leaning into me, it feels all too real, and a thrum goes through my frame. A *thrum*. I am thrumming for this female.

This is no dream.

This is reality.

Her soft body against mine, the feel of her breath against me, the sensation of her soft tongue flicking against my lips...

I groan as I grip her closer to me, crushing our lips together.

Soh'fee pants, whispering my name as her tongue darts out once more, brushing against mine and a shudder goes through me that has the beads of water falling off my ba'clan like shiny pebbles.

Her little tongue demands a dance I do not know, but want, oh so much, to learn.

I roll my tongue against hers, encircling it with my own as I pull it farther into my mouth and Soh'fee jerks, her eyes flying open. The tentacles at the sides of my lips snap to her jaw in a soft caress, not wanting her to pull away.

"Holy shit," she breathes, wide eyes staring at my mouth.

This is it. The moment she wakes up and realizes this is madness.

"Your tongue..." She stares at my mouth with that same shocked look but I don't know what has startled her so much.

My tongue is many times the size of hers. Perhaps I startled her with it.

"We can cease." The words ache as I push them past my throat. For I do not want to stop. Despite that I can never be the same after this, I don't ever want her to leave my embrace.

She meets my gaze again, her body heaving with labored breaths, and a growing look in her eyes that I cannot read.

"No," she answers, and her head tilts to mine again.

My pupils narrow so much, my vision wanes as a wave of need goes through me.

Soh'fee's tongue brushes against mine and this time, when I tentatively join in the dance with her, she doesn't pull away.

Instead, a groan erupts from her chest as I swirl the tip of my tongue around hers.

Her eyes fall closed but I cannot take mine off her.

Even with her eyes closed, the feelings erupting across her expressive face are scenes I wish I could have forever frozen in time. Does she know that with each passing moment, I am becoming addicted to her? Obsessed. That having her here with me now, like this, is a danger to her in ways she can never imagine.

For Fer'ro was right. My obsessions rule my consciousness. They are things I can never let go. And it is for this reason that I should pull away from Soh'fee. Because I was not making jest when I declared I wanted to consume her. Having her like this, I can imagine nothing else. I want her wrapped around me. I want to feel my sazi pierce deep inside her.

I want her *everything*.

The moment my claw slides over her midsection and she shudders against me, I know I cannot stop. Soh'fee whimpers into my mouth once more as I slip a claw underneath her lower garment.

Skin too smooth and soft greets my touch and another thrum rumbles through my frame. She is so incredibly soft, so delicate, that my finger pauses inside the waist of her garment, the warring factions of my brain struggling with what's right from wrong.

But at the moment I think to pull away, Soh'fee's fingers close over mine. I expect her to stop me now, but I should know to stop expecting things from her. Because Soh'fee is everything unexpected.

She guides me to the center of her lower garment, her hand slipping underneath the waist and into the space at the center of her thighs.

I hesitate for only a moment before I dip my claw in, a shudder going through me as I feel the warmth there, my claw sinking into a mat of curls, and I stop breathing. When I hit something too soft to describe, Soh'fee jerks against me.

She pulls a deep breath into her nose as she swallows hard. "That's uh..."

"Your *suu'ci*."

"My pussy?"

Rek, she can give it any name she likes. I don't care. For it is magic. Unbelievably soft. And that sweet scent rises even higher now with the gap in the garment from the intrusion of our hands.

Soh'fee shudders as she directs me lower and wonder fills me.

There is no protective covering. No pouch. No flap.

Here, at Soh'fee's center, is pure softness and warmth.

There are folds that open like a bloom. So soft against my fingers, I momentarily worry that I might hurt her there.

But the look in her eyes is far from pain.

Soh'fee's lids are low as she watches me, her bottom lip sliding between her teeth as she directs me lower. "And this..."

My fingers stop at the bottom end of her folds. I do not dare to open my mouth and speak. I will surely growl, scare her away, and this moment is one I want to last forever.

She holds my fingers at that spot and I take the liberty to brush them over her soft flesh.

A breath shudders through her as she hangs on to me, letting me feel her.

But confusion has me pausing. I do not feel an entrance.

My ears twitch and twitch again as I swirl my finger.

And then I feel it. So small, it was missed the first time. Wonder and immediate disappointment fill me.

We will never mate.

There is no way she can fit me there.

But that disappointment disappears almost as soon as it arrives. Because here, this little female is giving me something I never thought I'd ever have. Her touch. And herself. It is more than I could ever hope for. More than I need.

Soh'fee releases my hand and wraps her arm around my neck once more as I lift my fingers, traveling up what feels like a central channel straight to the soft nub at the apex of her sex.

As soon as my finger brushes over it, she jerks against me, her breaths becoming uneven.

I keep my finger there, flicking the little nub and watching her eyes roll back as her jaw goes slack, her mouth falling open as she takes deep breaths.

Mm...a pleasure spot.

And when I brush my finger across her folds, I watch the way her brow furrows as she moans against my lips.

My tongue slips into her mouth as Soh'fee sucks on the tip of it, sending shockwaves of pleasure I never knew could occur from tongue-sucking.

Torrent around us forgotten, I surrender to her as she bobs her head on my tongue, relishing in the feel of her warm mouth, her soft body pressed against mine, and the heat between her thighs.

Splaying my fingers, I use the tip of my index finger to brush against that nub that made her groan earlier.

Soh'fee whimpers on my tongue and when I twist my hand, using one finger to slowly pierce her entrance while the other rubs against the nub, she trembles against me.

Soh'fee moans, her body quaking as I slip inside her.

By the gods...

There is no way her entrance could handle my hard sazi, but even knowing that, I'm throbbing in my pouch, aching to extrude and claim the female in my arms.

But as I work my way in, I feel her suu'ci welcoming me, and when my finger goes deep inside her, the warmth around me pulses as her suu'ci tightens around the digit.

The thought of the pulse squeezing my sazi has me partially extruding and I almost growl loud as I force myself under control.

Soh'fee releases my tongue, her head falling back before she lifts it and meets my gaze.

There is pure lust in her eyes as her body jerks with every brush over her nub, every thrust of my finger within her.

She moves her hips against my hand and soon there is a rhythm that goes in tune with every breath she takes.

Soh'fee holds my gaze, her mouth forming a circle as her chest heaves and when I bend and take one of the mounds of her chest between my lips, sucking on the pebbled flesh there through her soaked clothing, she screams, stiffening against me.

For a moment, I think I have hurt her and horror fills me, but when her vision clears and she looks at me, I realize I have done nothing of the sort.

Soh'fee just reached her peak on my fingers and I realize something that brings another level of horror in me.

I realize...I want her for my own.

She is mine. I knew that.

But now, on top of that, I *want* her too. I want to have her. Need to.

But...that is the most selfish thing I could ever do.

CHAPTER TWENTY-FOUR

SOPHIE

I...came.

Fuck.

My chest's still heaving as I come down from my peak, the reality of what just happened between us hitting me like a brick.

He'rox is a being from another planet. Fuck that. He's a male I just met. And I had his fingers in my pussy while I moaned and panted his name. But what's worse is that none of that embarrasses me. What's embarrassing was my lack of self-control, so much so I don't know if I can meet his gaze.

But I can't run away from it either. I can feel his attention even as I'm unable to look at him.

I was staring into those eyes as I came. Thinking about how hot and sexy and forbidden he is. Yet, here I am in his arms. Wanting him more than I've wanted anyone ever before.

Shit.

Fuck!

He'rox lifts his hand away from my pussy almost hesitantly, his fingers brushing over my clit as he slips his hand out of my jeans, and I try not to squirm.

A shiver goes through me, the rain having soaked through my hair and my clothes, and I automatically snuggle closer to him.

He's so warm, I forgot about the fact that we're crouching in the rain.

Against my fingers, his ba'clan attach to me like a web and I lift my hand, blinking away the water running into my eyes as I look at them. Hard to believe this substance that looks like white ink, or maybe streams of thick paint that haven't dried yet, is a living organism. One that's interacting with me almost as if it...*likes* me.

I clear my throat, glancing at He'rox.

What now?

Despite the icy rain, my body's still burning with need. Do I reciprocate?

My gaze slides down his sculpted frame, my heart thumping in my ears as my breath catches the lower I go. He's all muscle and strength. Just the thought of going further with him makes a flush go through my entire being.

Does he even have a dick?

There's a noticeable bulge pressing against my ass. So delicious and thick, I want to squirm against it. Another wave of heat goes through me, making me shiver—a contradiction that's like everything else since I've met this being.

When I lift my gaze back to his, my throat goes dry.

The raw hunger in He'rox's eyes is startling. Like a lion that has its prey in its sights, he stares down at me, unmoving. Electricity crackles between us, and I fear that if I look away for even a second, he'll press me into the ground and take what he wants.

Another shiver goes through me.

...I want him to.

The realization hits me hard and I have to force myself to breathe; otherwise, I'd pass out.

Bracing against him, his ba'clan remain against my fingers, telling me more than the alien himself ever would.

The ba'clan want me to stay. They don't want me to move.

Slowly, I lift my gaze back to the alien. To He'rox. And our eyes meet once more.

"He'rox," I whisper.

"Don't leave," he says, giving me exactly what I didn't expect.

My heart stutters a little. Gazing at him, the rain powering down around us, I realize I don't want to be anywhere else. Just here. Right now.

It's just me and this being from another world. Out here. Alone in the wilderness. Just me and him. No masks. No pretenses.

And for some stupid reason, this is the moment that it all comes crashing down.

Leaving my bunker. Walking outside for the first time and seeing all the destruction. The stench of death and decay that hung on the breeze. Feeling utterly and completely alone. And then seeing that flyer and thinking that maybe, maybe there's still a place for me here on this planet. A purpose. Something to do. That I wouldn't live my last days in a dark little hole while the world ended around me. That life could go on.

The tears slip from my eyes without me being able to hold them back and I'm happy the rain is still pouring down on us. Happy He'rox can't see this lapse in my constitution.

"Waters come from your eyes," he says and I stare at him, stunned. "You feel sorrow." That icy gaze slides down my frame with a slow movement that makes me feel his attention almost as if he was touching me there, right until his focus ends at the center of my thighs. "Because of what we just did?"

I swallow a sob and a laugh together, shaking my head, my wet hair plastering to the sides of my face as my expression crumples. Somehow, him realizing I'm crying has made it worse.

I don't know why, but I turn into him even more, wrapping my arms around his neck as I plaster myself against him. It's a hug I didn't think I'd need and one I don't expect to be reciprocated.

It's pathetic, seeking warmth from a stranger, and yet I do it all the same. He'rox hesitates. Stiffens. I don't expect he understands what I'm doing. So when his arms envelop me like two thick tree trunks that plaster me to him, another sob slips through my frame.

"I have harmed you in some way," he says.

"No," I croak, unsure if he can even hear me over the rain. "You've done the opposite." I sniff. "You've healed a part of me I didn't even realize was broken."

He's warm and I plaster my face into his neck. He isn't human. All this must be strange to him and I know I should pull away. Give him some space. And yet, I can't.

I take from him all that he's willing to give.

"Sophie..."

I snuggle deeper against him, hiding my face from the rain.

"You have not shunned me."

I shake my head against him. "Why would I?"

"You saw what I have become..." He pauses and I sense he has more to say. Something that's weighing on the air around us. "Many of my people have not seen that side of me."

I want to lift my head so I can look into his eyes while he tells me this, but I remain where I am, listening.

"The monster I have become...and yet, you have not asked what I am."

I lift my head at that, facing him. Through the haze of the rain, he is even more beautiful than before.

"You are a hybrid."

His ears flick off the side of his head in a way that makes him look almost like a cute, harmless animal and not like the vicious killer that protected me in the forest.

"A monster."

"I wouldn't call a hybrid—"

"I am no hybrid." His sudden growl makes me freeze, and at my reaction, his ears flatten to the sides of his head. "I am no hybrid," he repeats, his voice more even, and for the first time, He'rox's gaze moves away from me to look out into the forest beyond.

"What I am," he continues, "is unnatural. An aberrant being."

I don't know what to say and a breath shudders from him, making the water pebble and fall off his shoulders in large drops.

"I was not always like this." His gaze shifts to mine. "Possibly...if I had not done what I did...sacrificed what I did to save my people... you would have found a worthy mate in me. But now..."

I search his gaze, desperate to fill in the blanks he's leaving unfilled. "But..." I lift a hand, clasping his jaw, and he stiffens underneath my touch. "Who says you're not worthy?"

He'rox stares at me, his gaze so unreadable I'm not sure what he'll do or say next. When he closes his eyes and his ba'clan shiver against me like a wave, so much they almost cover my arms, my eyes widen as my gaze snaps to them. It is almost as if they're trying to escape his frame. I can't understand it, and then, my breath stops in my nose as my gaze meets He'rox's once more.

Gone is the pale blue I'm used to, replaced by that soulless darkness that I've only seen in his eyes a few times. All when he seemed to be different altogether. His fangs extend, sharp as knives. And at his back, quadruple tentacles grow from his spine, twisting and turning in the air, so long my head tilts back a little as I watch them twist and curve. The tips, soft and fleshy, suddenly sharpen like blades as they curve around him and suddenly freeze, the business ends pointed directly at me.

I gasp but don't back away. I don't even move.

He'rox watches me carefully, waiting for a reaction.

"I am a creature twisted by experiments, forged into a weapon," he says, his voice even rougher than usual. Completely inhuman. "This is my true face, the monster I became to save my people."

I stare at him. Stare at the "monster" he's showing me, and realize that even though he has his weapons pointed against me, his arms that still hold me close remain gentle against me.

"Who did this to you?" I whisper.

For a moment, he doesn't respond. "To know thy enemy, one has to sometimes become them." He tilts his head, menacing with those dark eyes, and yet, I remain unmoved. "It was the only method I could think of to find their weakness." He leans in, nostrils flaring slightly as he sniffs at my cheek, almost like a predator sniffing out its prey. "After all other avenues failed, I did the only thing I could think of to save my people from the scourge that descended upon us."

"You did this to yourself," I whisper, realization dawning slowly. "You experimented on yourself. To beat the Gryken...you sacrificed yourself."

He rears back suddenly, tentacles sharpening all along their length as he stares at me.

"That's nothing to be ashamed of," I whisper.

"I failed." His growl is like two separate voices intertwined. The monster and the alien. And my gaze falls to his lips, to the two tentacles curling there. He shifts, almost like he winces under the attention. Under the fact I see the correlation between that part of him and the monstrous bits he hates so much.

"Edooria no longer stands."

My heart aches, the reality of it all leaving me stunned. "But Earth does."

His head snaps, his movements not as smooth as they usually are as he looks at me.

He'rox stares at me and for a moment I see raw pain in those dark eyes. The only emotion that shines through from the abyss.

"Earth is not my home."

Reaching up, I trace the ridged texture of his skin.

"No, but you protected it," I say softly. "You protected me."

He'rox remains silent, so I continue. "You did what you had to do. Became what you needed." I meet his gaze, staring into the darkness. "But it does not change who you are inside. You're still He'rox to me. The one who saved my life...the one who saved my world."

For a moment, silence descends between us, only the sound of the dying rain pitter-pattering on the dead leaves on the forest floor playing a symphony in the background.

"This form is all I have left," he says, and finally, the tentacles soften and begin waving softly in the air behind him.

"Then use it for good. Make a new purpose."

He'rox blinks, his eyes slowly bleeding back to blue. "You do not fear me."

"Why should I fear those who help the helpless?"

He stares at me for a long moment before, slowly, his fangs shorten, the tentacles at his back growing smaller as they sink and disappear.

"I do not deserve such trust." His words make me laugh through my nose. My fingers stroke against his jaw, enjoying the velvety feel of his skin and not wanting to interrupt this moment between us. Lifting his hand, He'rox closes it over mine against his jaw.

"For so long I lived with this hatred inside me," he murmurs. "For what I'd become. What I'd done."

I smile at him, tears brimming once more in my eyes, because now I understand it all. And it all makes sense. "You are selfless."

"You give me a gift, Sophie of Earth," he says softly. "Perspective I'd lost."

I nod. Leaning into him as his arms tighten around me. "And your ba'clan?" I whisper. "That is why you don't use them anymore... because of the sacrifice you had to make..."

"They are dying."

My head snaps up, wide eyes on him. "What?"

"The Gryken genetic material warred with mine. The ba'clan fought to keep me alive. Keep me Vullan. They fought until they were almost depleted."

I stare at him for a few moments. "What happens if they die?"

For a few moments, he says nothing. And then...

"Then, Sophie, I will die too."

CHAPTER TWENTY-FIVE

HE'ROX

Soh'fee looks stunned. She blinks at me with eyes that are too wide before they unfocus, her gaze moving all over my ba'clan.

"What—" Her throat moves, bobbing as she takes a deep breath. "What are the chances that will happen?"

As I gaze at this strange female who has defied all the odds and found a place at the center of my world, I wonder if I should reveal the exact truth. The care in her gaze awakens something deep within me that calls to protect her at all costs. Even from myself.

"A Vullan's ba'clan are tied to him from the moment he takes his first breath...and his last. When mine die..." I stare at her, unsure of how I want to continue.

"You will die too?" she whispers it, gaze dipping as if she's heard terrible news.

An answering thrum begins in my chest to comfort her.

"He'rox the Vullan will die."

Her chin lifts as she pierces me with her gaze again. "What does that mean?"

But I will have to answer her some other time, for my senses tingle.

"Beings are approaching."

Soh'fee stiffens, head turning in the direction in which I'm focused.

"Hyu'mans?"

She has a right to ask, and opening my senses further, I sniff.

"Three beings. Moving swiftly." Too fast to be purely hyu'man. But there is no time to warn Soh'fee as one of them breaks into the small camp we've made.

I camouflage, resting Soh'fee on the wet earth, and I hope she understands why.

We must be careful.

"I am still right here," I growl near her ear and she gives a discreet nod as she rises to her feet to face the beast of a hyu'man before her.

Tall. Male. Twice Soh'fee's size. I dislike him immediately—and that is before I catch the full extent of his scent.

Rotten. Corrupted.

Another growl slips past my lips for a whole other reason, and I can see when Soh'fee clenches her jaw. For she can see it clearly. There's no guessing this time.

Dark veins thread up the man's neck, traveling over his jaw to network over his face.

"Shit," I hear Soh'fee mutter as she takes a step back and into my camouflaged frame.

At the male's back, two more adult hyu'mans come through the bushes, pausing as their eyes land on Soh'fee. All corroded. Corrupted with the same filth that has warred within me for revolutions.

"Three of them," Soh'fee whispers, her gaze darting to the little shelter. To her weapon there. But it is too far, and her weapon is useless. If they charged now, she would not get there in time.

"I am at your back," I lean in, keeping my voice low. Her scent envelops me, thick with the sweetness left behind by her arousal and laced with her fear. My gaze flies back to the corrupted hyu'mans.

In this short time, Soh'fee has become the most important thing to me in this universe. If they dare to move, I will split them in two before they even take a step in her direction.

Maybe she senses my craving to end them, for she reaches back, pressing into me as she tilts her chin up and smiles at the hyu'mans. Two males. One female. All look back at her with blackened eyes that no longer see her for what she is. The only thing ruling their mind will be hunger and thirst.

For my Soh'fee.

"It's okay." I don't know if she says it for my or their benefit, but she smiles again.

They have said nothing. Not even moved, and my senses war. Something is not right here.

"They're not doing anything," Soh'fee whispers.

"Are you guys okay? Didn't think I'd meet anyone out here." She brightens her smile and lifts her voice. Over the silence of this forest, her voice carries and the corrupted hyu'mans tilt their heads almost in unison.

I can almost hear her swallow hard.

Right. This will not do. I should cut them down before—

Movement shifts behind the group of hyu'mans and I freeze, wrapping an arm around Soh'fee to keep her with me. There is something else there, and as it reveals itself, it is my turn to tilt my head.

A small hyu'man.

The moment the child reveals itself, I can tell Soh'fee startles. Her body jerks immediately as she twists to take herself from my grasp, but I hold on to her fast, my lips curling as I stare at the little hyu'man.

Something is wrong with it.

And why did I not scent it?

"He'rox," Soh'fee hisses under her breath, and with much willpower, I let her go.

She moves toward the group semi-cautiously, almost as if forgetting the three fully grown hyu'mans before her, her entire focus on the child.

"Hey there, princess," she smiles at the little hyu'man. "I'm Soh'fee." Her gaze darts to the adults the child hides behind, before placing her focus back on the small thing.

It is skinny and dirty, its hair tangled and knotted. Wide eyes stare back at Soh'fee from behind the leg of the massive male and Soh'fee stops a few lengths away.

"Come here, princess." Soh'fee smiles but the child doesn't respond. Eyes that have seen too much terror stare back at Soh'fee, unblinking.

Soh'fee gulps, glancing in my direction, but I do not reveal myself. Not until she needs me. And I can see it in her gaze. That silent pleading for me to wait.

Patience is not a trait I have. Especially not concerning her.

"Is that your dad?" she asks the child.

For the first time in the whole interaction, the child shakes its head almost hesitantly.

Soh'fee smiles, eyes warm.

I want to reach for her and pull her back against me where she will be safe. To take all of this away and return to the moment we shared before. For the world to fade away and it all to be well. Just me and her. Here. No one else.

Yet, I can't deny that her inner purpose is one I share.

Gazing at the Corrupted before me now, seeing the small hyu'man within their ranks, I can already tell Soh'fee will not turn her back. For she is too pure.

But me...I have been blackened. She is now my priority. My purpose is to keep her safe.

I take a step forward at the same time that Soh'fee rises.

"It's okay," she says again, as if sensing my nearing presence. She moves to the small shelter, keeping the Corrupted in her sights as she rolls her strange bedding and secures it to her pack before digging inside the pack itself. Out pops a small packet. A meal bar. She smiles as she slips her pack on her back and retraces her steps to crouch on the level of the small hyu'man. She stretches the meal pack toward the child, but the child does not move.

"It's okay," Soh'fee smiles again. "It's food."

She strips the protective covering from the meal bar and breaks a piece, popping it into her mouth and emitting a deep, overindulgent moan that has my sazi forgetting the position we are in.

"It's yummy." She smiles at the child. "Strawberry yogurt flavor." She stretches it in the child's direction again. "You can have the rest. I'm already full."

Her throat moves as she watches the child, her scent filling with hope. She wants the little hyu'man to bite. I want the little thing to stay away. For her three guardians stand ominously still. Silent. Watching. *Waiting.*

The child moves forward slowly, eyes on Soh'fee the whole time, until she is standing right before her. Eyes far too big for her face stare at Soh'fee as she reaches forward and takes the sustenance in her small hands. She brings it to her lips, taking a bite and chewing so quickly, I do not believe the flavor had time to seep into her tongue.

Something like a sob jerks Soh'fee's frame as she reaches for the child, wide eyes on the adults behind the little being as she takes the child into her arms.

"It's okay," she whispers. "Let's get you out of here."

The child stiffens, suddenly struggling in Soh'fee's arms, a scream that shouldn't be possible from a being so little piercing through the forest as she twists in Soh'fee's arms. At her back, the corrupted start moving, seemingly called by the child's growing distress and I'm about to cut them down when Soh'fee screams, "Wait!"

She sets the child down, eyes wide as she glances over her shoulder at the Corrupted who have frozen once more.

"I won't harm you," she says to the little being. "I have more food at another place." She glances behind her again at the Corrupted still standing there. "And people who can help. There are even other little boys and girls you can play with."

Unity. She's referring to Unity. But Soh'fee must know she cannot truly integrate this child there. It is corrupted. Just like the female she chased through the trees.

But from the way a breath shudders through her shoulders, I can tell she knows this and that it weighs down on her.

"Would you like to come with me?" she whispers, hand outstretched to the little hyu'man. "You don't have to be alone anymore."

The child stares at her for long, slow moments before she nods. A hesitant movement of her chin to her chest.

Soh'fee forces a smile across her lips before she finally looks up, eyes scanning the area before they somehow land in my direction.

"Unity," she says. "Let's go to Unity."

CHAPTER TWENTY-SIX

HE'ROX

Traveling alongside the Corrupted would be easier if I wasn't constantly watching Soh'fee.

Soaked from the torrent that had rained down on us, shivers go through her frame now and then as she holds hands with the little hyu'man and we make our way through the underbrush.

Still camouflaged, leading them is difficult. Discreet brushes against low-hanging vines and bushes tell Soh'fee which way to go. For only she is looking for such signs. The Corrupted at her back walk like mindless beings, controlled by something else entirely.

The child.

The network needs a host in order to control others. Feed off them. Spread. It makes sense. The Gryken did the same. They used the veins to control hyu'manity, turning them into mindless beings.

Now, with them gone, the network is evolving to survive without them. But one thing is clear: this early in the evolution, it is still trying to figure things out.

Soh'fee trudges on, leading the group through the underbrush.

When the child begins to slow down and stumble, she pauses.

"Can I carry you?"

The child looks up at her, wide eyes bearing no emotion, and nods.

As Soh'fee crouches, I watch her wince, the pain in her shoulder obvious. Yet, she lifts the child and we continue on.

I wish I knew what her plan is, for the dark cycle draws nigh. The thought of her being among these beings throughout the night is one that makes my ba'clan rise along my shoulder blades. They hate the idea as much as I do.

I cannot lead her when it becomes too dark for her to see my subtle cues. We will have to stop. Rest. Stand guard.

Still, I remain camouflaged, guiding her discreetly, eyes on her as the child rests its head on her shoulder. Its eyes focus in my direction and it stares, almost as if it can see me. And for a moment, I wonder if it can.

Though innocent in appearance, her powers are formidable enough to control the Corrupted following behind.

I watch Soh'fee carefully. She knows the child cannot truly integrate into Unity, yet she continues forward, unwilling to abandon her. I can see the wheels turning in her head, trying to figure out a way to save this small hyu'man.

I have done nothing to deserve a female with a soul as pure as this.

But then something catches my attention. The child, as it lifts its head and sniffs.

I stop moving, watching as it tilts its head, something akin to life firing in its eyes as it focuses on Soh'fee's wounded shoulder.

Soh'fee's blood.

A snarl rises on my lips at the same time that the child places its hand over Soh'fee's wound.

"You are bleeding here," the little creature says, voice small and soft.

Soh'fee turns to face the child, a smile on her lips. "Oh, you can talk, and such a beautiful voice you have." Then she smiles even more. "What's your name?"

The child stares at her for a moment. "Asha."

"Nice to meet you, Asha. We'll get home in no time and then you—"

"I will help you…"

I see it the moment before my world stands still.

A singular dark vein pulses down the child's neck, disappearing behind the filthy garments hanging from her slight frame. It lights up under her skin, running through the arm that's connected to Soh'fee's wound, too fast for me to stop.

I lose my camouflage. The universe ceases to exist.

"No."

Soh'fee staggers as the child's palm lifts from the wound. It is already done. There, like a sticky web, a mass of thick veins snap from the child's palm to disappear under the bandage.

My roar echoes through the trees, chilling the darkening sky at the same moment the child's eyes widen as she turns my way. For the first time, I see fear in those wide eyes, but all I can focus on is Soh'fee. She stares ahead as if experiencing something inside that she can't quite explain. As if her mind is taking some time to catch up with the sensations going through her.

And then she looks at me.

It's a look filled with regret and sorrow. As if she's *apologizing* to me. In that one moment, it's as if she's realized and accepted the inevitable. That something unchangeable has just occurred.

The child screams, and Soh'fee seems to knock back into herself. She turns, running in my direction at the same time that the Corrupted charge at her.

No. *At me.*

They're focused on me now.

My gaze snaps to the small screaming hyu'man.

They're focused on me because *she* is focused on me.

"He'rox!" Soh'fee screams, but I am already there, grasping her and thrusting her behind me as I unleash my tentacles, swinging them forward and toward the charging terror.

I cut down the first Corrupted even before they realize I'm there, another tentacle wrapping around the female Corrupted's neck and pulling her back and away from my Soh'fee.

But that's when I hear a sound I don't want to ever hear again.

Soh'fee screams. Bloodcurdling and filled with pain. At my back, I feel when she falls to her knees and my tentacles slice through the air as I spin, cutting through the tower of a male that's reaching for me. But he isn't the reason she screams. He isn't the reason she's fallen on her knees in damp earth, blood seeping from the wound in her shoulder.

A roar rumbles through me, stilling the air as my gaze snaps to the hyu'man child. The tang of copper fills the air as Soh'fee releases her, the pain wracking her frame too sudden and too much for her to control her grasp on the child.

And those wide juvenile eyes turn on me, fear so thick I can taste it, as she turns and disappears into the bushes.

"No!" Soh'fee calls, staggering to her feet, but I am already there. I brace her up, fury going through me as I see the pain on her face.

"I'm f-fine," she stutters. "Save her."

I stare at her in disbelief, knowing my gaze has bled to black and that the smell of her blood is calling to that other part of me. But something supersedes that call. *Soh'fee* supersedes that call.

"Save her, He'rox. Don't let her get away." She says this, even as she grits her teeth against the pain and I see a flash of darkness pulse under her skin, leading from the wound toward her neck.

My nostrils flare as my gaze lands on the wound at her shoulder.

No.

This is not what's supposed to happen.

I'm supposed to save her world. Save *her*.

"He'rox! Please! Go!"

I did not sacrifice everything to be unable to save the one thing I truly care about.

Back on Edooria, my people and my work had been my life. I'd thought they were my reason for living. For being.

I was wrong.

With just one touch, this female taught me I'd been living a hollow existence.

The universe wouldn't dare take her away from me now!

"Go!" Water's in her eyes as she grits her teeth and looks up at me. "Find her! She might be the clue to all of this."

And at that moment, I realize one thing.

Soh'fee was wrong.

"My sacrifice was not selfless."

She blinks up at me, even as my tentacles grow longer at my back. Even as I allow the monster to claim what's left of me. And still, she does not flinch.

"You were wrong, Soh'fee." I crouch, gathering her in my arms as I hold her as gently as I can. "When I tried to save my world, I acted out of selfishness."

"He'rox." A tear slides down her jaw as she looks at me. Pain tightens her features as another dark pulse spreads from the wound in her shoulder.

"And when I saved your world, it was for the same selfish purpose." I lean in, face level with hers. "And I'm about to do it again."

For I am no hero.

A tear slides down her cheek as the infection spreads within her. I gather her gently in my arms. She is my light in the darkness, my beacon of hope.

"I'm about to save you again," I vow, my gaze level with hers. "Even if it means this world burns."

For I will become the monster to keep her light alive. Commit every atrocity, cause every destruction, if only it means she will survive.

I will tear down stars from the sky if that is what it takes to save her. For her, I will sacrifice anything. Even my own soul.

CHAPTER TWENTY-SEVEN

SOPHIE

Pain shoots through my shoulder, searing my veins as I grit my teeth, gripping the wound. The world spins.

He'rox gathers me in his arms, holding me ever so gently as his tentacles writhe and snap at his back.

"Find her..." I whisper again, pleading with him through the haze of pain. "The girl...she was controlling them. She might be able to help us. Maisie died, but maybe this little girl...Maybe she can..."

He stares down at me, his gaze black and filled with purpose. "I must save you first."

The ground shifts under us as he moves, swiftly cutting through the forest. My head lolls back, darkness creeping in at the edges of my vision. I can feel the cold seeping through my veins, followed by fire. As if I'm freezing and burning at the same time.

"I could amputate it. Stop the infection." But even as I whisper those words, I know that isn't the right solution. It's too far gone already. I can feel it in my neck, traveling down my spine, the speed at which it moves sending more than fear through my bones.

I stiffen against the pain, unable to breathe, my eyes fluttering open to find He'rox's dark gaze on me.

It's cold. So cold. And I recall the words he'd said before he took me into his arms.

"The girl," I whisper again. "Please, He'rox."

Movement stops as he halts, eyes focused on me and I phase out of consciousness for a moment, only to reopen my eyes to us moving again.

There's a cold reality creeping in at the corners of my mind. A surety, as if the universe itself is talking to me.

I'm dying.

So...this is how it feels.

I could almost laugh.

So, my father was right all along. The end of the world does end in disease. At least, the end of *my* world. And his. But there might be hope for the rest of humanity. And I'm confident the alien holding me now can find the key.

My eyes flutter open again and I'm dimly aware that we're high in the canopy, swaying gently even though we're moving at incredible speeds. He's walking on his tentacles, using them like four stilted legs.

"The girl," I whisper again, lids low as I focus on him. He'rox. The alien who has taught me so much in such a little time.

All my problems, all I've been through, have been nothing compared to what he and his people have endured. And still, they fight. Still, they came to save us.

Save *me*.

A smile curves my lips despite the pain, and He'rox's gaze snaps to mine.

"I'm going," I whisper.

His eyes flare with something I don't have the energy to understand. Only accept.

"I'm glad I got to spend my last moments with you..."

I think he calls my name, swear he roars in distress, but all else fades as my head lolls back once more. And as my consciousness wanes one last time, I'm aware of something moving over my skin.

Like water, but not.

Maybe I'm dreaming.

But something crawls over me, slick and cold. I wish I could, but I'm unable to even react. Whatever that child put inside me is leeching every energy reserve I have.

It was physical contact after all. That's how the virus spread. Or maybe I'm still getting it wrong. Maybe it's more complicated than that.

I might not be able to finish this fight. I might turn into a mindless husk. A shadow of myself. But I hope He'rox can take what we learned. Defeat this new threat. Save us.

That cold wave spreading across my frame runs under my clothing, reaching every inch of my skin and a flash of consciousness shoots through me as it slips under the bandage on my shoulder, covering the wound, what feels like tendrils of ice burrowing into my flesh. I scream at the violation, tears slipping free as a flash of heat erupts from the contact point. The world spins and the only thing that keeps me tethered to reality is He'rox's voice as it echoes oddly in my ears.

I drift in and out of consciousness as we race through the darkening forest. At every point when I awaken, I mutter to him that he needs to find the child, and he answers with a comforting deep vibration in his chest.

Time ceases to exist. Minutes, seconds, hours mean nothing as my world fades in and out. When my eyes flutter open next, the pain in my shoulder has dulled to a throb, and a cool wave moves over my skin. But with every heartbeat that thunders in my ears, it's almost as if I can feel the darkness. Feel it encroaching. Feel it ready to take me away. Forever.

"He'rox," I whisper.

That comforting vibration beats against my ears as he responds.

"I have done as you wish, my mate. Rest now. It will be over soon."

Done what I wish?

My consciousness wanes then comes back.

His mate?

I open my eyes to focus on pure white ridges with an underside of gray. Smooth. So smooth. He'rox's skin.

I blink at the sight before me.

He's no longer wearing his ba'clan.

"Your ba'clan..." I whisper. I didn't know he could remove them. But instead of awe, panic rises within me and that wave that I imagined over my skin shivers like a thousand small beads at my sudden response.

He said he would die if he lost his ba'clan.

But when I lift my gaze, the dark night suddenly no hindrance to my eyes, the male that holds me close looks far from near death.

He'rox is big. Imposing. Magnificent. He walks like an otherworldly being, keeping us above the forest floor and the obstacles on the ground as he moves over the space with ease. And there, in the corner of my vision, something catches my attention.

My head feels heavy as I turn it and I wonder if I'm dreaming.

There, in one of his tentacles, hangs the little girl. Asha.

The monster, she says. *The icky bug is gonna eat me!*

I blink at her, trying to focus. Icky bug?

He'rox.

No dear, he's not a monster, baby. He won't ever hurt you.

Even from the distance between us, I see the tear slide down her cheek and I hate it. I hate that a child as young as she is has had to go through all this. Has had to face this alone.

He killed Sonny and Bertha. Greggy too.

Sonny, Bertha, and Gregory. I can only guess those were the people she'd been walking with.

They were my friends. Another tear runs down her cheek. *And now the icky bug is killing you. And you're my friend too.*

It's only then that I realize her mouth's not moving. That she's somehow talking to me without actually speaking. I blink at her, unable to understand how. Convinced I'm hallucinating.

And, as if she's heard my thoughts, the child continues. *You're my friend now. We don't gotta use our mouths.*

I swallow hard, trying to ease up, but He'rox's arms tighten around me.

But you gotta do what I say, right? Since you're my friend now?

I blink at her again, fighting to understand how the fuck I can hear her.

You can kill the icky bug.

Her words chill me and I fight against the pain and grogginess so I can focus.

"Kill the icky bug?" I whisper. And even though I've spoken out loud, she nods slowly.

So I wasn't hallucinating. She was really talking into my mind. This new development sends both anxiety and trepidation through me.

He'rox glances down at me, features etched in stone, and I swallow hard.

Why aren't you listening to me?!

Her scream, though it is in my mind, makes me wince.

My friends always listen to me! Why aren't you listening to me?!

"I—" Pain and grogginess make it hard to focus. "He'rox," I whisper.

It is only then, when a new wave of pain goes through me, that I catch a glance of myself. Consciousness wanes before I come back.

There's a pulsing against the wound in my shoulder and I lift my hand to the spot.

The whitened suit that covers every inch of my skin reflects in the starlight, and I pause.

The ba'clan?

My eyes snap to He'rox and I see the cosmos in those dark eyes.

I understand now. What he has done. Why I am still here. Sane. Alive. Conscious. And most of all, *myself*.

"You've given me a piece of your soul so I can survive a little longer," I whisper.

I lift my gaze to his, seeing the truth reflected there. And at that moment, I know that whatever's happened between us cannot be undone. Will *never* be undone. My life's forever changed by this being from another world. He has sacrificed for me again.

My life is his, in its entirety. A debt that can only be repaid one breath at a time.

CHAPTER TWENTY-EIGHT

SOPHIE

My vision comes in and out of focus as He'rox carries me through the forest. Pain still flares through my wounded shoulder, though it is now more of a distant ache than the searing fire from before.

When I open my eyes again, I am staring at the smooth white walls. There is a warm liquid surrounding me and that realization sets me in a panic. I struggle to swim to the surface, but it feels like lead is strapped to my ankles, pulling me down. Anxiety rises inside me as I realize I am trapped inside this watery tomb. But I notice something else.

I finally see the room around me...and the double pits of terror staring straight back at me from the other side.

The Gryken floating in the huge cylinder.

I'm floating in a huge cylinder.

Memories rush back. The Corrupted. The little girl, Asha. When she'd tried to help me and the searing pain that came straight afterward. He'rox carrying me through the forest. Giving me his ba'clan. *Saving my life*. Again.

We must have made it to Unity. And I am in his lab.

I focus on calming myself. To think rationally.

If I'm here, it means He'rox put me here. And if I can make sense of all this, that means I'm not a mindless husk. I'm still me. Somehow.

Spinning slowly in the fluid, I look around, my gaze snapping to the Gryken across the room.

Part of me wants to stay, to let the warm liquid soothe my injuries and my fractured mind. But another part needs to break free, to see He'rox again and understand what happened between us in those final moments in the forest.

I ball my hands into fists and summon what little strength I have left. Pushing with everything I've got, I fight through the thick liquid, heading to the top. Bracing against the walls of the tank, I slowly force the lid open. Liquid spills out as the seal breaks and cool air rushes in.

I tumble out of the tank, landing on the floor in a coughing, sputtering heap as pain shoots through my bones from the distance of the fall. As consciousness threatens to slip away again, a familiar pair of dark eyes appears above me.

"He'rox," I manage, reaching a hand toward him.

He takes my hand gently in his, and I know in that moment that I will always crave his calming touch.

He'rox clutches my hand softly, as if I am something precious and fragile. His dark gaze bores into me, filled with sorrow, guilt, and a hint of hope.

"Forgive me," he whispers. "I had to save you."

Forgive him?

I try to speak, but all that comes out is a hoarse croak. My throat is raw from the regen liquid.

Asha!

"She is safe. Confined in her quarters. But safe."

He'rox gently scoops me up in his arms, moving me away from the spilled liquid on the floor. My vision blurs as he carries me, the trauma and blood loss finally catching up to me.

How am I...how am I alive?

Turning my hands, I blink at my skin. I'm...*me*. There's no ba'clan covering me as I thought. No dark veins threading through my skin. But even as I think this, there's a comforting pulse all along my spine. I blink, looking up at He'rox as the wall opens before us and he takes me from the room with the regen tanks. Cool air brushes over my skin and I shiver against the sudden cold.

Almost immediately, a wave moves all across me like a warm embrace. Almost like watching white ink run over my skin, He'rox's ba'clan flood over me, warding away the chill.

"They're still here," I whisper.

"Enough to heal your wounds and keep the darkness at bay," He'rox says softly as he sets me down on a floating table. The warmth from his "gift" spreads through my body, chasing away the pain and cold and I stare at my skin in disbelief.

"How is this possible?" I whisper.

He's quiet for a moment, as he walks over to a section of the wall and activates a light matrix. A three-dimensional image of myself pops up, with He'rox moving through the scan right down to the nervous system. "It means we are forever bound, in a way I could not have foreseen. But not unwillingly." He meets my eyes. "I would not undo what I have done."

I swallow again, for the first time noticing him properly.

Without his ba'clan, it is surprising that he looks...*naked*. The ridges along his body are more pronounced. His muscles. His strength. Every dip and angle of his is more defined.

White from head to toe, with completely black eyes, he is even more remarkable than before.

"Your eyes," I whisper.

I meet He'rox's gaze, but something has changed. The calmness is gone, replaced by a storm I do not recognize.

He turns to face me fully, and I see a struggle raging within him. From the way he stands rigid. From the way he'd put distance between us.

I don't move, sensing a predatorial energy emanating from him, and all along my body, the ba'clan pulse like an external heartbeat. In comfort? As warning? I do not know.

"Something's changed," I whisper. "Hasn't it?"

He'rox closes his eyes for a moment. When he opens them again, they are blacker than ever. Slowly, he nods.

I stare into those eyes, just as something snags my attention.

Sound. On the other side of the wall.

I turn my head almost too slowly, gaze snapping to the white wall. In my periphery, He'rox stands like a shadow, unmoving.

And there, across the wall, somewhere on the other side, the raging voices of Fer'ro and Adira, Sam and Ga'Var, filter through. They are trying to get in. Something about He'rox losing his senses and the change having taken full effect. Something about not being able to trust him fully now.

Something about him being a danger to himself, to Unity, and most of all, to me.

They do not know how to get in. Or maybe, He'rox has locked us both in this lab. Shutting them out.

"The darkness you call the monster..." I whisper. "It has overtaken you."

I turn my gaze back to He'rox and his ears twitch.

He may think he is a monster, one he's been chasing away all along, but that little movement tells me more than he knows.

He nods once, chin jerking sharply to chest.

He doesn't move. As if he is afraid of coming even an inch closer to me.

"Why did you do it?" I ask softly. "Give me your ba'clan, binding us together?"

He'rox is silent for a long moment. Then, "You were dying. I could not save you any other way."

"The same way you've been preserving yourself," I whisper, the extent of what he has done for me becoming even clearer. "The only way you've been keeping yourself whole."

He doesn't answer and I don't expect him to.

"But at what cost?" I whisper. "You said if you lose the ba'clan… you die."

We stare at each other for long moments, his black eyes fathomless. "Some costs are worth bearing, if it means the one you care for lives."

It's unexpected, the small smile that twists my lips. That makes me want to reach out to him, even though he's put a huge warning sign between us.

Because I never expected this. To find someone who would care about me as much as this male does in a world that's falling apart.

When I exited my bunker, I expected to be alone. To maybe find a group, but in essence, still be on my own. Every man for himself.

He'rox represents none of that.

"But if you're dying…"

"I am already gone," he says. "I cannot…"

He cannot undo the change. The fact his eyes have remained that black color is evidence enough. And this is all because he's tried to save me. *Has* saved me.

"And if I give the ba'clan back to you—"

I'm unable to blink before he's right before me.

A breath shudders through him. "You *must* not. I beg you, Soh'fee. They must remain with you."

Tilting my chin, I meet his gaze once more. "Or else…I will die…"

He doesn't answer. He doesn't need to. The answer is already clear.

"Asha," I whisper. "Where is she?"

"She is unharmed," he assures me. "Deja has her. Is keeping her company."

"Will she be safe?"

My eyes fall to his lips and I watch a shudder go through him as he grips the table beneath me so hard I swear I hear the material crumble. As if being so close to me is really testing his limits.

"Deja has the protection of fully operational ba'clan. She will be fine."

Outside, the conversation grows more intense and He'rox raises his hand. Another layer of white material slides along the wall, dampening the sound and sealing us in.

Lifting a hand, the ba'clan rear against my skin, forming spikes along my outer arm as I stretch toward He'rox, and even in that dark gaze, I can see the pain there.

His own symbiotes are unsure of what he now is. Are aware that he is no longer himself completely and are willing to defend themselves against the tainted part of him.

It must have been so hard for him.

Tears well in my eyes that I don't allow to fall. Because He'rox doesn't need pity. He needs strength. Because I know what it's like carrying a load all on your own. I lived most of my life alone, afraid to form any lasting relationships from the deep-seated terror my father instilled in me since I was a child. Everything was going to end, anyway. Why try to fall in love when it was going to be ripped away painfully, whether by death, disease, or destruction?

As my hand makes contact with his jaw, he stiffens, those dark eyes swallowing me.

"Sophie," he warns.

But I am far from afraid.

In fact, I feel stronger. Wiser. More in tune with everything around me. I can almost...I can almost hear his heart beating in his chest.

I don't think, I just do.

Tilting my chin, my lips press against his and there's an immediate growl that rattles through me, sending shockwaves of want, pleasure, and need straight through my bones.

He'rox's hesitation disappears as he grasps me and lifts. My legs automatically wrap around him as he cradles my ass and takes me across the room.

We don't get to wherever we're going because the moment my tongue slips against his, he growls again, the sound vibrating the air in the room as he stops walking and presses my back into a wall.

His lips crash against mine. Eager. Demanding. And I give in, opening my lips to him as his tongue slips into my mouth.

He tastes like fire. Flaming, burning and scorching, his tongue dances against mine, his mouth eager and hungry. A hunger I know all too well because it rises within me now, pushing me forward, making me hang on to him, my fingers clawing into his back as if the taste of him is not enough.

I can feel myself being lifted, my back sliding along the wall as He'rox continues to kiss me, my legs tight around his waist. His hands grip my hips, pulling me closer to him, our bodies grinding against each other. I moan into his mouth at the same time that something hot and hard seems to spring out between us, pressing against my core.

"Tell me this is what you want," he growls against my lips, his voice rough and low.

I nod, unable to form words as he tightens his hands against my thighs, the tips of his claws pressing in almost painfully, as if he's afraid I'll run away. I pant against his lips, my tongue flicking out to brush against one of his fangs in a way that makes him growl against me, sending a surge straight through the center of my being and down to my core.

I need to be filled by him. And as if he can read my mind, something writhes between us, brushing against the intense heat of my core as it begs to be filled by him. Even the shadows at the edges of my vision dance with a life of their own.

The dryness of the air sticks to my skin, making each one of my senses more heightened than they already are. The fire of his lips burning against mine, his hands gripping my skin, the tension building between us... A low moan escapes my mouth as He'rox pushes himself against me, my nipples pebbling almost painfully as he slips his tongue from my mouth, those dark eyes swallowing me as he curves his tongue under my jaw, tilting my head up to face him.

The thought of him putting himself inside of me is so strong that I don't even notice when he spreads my legs wider and inhales deeply.

"They are right, you know, dear sweet Sophie," he says, swiping his tongue down my cheek before it disappears back into my mouth. A whimper leaves me that I don't even try to hold back. I don't know who he's referring to and I don't even know if I care. All I can feel is the heat spreading through my frame. That clawing need for him.

Through the edges of my vision, I see the tentacles at his back rise like thick tendrils behind him, his gaze going bottomless as my lids lower and I look at him.

"You are not safe with me."

Wrong. I have never felt safer in anyone's arms.

A hand comes up, clasping my neck as he supports my ass with the other.

"I crave you," he growls. "Your scent drives me to insanity."

He dips his head to the other side of my neck, fangs extending. "Your blood..."

My breath stops in my nose as he freezes there, his fangs hovering over my neck and...I open to him.

Swallowing hard, I remove all barriers. I go limp in his arms, trusting that this being will take care of me. Because deep down, I know He'rox won't hurt me. Despite what he thinks, despite what he believes about himself, even when I was down in my bunker, I never felt this safe. And that's all I need to know.

The mental removal of barriers must manifest physically, because almost immediately, the ba'clan flood away from my skin, disappearing as if they were never there as they move to pulse along my spine.

He'rox growls, realizing what I've done.

"Sophie..."

The way he says my name only makes my head tilt back as I smile at him.

Because there's something thrumming through my veins too. A darkness that calls to me. Telling me we are meant for each other.

I should be afraid of it. Afraid of the potential of this union, but all I can feel is anticipation instead.

He'rox's head dips, pulling a line along my neck that's led by his fang pressing into my skin. The ba'clan pulse at my spine and I get their message. They will intervene if I need them to, and yet, I feel no fear.

Instead, all that happens is a slight twinge of pain that makes me clench at my center. And the moment He'rox slides his tongue over the narrow wound, I whimper his name.

"Across the universe," he growls, "I have met many gods. But if I had to choose, I would only worship you."

He pulls away for a mere second, savoring the sight before him. But then, his lips are on mine again, his hands gripping my ass as he spreads my legs even further. He lifts me higher and even though I know he is strong enough to hold me like this for more than a few seconds, I let out a small yelp.

Two thick tentacles swerve from his back and grab each of my ankles, keeping my legs spread as wide as they can go as He'rox dips, tongue trailing down my neck, the center of my breasts, and down lower as he shifts both hands to balance me under the ass.

His fingers come around, spreading me enough that his thumbs open my lips, baring me completely as his palms splay across my ass.

My hands fall, lids lowering as lust consumes me the moment I realize what he's about to do. They thread into the locs atop his head as He'rox dips his face into me.

The heat of his tongue is the first thing I feel. So hot, slick, and smooth that I shudder at the contact, a whimper slipping from my lips.

"Greatest gods," he groans, his voice a deep rumble that speaks of dark, tantalizing things.

His tongue dips against me again, the flat of it pressing into me, starting from the top and descending in a fluid, slow drag. It pulls at my flesh, urging my lips to part for him. The moment they do, he sucks me between his lips, pulling me inside of his mouth. The suction is intense, a gentle pull that makes me moan. He'rox releases me with a wet pop and starts all over again, his movements growing more intense at each passing moment.

My mind reels, senses overtaken by the sensations that are running across and through me. I'm hot. Flushed. I'm so wet, I know He'rox has to be able to scent me. He can probably smell a drop in the ocean that's running down my ass, soaking my entrance and dripping onto the floor below us. And when he pulls me into his mouth one more time, sucking and licking and flicking his tongue over my clit, I know I'm gone.

Two more tentacles grab my arms, lifting them and pinning them above my head as He'rox growls against my clit, the vibration making my eyes roll over. And just when I think I can't take it anymore, something hard, hot, and thick presses against my entrance.

My vision returns, flying to the male between my thighs as He'rox holds my gaze, his tongue swirling before he sends it forward.

I cry out, my legs spasming in the hold his tentacles have on me as his tongue pierces me deep. Swirling, as he pushes it deeper, filling me up more than I ever thought any tongue could.

If this is his tongue...what will his...

But the thought doesn't get to finish.

Fingers splay my cunt, spreading my lips as they work on my clit, just as He'rox slides his tongue out, slurping up the juices that have moistened my skin before sliding back inside. He pumps as he holds my butt with his hands, squeezing and pushing me into his mouth. The sensation is so great, I feel like I might explode. I want to scream and yell, but I am silent, only pants and deep moans leaving my throat, my voice captured by the moment.

My legs shake as I lose all control and my body sags completely in his arms. My stomach tightens and the muscles between my legs begin to spasm as my whole body tenses. I try to stop it from happening. I don't want it to end yet. But it is useless. A scream erupts from my lips the moment the two thin tentacles that hang near his lips find my clit and curl around it, just as He'rox's fingers tighten on my bum, his tongue plunging deep one last time as I shatter around him.

CHAPTER TWENTY-NINE

HE'ROX

She is perfection.

But I already knew this.

Now, she is my everything.

I rise, Soh'fee's sweet juices slathered over my lips and tongue. A taste I never want to forget. She is truly something special, *and she is mine.*

I now know what it feels like to have your mate come apart in your arms. And I want her to do it again. And again.

I could get lost in the symphony of Soh'fee's little whimpers and cries.

Running my tongue over my lips, I bring her taste into my mouth once more as my gaze slips to hers. She is open before me. Soft perfection as her body shudders in the aftermath of her release. And as I stand now, my sazi throbs and bobs in the air, eager to sheathe itself inside her warmth.

Her breath catches and her eyes go wide as they land on my shaft, and I pause.

This is the first time she has seen me. The first time I have seen *her*, but for her it must be incredibly strange.

My sazi is not like it usually was before the change. This side of me has added...externalities. The thick shaft, wider at the base than it is at the tip, bobs in the air nestled between four thick tentacles that writhe around it, searching for her, wanting to *embed* themselves inside her.

"Oh fuck," she whispers, a tremor going through her legs as her tongue runs over her lips.

Soh'fee stares at me with the same hunger that's reflected in my eyes before another shudder goes through her as she lifts those eyes to me.

I cradle her jaw gently as I step forward, the other claw running along her leg and up her shuddering chest to cover one of the soft mounds there.

Her breath comes in deep as she tilts her head toward me, nose brushing against mine before her scent drives me over the edge.

I pin her back, capturing her lips as I surge forward.

She's so slick, just the first sensation of her walls closing around my tip, welcoming me inside her, has me groaning into her mouth.

I pierce her, opening her wide to accommodate me, and Soh'fee accepts every bit of me, writhing as she takes me inch by inch, not perturbed by the tentacles that grip her ass, wrapping around her backside, curling through her folds to rub against the little bud there even as they seek entry to her warmth.

When my hips settle fully against her, I pause for a moment, wanting to just savor this moment for what it is. She accepted me. This tight little hole has taken me.

I have never had a female fit me so perfectly. But hunger does not make me stay still for long.

I shift, pulling back and sliding deeper into her warmth. Soh'fee gasps as I thrust inside her, feeling her walls quiver around me. Each move I make seems to make my sazi thicken even more inside her, meeting her needs as her thoughts, her emotions, all seem to merge with mine.

Soh'fee moans deep, braced up by the wall as I drive into her with a passion that all the stars in the universe would be jealous of.

My cock throbs, and each movement of her body to mine, each convulsion of her muscles, each gasp of her lungs, each heated moan, makes me feel like coming undone.

My claws dig into the skin of her hips, keeping her in place as we mate. My thrusts are harder and faster than before, and she matches my intensity, our moans and grunts filling the air in a song that will stay with me for all time.

There are no words in this language.

Words are unnecessary.

For Soh'fee is now at the center of my soul and I can feel her there.

Lightning feels like it strikes as Soh'fee shudders around me, her body becoming undone once more and just the scent of her channel flooding with slickness drives me over the edge.

I slam into her, driving her against the wall at her back as spend shoots from my tip, pumping into her, filling her to the brim.

I shudder with every jet, pressing into her, never wanting to let her go, and when the tentacles holding her arms release her, my mate leans into me. Arms around my neck. Face pressed into my skin.

My life organ swells with her unconditional acceptance, and when she finally lets me go and places her palms on my cheeks, her eyes now blue with black flecks that pull me back to reality, a hole opens up in my world. One filled with despair and fear.

For my last mission isn't one I thought it would be.

And I will save her.

If it is the last thing I do, I will save her.

That...is my promise.

CHAPTER THIRTY

SOPHIE

He'rox releases me slowly, catching me in his arms as he brings me back to the floating table and sets me down. He doesn't move, and as I cling to him, I realize I don't want him to.

If I could stay here like this with him forever, I wouldn't change a thing.

But such ideas are dreams. Even I know that.

As my breaths begin to calm down, I inhale deeply. His vanilla scent fills my lungs, but now it's laced with something else. Like dark smoke. I breathe him in still, enjoying this new scent, because, despite what he thinks, he's not the monster he's painting himself to be. Never has been. Even the way he made love to me tells me that.

I drift in the silence, a smile coming over my lips as I realize I can still hear his heart beating. But that realization soon makes me stiffen. Lifting my head slightly, I freeze.

I can hear his heartbeat.

I've never heard his heartbeat before.

"I can hear the blood rushing through your veins," I whisper, lifting my gaze to his. "I've never—"

And then I hear something else. Tilting my head slightly, I realize I can still hear the people outside the room as well. Their arguing has stopped, but I can hear...pacing. Small feet. At least, smaller than a Vullan's. A human female then.

She's pacing so hard, I can almost hear the agitation in her footsteps.

"And...the others outside this room," I whisper. "They want to get in." I turn my gaze back to him. "You locked them out."

He'rox's fist clenches on the table, a fine tremor running through it. A reaction he couldn't control. A memory flashes through my mind—my own shaking hands as I stood before the Corrupted, terrified yet determined. And he'd stood with me. There'd been no tremor then.

Frowning, I focus my hearing, tuning into He'rox's every inhale and exhale, the faint rustle of his tentacles waving in the air at his back as he shifts his stance and they slowly begin to recede. Sounds I shouldn't be able to detect so clearly.

"Is this...the ba'clan?" I ask. "Is this why I can sense all these new things?"

He'rox's black eyes study me intently. Slowly, he shakes his head.

A tremor goes through me as I lift my hands, turning them over. No dark veins.

My neck?

As I shift, He'rox allows me to slide off the table and, as if reading my mind, he activates a section of the wall that transforms into a mirror.

I stand naked before it, He'rox at my back as he meets my gaze in my reflection.

Soft bruises where he gripped my hips stand like a witness to our lovemaking.

At another time, I would blush. But greater things weigh on my mind.

I tilt my head, examining my neck for the telltale signs of the infection.

There is nothing. Not even at my shoulder, the contact point.

Gone is the bullet wound that had been there. Completely healed. And I run my hand over the spot, amazed yet terrified at the sight.

Was I healed because of the ba'clan? Or that other thing?

My legs are shaky as a lump forms in my throat the moment I decide to turn around. I do so slowly, eyes on the mirror until I'm looking over my shoulder at my back.

What I see there has me unable to move.

There, at my back running in a neat line down the center of my spine is a thin white column. He'rox's ba'clan.

But directly behind them, like a festering shadow, is a thick vein that looks like black ink, pulsing to every beat of my heart. Like a thick, black snake. Lurking. Waiting.

Terror shoots through me and I can't stop myself as I reach for it, clawing at myself, the urge to remove the corruption too strong to deny. Blood springs from where my fingers dig into my skin and I only realize He'rox is holding on to my hands when I try to pull them to rake my skin once more and my whole body jerks toward him instead.

My heart pounds in my chest as panic rises in my throat, while the black vein pulses, as if laughing at my terror.

"Get it out." My voice is deceptively more level than I feel inside. "Please, He'rox. Get it out of me."

His grip on my wrists tightens. "Doing so may kill you."

I shake my head. "I'll take the risk. I can't have this—this thing inside me."

The urge to claw at my back returns. To rip and tear until the corruption is gone. He'rox pulls me close, wrapping his arms around me to still my hands. My breath comes in short, ragged gasps as I stare at my reflection. At the vein.

At the thing that will be the cause of my end.

"Listen to me, Sophie," he says. "I will find a way to remove it." He says. "But I need time."

Time. The one thing we may not have. I squeeze my eyes shut but the image of the vein is seared into my mind.

"We have to get it out now," I plead. "Before it spreads. Before it—it takes control."

I cannot imagine walking around like one of those things out there. I'd rather die.

"If I were to cut it out now, you would bleed to death." His voice is steady, his tone almost unreadable, but I hear it anyway. The anguish underneath his words. Anguish *for me*. "The network has attached itself directly to your spine and major blood vessels. Removing it without precision will destroy you. And I refuse to let that happen."

A sob escapes me. I can't help it.

To survive the Corrupted only to become host to this sinister thing. He'rox strokes my hair, my back, holding me as close as he can. His warmth and the beat of his heart the only things offering me any semblance of comfort.

"I can't live like this," I whisper. "With this inside me, waiting to turn me into—into one of them."

He'rox growls. "I will not let that happen."

The conviction in his tone gives me pause. I lift my head to meet his gaze, finding determination swimming in the black holes there. "I refuse to lose you." He pauses. "This is my final oath. I will free you of this."

The tears spill over, trailing down my cheeks. I cling to him, needing the solidness of his body against mine. His promise is all I have to cling to, for I have nothing else.

"And if you can't?" I have to ask. I have to prepare for the possibility, as grim as it is.

He'rox holds me close, pulling me against him. "I will find a way."

His words hardly have time to settle before the room erupts with a blast so loud, my ears ring. Shrapnel fly inward, narrowly missing me only because He'rox spins with me in his grasp, putting his body in front of the flying debris.

A roar barrels from his chest, shaking the room and everything in it, only to be matched with answering roars that thunder through the air, vibrating my bones. I can almost feel He'rox change, the tentacles springing from his back as he releases me and spins to face the gaping hole in the wall.

Three Vullan stand there, blades trained on He'rox, ba'clan spiked all around them in agitation. My heart leaps into my throat as He'rox's ba'clan respond on *me*, pulsing at my back as if waiting for instructions.

Fer'ro, Ga'Var, and San'ten. And from the looks of it, they've come prepared for a fight.

"He'rox," Fer'ro growls, taking a step into the room. The other two follow, fanning out to surround us. "Tell us we have not judged you incorrectly. Tell us you have not been experimenting on the human and on that *child* you brought."

He'rox shifts, blocking me from view, a growl rumbling in his chest.

"Lower your blades," he growls.

They do not. Instead, Fer'ro's lava eyes narrow. At the same time, one of the others speaks. San'ten.

He's moved to the side enough that he's looking right at me, and I can tell the moment he spies the vein at my neck. A hiss escapes him, his eyes going even blacker than He'rox's as his fangs extend.

At the sight of his snarl, the ba'clan shoot over my body, covering me from head to toe. San'ten's ears flick off the sides of his head and his snarl hesitates for only a moment before he turns to Fer'ro.

"She's *infested*." I can almost hear the blades on his ba'clan sharpen as his shoulders hunch in a stance that looks like he's about to pounce at any moment. "But she holds his ba'clan," he continues. "He has mated her and given her his affliction."

"No!" I shout.

"Wait," someone else says.

It's Adira. We speak at the same time as I dart out from behind He'rox before he can stop me, throwing my hands in the air. The Vullan's eyes flick to me in surprise, even as Adira, Sam, and Mina glance at each other.

"He didn't do this to me."

Silence falls in the room, and I take a shuddering breath.

There's no use hiding it. I'll only put the entire camp and all they've built in danger. The future of humanity in danger.

So I begin.

"We found something out there." The air becomes so thick, I can cut it with a knife. "Those veins we went to investigate. They're..." Glancing behind me, I see He'rox's gaze locked on mine. His tentacles wave at his back as he gives me a slight nod to continue. I take a deep breath, pushing forward. "They're growing. Creating a network underground. Vast, more vast than you can even imagine. Already..." I gulp. Memory of what happened at that camp rushing back through me. Memory of what I saw. What I experienced. "People are infected. The network. The parasite...it's..."

Fer'ro's pupils narrow, blades still pointed at He'rox. His disbelief is palpable. I take a step forward, steeling my nerves under his scrutiny.

"It's worse than we thought. We found some people in a camp. They all seemed normal except—"

"Except they've been changed." Mina steps forward, piercing gaze on me.

"*Mina*," San'ten warns, as if telling her not to come too close to me. As if I'm a threat. His overprotectiveness would be heartwarming if his distrust wasn't directed at me.

And then I realize something.

In that pause, as I shift my gaze to Mina and she swallows, I hear the sound of her saliva going down her throat. My gaze flicks to everyone in the room. One by one. And with each one, I can hear their heartbeats thumping in their chests.

I can hear what I should not.

"We can block the signal," Mina says, gaze still focused on me. "You can hear them, can't you? The Gryken. You can hear their whispers."

I swallow hard, shaking my head slightly.

"I can't hear them," I blink. Mina's heartbeat rises and I hear it thumping hard in her chest. My gaze flicks to the spot as an urge rises within me, one that makes me want to claw at her chest just so I can see the organ beating there. The thought sends bile rising even as the urge grows and I stagger away from her, back pressing into He'rox.

Mina steps forward and my eyes widen in horror at the track my thoughts have taken. I stretch an arm toward her to ward her back.

"Don't come closer."

Her gaze flicks to her mate before refocusing on me. "What's happening, Sophie? You can tell us."

But I can't. How can I tell her that as the moments tick by, all I can hear is the blood rushing in her veins and the sound is slowly driving a thirst in me I wish I never had.

"I..."

"She cannot hear the Gryken," He'rox says, an arm snaking around me. "She can hear something else. She can hear *you*."

I swallow hard.

Is this what he's been fighting all along? Even now? This is the call that's been at the back of his mind all this time? To consume. To devour. And yet still, he never tried to hurt me?

"Your breaths," He'rox continues. "Your lifeblood. She can hear it all. And it is telling her to take. To control."

The horror of his words is even more terrifying because *it is true*.

I'm...turning into a monster, and as I glance up at He'rox, the irony isn't lost on me. Now more than ever, I want to tear this corruption from my veins.

"There must be something you can do," Fer'ro's blades disappear as he takes a step forward. "Brother." The utterance is obviously an olive branch. An apology for their fears. Their assumptions.

"Can you control it?" Adira asks.

I shake my head. I'm not sure. I want to say yes...but every moment that passes, my senses tune in to new things. I can even feel the air shift in the room as she steps forward.

"Fuck," Adira whispers. "Okay. Listen. We're not going to let it take you. We'll find a way." Her gaze meets He'rox's over my head and I assume he jerks his chin in affirmation.

"And you, brother," Fer'ro's gaze slips over He'rox. His ba'clan wave as if ready to spike once more but he manages to keep them down. "Your fears were incorrect." His gaze flies to the tentacles waving at He'rox's back. "You are in control."

"I am...not." He'rox's utterance makes Fer'ro's ba'clan wave, and off to the side, Ga'Var clicks something in an alien tongue.

Fer'ro clicks back before San'ten joins in. From their snarls, fangs baring, I can tell the conversation is heated before He'rox growls. "I'm *not* leaving Soh'fee."

"What?" I startle.

"She is mine. My ba'clan have claimed her. *I* have claimed her. I will not leave until she has turned me away."

I blink at him, shaking my head. "I won't..."

His gaze locks with mine before he continues. "There is one final experiment I can conduct. But for its success...something must be sacrificed."

A tense silence follows, before Fer'ro snarls. "We sacrifice nothing," he steps forward. "This time, not even yourself."

"I am afraid, brother," He'rox says, "that there is no choice."

My mouth falls open and I'm about to protest when a fifth Vullan rushes into the room.

Fi'rox, Deja's mate, skids to a halt, taking us all in before his gaze snaps and holds on to He'rox. His ba'clan react immediately, spiking all along his skin.

"A group approaches. Several humans. All carrying weapons," he growls, voice impossibly deep. "No response to the scouting drone." His gaze flicks to me before going to Fer'ro. "They shot it down."

"Hostile," Fer'ro says.

"Oh fuck," Adira mutters. "Alright, come on girls, let's go—"

"No!" I step out of He'rox's grasp. "You can't go out there. Warn the others in the camp. Get them to safety. Those humans approaching are..."

"Corrupted," Mina says, eyes widening, and for the first time I realize something that should be obvious from the first meeting we all had together.

Mina is not like the others.

Mina is different too.

CHAPTER THIRTY-ONE

HE'ROX

My gaze snaps to the vein pulsing down Soh'fee's spine, visible even under the ba'clan.

Even facing the Gryken alone on Edooria. Capturing one. Experimenting on it. On *myself*. Never have I felt such fear.

My ba'clan are slowing the corruption's spread, but their power is weak. Having sustained me for so long, there is not much they can give, and at the rate it is progressing, Soh'fee's system will be entirely corroded before long.

I am running out of time.

And now a new threat approaches.

Everything within me wants to retreat to the inner room within the lab. To start working on a cure. To find it. To save my Soh'fee. But she turns and looks up at me, the blue still shining through amidst black specks encroaching in her eyes. She knows the truth.

She can feel the abyss. The end approaching.

And I no longer hide. Not from myself. Not even from my brothers.

My tentacles curl around me, brushing against her back in a soothing caress as my mind races, grasping for solutions. There must be something that can be done to save her, to protect these hyu'mans and the fragile Unity they have forged.

"We have to go," Soh'fee says and once again I'm impressed by her resilience. Her bravery even though she is terrified within. "We have to go down."

My head tilts toward the inner lab, my thoughts moving to the Gryken and the female floating there.

I will use them if I must. Use myself.

I will find a way.

Soh'fee must realize where my mind's gone because she grips my claw. "Come with me. We'll deal with this later."

No. I must go to the lab. Find a way to end this. But I cannot dismiss her from my sight either. So I pray to the gods of Edooria. I pray my ba'clan can stave away the corruption as they did for me. I pray they grant me time.

I don't know how I move. How I follow her, my brothers, and their mates through the corridors of our ship. Into the lift. Down to the surface.

In the distance, shouts echo through the trees, and the camp becomes alert. The scent of panic begins to taint the air, grating against my senses and I growl, fists clenching.

Unity will stand.

These hyu'mans did not come this far, survive this long, only to fall now.

Beside me, Soh'fee stiffens. Her head tilts as she listens to sounds only she can detect, my gut coils at the changes already evident in her. Changes that fill me with equal parts despair and thirst I dare not dwell upon.

I clench my fist tighter, ready for the onslaught of fear scent that will fill the air as soon as we hit the ground and the camp devolves into utter panic. Moving closer to Soh'fee, I inhale her scent, her warmth. Using her as my anchor.

For I cannot lose her. Not to the Corrupted, not to this sinister thing transforming her from within. But even as I lean into her, the hyu'mans within the camp do not do as I expect.

It is only when we hit the ground that I am brought back to the fact that I have revealed for all to see. This part of me that I hid for so long is now visible to their scrutiny. And the hyu'mans gathered in the camp stop what they are doing. Tasks forgotten, they stare.

I expect fear. Terror.

I am their greatest enemy and savior combined.

Soft mumbles rise among them, and all turn to face us.

One comes forward, a weapon in hand. I recognize him as a young male, one of the first to have come to our haven in Base Zero. Bih-lee.

"Ok, so what are we killing?" His gaze snaps to mine. "Nice upgrade, man." He grins, teeth baring in the friendly hyu'man gesture.

My head tilts, unable to believe this is the reaction of these people, and Soh'fee turns and smiles up at me. One of reassurance. In her eyes, there is hope that this will all be okay. That it will all work out.

And one thing comes to me. Something I'd forgotten in my time on this planet.

As I look at Soh'fee, and as her people begin to move, getting to safety, some gathering arms, prepared to fight, I'm reminded of one unique quality of this species.

Their ability to adapt.

My gaze snaps to Soh'fee, a plan forming in my mind.

She can adapt. Adaptation is the key. Not destruction.

I can't cure her, but I can make it so she lives.

I can make it so that they all live.

"We have to help the camp," Soh'fee says. Her gaze flicks to Fer'ro, to Adee'ra, and then to the two other females, Mee'na and Sa'am. They stand ready, hackles already rising, prepared to fight for this fragile Unity they have all sacrificed to build. "If we don't stop this group…"

She doesn't need to finish. I jerk my chin in a nod, turning to Fer'ro. He holds my gaze, our differences set aside for now in the face of this shared threat.

"We should be enough," I say. "Tell the others to evacuate any remaining hyu'mans in the camp and secure the perimeter. We will head out to intercept the Corrupted."

Fer'ro growls an assent, following my direction even though he is our leader. A trait I have always respected in him. His mission has always been to keep us and whatever world we save alive. He waves to the others before heading to one of the larger tents.

Turning back to Soh'fee, I take her face in my hands. Her skin is warm against my touch, the beat of her heart strong despite the changes within.

"Stay close to me." She nods but there's an undercurrent of something there, and I am positive she will disobey this order if she sees any vulnerable hyu'mans out there. Her life organ is too big, beating for more than her. But mine is hard and cold. Soft only for her. I will strike them down if they get too close. "Do not engage the Corrupted directly. Your…powers are still unpredictable, and I will not risk you further."

To my surprise, she smiles. A faint thing, but a smile nonetheless. "Only if you promise the same." Her hands cover mine, gripping tight. "We fight together, He'rox. You and me. We end this together."

Warmth infuses my being at her words as I lean down, pressing my forehead to hers.

Together. The word repeats in my mind like a sacred song. It is a vow more binding than any other, and I hang on to it as we move as a group toward the incoming threat.

The angry shouts get louder as a band of hyu'mans bursts through the tree line. They stop short, eyes filled with manic rage, all pumped up to wreak havoc.

There will be no persuading this lot.

This will be war.

And yet...Soh'fee steps forward, hands raised.

The leader of the group snarls, eyes glowing with an inner malevolent light only I can see as he advances.

"Stop!" Soh'fee shouts. Her voice echoes across the air, halting the Corrupted in their tracks. They stare at her, heads tilting. Assessing.

I stiffen, ready to lunge forward and rip them apart. But Soh'fee glances at me, shaking her head slightly. A warning to stay back. To give her a chance.

I do not understand what chance she thinks they will allow. They are too far gone. But I obey her silent command, though every step she takes toward the threat makes my tentacles sharpen. At the slightest hint of attack, I will end them.

"You don't have to do this," Soh'fee says, holding the leader's gaze. His lips peel back, a hiss escaping him. The others mimic his reaction, a ripple moving through their ranks. But still they do not attack. "This violence, this desire to destroy—it isn't you. We're stronger than this."

Rage fills the leader's eyes. "What do you know? While we're out there trying to build society again, you're here with these *freaks*."

Soh'fee shakes her head. Gesturing to the dark veins evident underneath his flesh, she meets his gaze once more. "That's the enemy. That's the problem. Not these guys. They came here to save us. And they did. They belong here as much as we do. Without them, we wouldn't have this planet to call home anymore."

"Traitor," one of them says from the back, and others join in, calling my Soh'fee despicable names in their hyu'man tongue. I growl, my patience wearing thin, but Soh'fee says those words she said back in the forest before she was attacked.

"It's okay."

I know she's talking to me, letting me know she's fine. But the last time she said that, she was infested with the same scourge that eats away at the hyu'mans before us. Her words give me no peace.

"You're all ill. You feel like something's taking over your body, but you can't exactly tell what it is, right? Something that's heightening your senses and even though that's great, you can't get rid of the pit of fear swelling in your gut." She meets their gazes. "I know what it is. We can help you."

She takes a step forward. The leader tenses, blackened hands flexing.

"You can fight it," Soh'fee says. "These aliens are here to help us. We'll find a way to get rid of this new threat. Come with us. Help us build. It doesn't have to be this way. *The Vullan are not the enemy.*"

A hiss erupts from the Corrupted—a sound of hunger and recognition—and I wonder if they realize how inhyu'man the sound is. That they are changing. That they *are* changed.

"I have something inside me too, and it wants the same as what's inside you. But we don't have to listen. We can be more than what it makes us." Soh'fee holds their gazes, giving them an out. Blaming their bloodlust, their urge to destroy the last hope of their world, on the parasite taking over their bodies.

They can take it. Dissolve the blame on something else. But I know the moment they won't. The same moment the leader snarls, shaking his head as if to dispel her words. But another, a female, blinks rapidly. Her hands clench and unclench on her weapon, warring thoughts hitting her mind.

Soh'fee takes another step, her hands still raised. Pleading. "You know me. Maybe not by name, but you know my face. I'm like you—hyu'man. We don't have to be enemies. We can all do this together. We can co-exist."

The female Corrupted whimpers. Her legs tremble, head shaking back and forth as if trying to dispel some inner battle and I can tell Soh'fee's life organ clenches at the sight; at the pain etched on her too-pale face.

Another Corrupted, a male, stumbles closer to her. He grasps her arms to steady her, meeting Soh'fee's gaze for a brief moment. There is a flicker there, a glimmer of the man he is underneath.

Not all of them want to fight us. Some have come simply because, for them, being part of a group is better than being left alone.

But there is still one problem. They are all Corrupted. And until I find that cure, they are all a risk. A risk to Unity.

A risk to Soh'fee.

The leader snarls, shoving the male Corrupted aside. He storms toward Soh'fee, weapon raised. "I won't listen to a traitorous bitch like you!"

Tension releases from my shoulders, the call of violence easing some of the strain. I can purge them now.

I surge forward to intercept him, a roar tearing from my chest. He whirls to face me, his weapon firing into my chest and I jerk as the projectile enters my frame. I have no ba'clan to stop his bullet and the pain makes my tentacles spike around me.

I roar again, my claws and fangs seeking blood, and it is only Soh'fee's shout that stops me from slicing him in two.

"Stop!"

Behind him, the others charge forward to join the attack and that familiar bloodlust rises, urging me to abandon restraint and tear into living flesh until there is nothing left.

I shake my head, clinging to purpose, Soh'fee's command, her scent still lingering in my nostrils, on my tongue. I cling to that as I knock the leader's legs out from under him. He crashes to the ground, limbs jerking as he struggles to rise once more. The glint of madness remains in his eyes; the hyu'manity Soh'fee glimpsed fading once more behind the sinister purpose that drives these hyu'mans.

There will be no reasoning with them.

The others close in. I cannot hold them back and protect Soh'fee both. As my tentacles spike and jab, keeping the Corrupted at bay, I know I will have to rip them all apart, one by one.

At the center of the fray, in a circle of empty space, stand five corrupted facing off against Adee'ra, Mee'na, and Sa'am. Fer'ro, Ga'Var, and San'ten are on the other side, wounding but not fatally harming the Corrupted as they come in waves, advancing without fatigue, without pain, focused only on their singular purpose.

Destroy. Consume. Spread.

"Stop!" Soh'fee screams again.

A snarl leaves my lips as I wrap my arms around her, my tentacles spiking around us as I prepare to tear into the Corrupted's ranks. To protect Soh'fee. To stop this madness.

But Soh'fee releases a cry of pain. My gaze snaps to her, and I go still at the sight of the vein spreading up her neck, tendrils of inky black corruption racing across her skin.

"No." This is far too soon. Advancing faster than it should.

Soh'fee whimpers as the vein pulses, and I forget all else.

There is a shout behind us and I'm aware of a Corrupted charging toward us with a scream. My tentacle hardens, slicing through the air like a blade. But before I can reach my mark, the Corrupted stumbles as if shoved from behind. He rises again, trying to right himself, only to stumble and fall to his knees with an agonized groan moments later.

His head jerks to the side at an unnatural angle as the other Corrupted cease fighting, turning as one to look behind them.

The silence. Is deafening.

And in the midst of it...my Soh'fee.

The veins have spread down her other arm, devouring her body at an alarming rate. And her eyes—her eyes shine with the same dark power I've felt within me.

Silence reigns as the hyu'mans, the Corrupted lower their weapons and turn to face her.

"Stop," she says. Voice level.

And they do not move.

Turning to face me, there is only a moment where our gazes lock and the darkness fades from her eyes, the brilliant blue reclaiming her iris before she smiles faintly and her legs give out.

I catch her before she falls, cradling her to me, even as my tentacles remain trained on the threat around us.

"Soh'fee." I call her name but she barely responds. All along her neck and arms, the dark veins fade, almost as if they weren't there in the first place. All that remains is the one pulsing on her spine.

"Did I do it?" she whispers, head rolling back. "Did I make them stop?"

My throat tightens.

"Is anyone hurt?"

Despite all that's happened, her hope in her species still comes to the fore.

"They have ceased," I tell her, catching her head as it rolls back once more. She is weak. Weaker than before. But her display of strength has revealed one thing.

My Soh'fee is not a follower. She is a leader. Like that little child. Like that female back at the camp.

The network has chosen her as a conductor.

She holds the key to ending this scourge.

CHAPTER THIRTY-TWO

SOPHIE

I feel sleepy. Oh so sleepy, even though I know I shouldn't.

This isn't simply tiredness from overwork and lack of rest. This is something else. As if the energy itself is leaching from my bones.

I'm moving. Somewhat aware that He'rox is carrying me and that all around us, the Corrupted move as one, coming after us.

"He'rox!" Adira shouts, but he doesn't stop. He doesn't pause. I'm mildly aware that alarm rings through her and the others as they try to intercept the Corrupted who are heading our way, to no avail. They're hitting them with non-lethal blows, trying not to harm them but push them back, and all that's happening is the Corrupted stand after being struck down and continue on. As if they have one singular purpose.

But even as they come after us, they don't attack.

They're simply...following us. Following *me*.

The realization makes my head swim.

Adira appears alongside He'rox, somehow managing to keep up with him.

"Where are you taking her?"

"To my lab."

"He'rox, you can't—"

"What you believe I can or cannot do is none of my concern." He growls hard enough that she backs off, gaze flicking to me.

I want to tell her it'll be alright. I want to tell *him* it'll be alright. But I'm not so sure anymore. Even as the seconds tick by, I feel like I am losing myself.

The moment He'rox reaches the center of the camp I hear the exclamations of the people standing there, weapons ready.

"Don't fire!" Adira shouts, even as the Corrupted flood the camp behind us. "Don't shoot unless they attack first. Stand guard!"

"What's happening?!" one soldier asks and even in my state, I realize just how much power this woman holds. How much things have changed for humanity. This woman must have been just a regular civilian like me before our world changed. Now, she commands soldiers.

"Nothing," she replies. "I hope."

Her gaze flies to He'rox but he doesn't see. His whole focus is on me.

As they step into the lift and it closes, I spot the Corrupted skidding to a halt, eyes on the device as it rises into the air.

They tilt their heads, watching us, an eerie stillness going through their ranks.

"Think they'll just stay there like that?" Adira asks.

"They will do as Soh'fee commands."

Me?

I blink at He'rox, my hand trembling as I lift it toward him. He grasps it tight and it's all the communication we need. He's here. I'll be alright.

We move through the ship, the walls a blur until the familiar white walls of He'rox's lab come into view. He steps in through the hole the others had blasted into the wall before heading straight for the other side. That wall opens, leading to the inner chamber, and I catch the eyes of the Gryken floating in the tank before He'rox sets me down on a table that materializes from the wall.

I lock eyes with the creature, as if I'm unable to pull my gaze away, and I swear I see a shimmer of light in its eyes.

Interest.

It is *interested* in me.

"Strap her down."

My gaze snaps to He'rox the moment the words leave his lips.

"He'r—" I don't get to protest. Whatever AI is in this room obliges immediately, and stiff restraints pin my arms and legs to the table.

My eyes widen at the same time that Adira's do and she rushes before me, putting herself between me and the alien I've come to love.

Love?

My heart hammers in my chest at the word, and through blurred vision, tears forming in my eyes as I look over her shoulder at He'rox, I know it is true.

There is no other word for it.

I've never felt this way about anyone. He'rox is...

And that's when I catch the look on his face. My unfathomable alien lover, stoic in all there is, looks *pained*. He'rox's attention isn't on Adira, even though her ba'clan have created spikes all along her arms as she aims them straight at his neck. His gaze is on me.

"Forgive me, my light," he says, gaze locked with mine, and more tears spring into my eyes.

"It's okay," I say, and Adira looks back at me, eyes wide with disbelief.

"I don't know if you know this," she says, "but He'rox...he...the reason he's not exactly like his brothers is because he experimented on himself. He mixed his DNA with Gryken genes. Letting him experiment on you... There's a risk..."

"I know," I whisper, hating how much my eyes are threatening to close even though I'm fighting to stay awake. As if the moment I lose consciousness, this thing that's within me will rush through my veins past my last resistance and take over. "He did it to save them."

"Yes," Adira says, "but there has to be some other way to save *you*. We can...try taking the parasite out—"

"*I will end your life and that of any other being who enters this space and tries to do the same thing.*"

Adira stiffens at He'rox's words, blades getting longer, sharper, as she grits her teeth.

"Simple extraction is impossible." He takes a step closer, dark blood brimming from his neck as he walks straight into one of Adira's spikes as if they aren't even there. "Soh'fee will die, and that end is UNACCEPTABLE."

His tentacles coil and snap at his back, cracking the air like whips before they launch over him, all four pointing at Adira's crown.

"*Move,* commander."

Adira hesitates, blades withdrawing a little as she glances back at me even as He'rox advances. And I realize this woman who I hardly know is putting herself in danger just to protect me.

I smile at her, reaching weakly toward her even though only my fingers stretch in her direction.

"It's okay," I breathe. "I trust him."

She studies me for a moment before letting out a breath.

"Fuck," she mutters. "Fine. Do what you can." She pins He'rox with her gaze. "Save her if you can."

He'rox doesn't hesitate. "*I will.*"

Only when she steps away do I see the massive wound in his chest.

"You're hurt," I murmur, even as my vision wanes and I fight to keep a hold on consciousness.

"Not yet," he says, dark gaze locked with mine. "Only if I fail. And that is not an option."

There's a promise in his words that I cling to, knowing that if anyone can save me, it's him.

A light matrix appears above me in a language I cannot read.

Nearby, Adira paces, at the same time that there's a thump in the wall.

Adira's gaze snaps to where the entrance to the room is. "You locked them out?"

"I would have locked you out, too." He'rox's eyes remain on the matrix as his hands move like a whirlwind, the computer performing calculations every millisecond. Each formula he puts in comes back with a red flash against the screen. Every theory he tests comes back as a failure.

Adira's jaw tightens as she moves to where the door stands seamlessly in the wall.

"Open it."

"I must warn you, commander, if you let my brothers in they will try to stop me." He looks up at her. "And I will kill them all."

Adira's throat moves as they hold gazes. "You would attack them? Kill them? Your own Vullankin."

He'rox dismisses her with his gaze. "For Soh'fee, I will do anything."

I stare up at him, amazed as I watch him work, and hardly believing this is really happening.

To have someone fight so hard for me...not even the one person I could trust in this whole world fought this hard for me while he was alive. My father taught me to fight for myself. But now...

He'rox clicks something in his native tongue, not bothering to speak to us in English. The wall moves, long needles coming out of the wall as his gaze flicks to mine.

"Do not be afraid, Soh'fee."

But I am not. I am calm. Surprisingly calm as I watch the needles enter my skin, taking blood before they disappear into the wall.

"Tell me what you're doing," I whisper, energy so low, my voice is a whisper. "Maybe I can help you."

"Adaptation," He'rox says. "I cannot remove the network, but I can make you adapt to it. I am positive. Humanity has adapted to its changing world. Your species adapted to the ba'clan. You adapted to become mates for my kind. And when the Gryken created this network, they adapted to control your species. If I can reverse that adaptation..."

I watch him work, unable to take my eyes away as he desperately tries to find a winning combination that could save me.

His technology. His knowledge. It's all so advanced, I am in awe even as my consciousness wanes once more.

"I'm drifting," I whisper.

"*Stay with me, Sophie,*" he says.

"Leucochloridium paradoxum," I whisper.

"What?" Adira says.

"Parasite," I whisper. "Flatworm. Infects snails." I force my lungs to move. "Or...ophiocordyceps unilateralis. Fungus. Makes. Zombie ants. Both alter behavior." My tired gaze flicks to He'rox. "Maybe the key to beating this thing is here, on Earth."

He'rox pauses, gazing at me but not really seeing me. The inner workings of his mind going too fast for him to even speak.

"Or perhaps," he suddenly says, "it comes from Edooria."

My head lolls, turning to the side as my consciousness wanes once more.

Outside the room, I can hear the others trying to get in and I wonder if they will blast in here like before. Only, He'rox doesn't seem concerned.

His fingers are flying through the matrix once more as a tray exits the wall above my body. Samples of my blood spread out in tubes, all being mixed with different compounds.

"A new parasite," He'rox suddenly says.

"What?" Adira says, eyes wide. "No. No, we can't do this."

"I am not asking for your permission."

I nod at her, letting her know it's okay. I wasn't lying when I told her I trusted him, because I do. With all of my being, I trust him.

He'rox's gaze locks with mine as soon as one of the vials turns blue, lighting up in the center of the tray.

"Soh'fee," he says. "Forgive me for the pain." His voice almost breaks and it's the only sign I get that his warning is really and truly to be heeded. Because the moment he stretches his hand over me and the white ink of his ba'clan flood back toward him, pain lances through me, making my back arch on the table.

"Fuck, He'rox!" Adira screams.

"I need some of yours too," he turns to her and she fumbles as she stretches her hand to him, black ink running from her skin to pool in his palm. The black ink rises and shivers as if being so close to him is painful and He'rox deposits it on a tray along with the entirety of his ba'clan.

The tray disappears in the wall as He'rox's fingers fly through the matrix, lighting up his dark eyes with a white light that makes him look unreal.

Pain shoots through my being, not easing up even as I grit my teeth. My eyes widen and open, my mouth gasping for air that won't reach my lungs as I feel the pain searing through my veins.

All across my body, I feel the network spreading, no longer inhibited by the ba'clan.

"Hold on, Sophie, just a little more."

"I...I don't know if I can."

With each passing moment, the pain feels like it is burning me from within, even as I try to keep my hold on reality.

In the corner of my vision, Adira paces...and further beyond her, all I see are the twin eyes of the Gryken floating in the tube.

They remain locked with mine as if it had been watching me all along. And I don't know how I know it, but I *know* the creature is livid.

That's when I hear the crack.

Even with the pain and the rushing noise of my own blood in my ears, I hear it.

"It's...coming..." I whisper, hardly getting the words out.

"It what?" Adira stops, stiffening as she looks at me, right before the splintering of glass shatters the air around us.

Water floods the room like a tidal wave and I'm only aware of Adira's scream as she's swept up in the flood.

But He'rox doesn't falter. He doesn't wane. Not even when the water hits him and there's a deafening screech that splits my skull. His fingers fly across the matrix, performing the final calculations as the Gryken screeches once more.

"Fuck!!" Adira's scream shatters my consciousness as she moves like a blur, launching herself in the air as she aims for the Gryken. Her bravery is astonishing.

But the Gryken reacts as if it expects her. With one tentacle, it slaps her out of the air and she bounces off the wall before falling to the floor, the water from the regen tank draining almost as fast as she moves.

"No," I whimper, helpless in my state.

But the Gryken turns in my direction, those soulless eyes swallowing me whole as it advances.

And I hear it. I hear it in my mind.

"Little one," it says. *"You have adapted."*

And somehow I know, it's not speaking to me. It's speaking to it. The network. As if the mass of veins invading my being is its child.

This being that towers over all of us as it stands at its full height, sends terror through my veins.

And then...it reaches for me.

A tentacle moves through the air too fast for me to see.

Through the pain, a scream lodges in my throat as I wait for the impact.

But it doesn't come.

Instead, the Gryken screeches, splitting the air in two. And that's when I see He'rox has got a hold of it.

Two of his tentacles war with the Gryken's one as he grips the fiend and pulls, taking the thing away from me.

I fight to see what's happening. Fight through the pain. But all I manage to catch sight of is a deadly dance.

The Gryken thrashes and screams, its tentacles lashing out and

He'rox meets each one with his own. They're a blur of motion, tentacles striking and slapping only to be blocked by the other. The lab shakes with the force of their attacks, as He'rox throws the Gryken into the wall, only to be grabbed and slammed into the floor himself.

He'rox!

I want to scream his name. To help him somehow. But even as my body slams back into the table, I feel my limbs go weak.

So...this is the end. The real end. All those other times were just practice.

And yet, I am not afraid of it.

What I'm afraid of is seeing He'rox go down.

Adira gets to her feet and races towards me, ripping the straps from my limbs. "We have to get you out of here!" she shouts. But I can only watch the battle between He'rox and the Gryken, horrified and unable to move.

He'rox roars, a guttural inhuman sound, as his tentacles wrap around one of the Gryken's, twisting and jerking it until it rips from the creature's body. Black fluid sprays through the air, spattering against the walls. But the Gryken merely shrieks louder, shooting its remaining tentacles at He'rox with deadly speed. One strikes him across the chest, slamming him into the wall, and all I can do is stretch toward him.

"He'rox," I whisper.

This can't be the last time I see him. Not like this.

It cannot end this way.

And just as Adira gets me to my feet, supporting me under my arm as she heads toward the door, I only catch sight of the danger a split second before it hits me.

The pain is immediate. Different from the other pain shooting through my being.

This one is calmer. Sweeter. Sweet pain? But it is. I freeze, my chin dipping as I feel warmth spread across my chest.

The sight of the sharp tentacle sticking out from the center of my body is almost puzzling until I see the blood. And I realize what's happened.

The sound behind me will be etched into my memory forever.

He'rox's pained cry is filled with anguish and devastation, and I'm dimly aware that Adira is frozen in shock. As the Gryken's tentacle retreats, a sickening wet sound as it releases me, there's a deafening roar as the tentacle is sliced off and lands with a heavy thump on the floor.

I stagger, all energy leaving my frame as Adira staggers with me, my sudden deadweight pulling her down. My vision begins to blur and darkness creeps in at the edges but I will myself to stay conscious.

I have to see He'rox one last time.

And I do.

His beautiful sculpted face appears above mine, his eyes manic as he punches something in the light matrix. It blinks red and he slams his fists into it, going straight through the wall.

A tray slides out, a needle inside. Filled with thick black fluid, he grabs it, eyes locking with mine as he rears back and plunges it into my heart.

My body jerks, hot liquid filling my throat that tastes like blood.

"Thank you," I whisper, my voice sounding far, far away. "For caring about me so much."

He'rox releases another roar just as my vision begins to wane again.

But I see the moment his heart is pierced, a long tentacle coming through the other side.

I jerk, the last of my consciousness waning as another tentacle pierces straight through him.

And with a roar he turns, all four tentacles lashing forth.

The last thing I see is the Gryken's head being sliced from its body. Falling to the floor to roll straight to my feet.

And the last thing I hear? The deafening thump of the male I love as he falls to his knees on the floor.

CHAPTER THIRTY-THREE

ADIRA

I watch in horror as Sophie's body goes limp in my arms and He'rox's tentacles slice the Gryken's head from its body.

Everything seems to happen in slow motion—the Gryken's head rolling to a stop by Sophie's feet, He'rox falling to his knees, a wail of anguish tearing from his throat and his head dips to his chest.

Gently, I lay Sophie's body down on the floor. I can feel tears welling up in my eyes as I look at her peaceful face. She fought so hard, right until the very end.

I don't know this woman, but I've long come to realize that those of us who fight side by side, bleed together, grieve together, are one.

We are the closest thing to family in this new world.

I turn to He'rox. He doesn't move, and a sick feeling gathers in my chest.

No longer are my ba'clan crawling against my skin, warning me of the threat in the room. For there is none.

I sense no life in this space.

The Gryken is dead and He'rox... Sophie...

The three large gaping wounds in He'rox's chest are so big, they practically form one, his blood seeping out to settle in a pool around him.

This male who has given so much for my world, my people, lies right here, broken. The woman who is obviously his mate, unmoving at his back.

I have never seen his true form. All this time, he'd hidden. How he must have loathed himself. And I know, because I know how much the Vullan despise the Gryken.

It was their only reason for leaving their world, chasing the scourge that destroyed Edooria.

To be the very thing he hated most in the universe...

I turn my gaze away.

This is a scene I wish I didn't have to witness, and yet, here I am, grieving loss above the grounds that should be the beginning of a new Earth. A new world. A rebirth of the planet I once knew.

"I'm sorry," I say softly, not knowing what else to say. "You saved her...in the only way that mattered."

I stand there for a few moments, unwilling to believe this is really the end for this brilliant being. He'rox has always been different. Strange. But he was integral in everything we accomplished.

I have never seen a Vullan die, and it almost doesn't feel real.

I stretch my senses again.

If there is even the slightest heartbeat, we could rush him to a regen tank and hope for the best. But even as I hope, even as I wait, there is nothing.

He and Sophie both... are lifeless.

Pushing past the lump in my throat, I move toward the door as a noise outside the room draws my attention.

It opens for me, bypassing He'rox's commands now that his presence is no more, and I swallow hard, knowing I will have to face the others and give them the news.

As the door opens, I raise my hand to stop them. Fer'ro, Mina, and San'ten stand there. Ba'clan all raised. The blades only lessen in sharpness once they see it is me standing there.

"Adira." Fer'ro rushes to me, pulling me into his arms as San'ten storms into the lab.

"Sophie?" Mina asks.

I shake my head and her eyes widen as she rushes in.

Fer'ro holds me. No words are necessary between us. He can already feel the grief pulling me down. And as he turns, pulling me against him as he enters the room, I dip my head to his neck.

"He's not dead." I hear Mina say, and my head snaps up.

Hope rushes into me as my gaze snaps to find her on her knees in front of He'rox.

"I can still...*feel* him. Not his life force...but that other part." She gulps, gaze dipping before her eyes meet mine, uncertainty brimming there.

She's never quite liked relying on the powers...or rather, the effect of the trauma she'd endured at the hands of the Gryken. Carrying a Gryken spawn within her changed her biology. Made her senses more heightened.

A bit like with Sophie. And yet completely different.

"It's faint, but I can feel him. He's alive. Barely, but alive."

San'ten and Fer'ro's gazes lock and I don't protest when he releases me to rush toward his friend. They hoist He'rox up, lifting him together as they bring him to a section of the floor that has a faint circular outline on it. Setting him down, Fer'ro activates something and a cylinder rises from the ground, enclosing their friend and slowly filling with fluid.

I swallow hard as I watch his body begin to float. His tentacles and most of his body are colored black with the Gryken's slick blood.

Turning away from him, I move to Sophie's side, taking her limp hand in mine.

"Sense anything here?" I ask, but I know if Mina had sensed anything, anything at all, we'd be rushing Sophie into a regen tank as well.

Mina shakes her head.

Releasing a slow breath, I close my eyes.

"We should put her in a tank anyway," I whisper. "He will want to see her if he survives. He will want to say goodbye."

The others agree, a somber tone settling over all of us as Fer'ro lifts Sophie.

I watch as the tank rises around her, filling with fluid and she begins to float, her red hair fanning out like a halo. I can see why He'rox called her his light. He had never seemed so emotional, so truly alive, as when he was with her.

My gaze flicks to the one being in this room who holds my heart, and a part of it breaks.

If by some miracle He'rox does survive…I cannot imagine where he will go from here.

CHAPTER THIRTY-FOUR

HE'ROX

Darkness. Then the feeling of weightlessness. Fluid surrounding my body. My mind drifts in and out of consciousness.

Memories return slowly.

The battle. The Gryken's tentacle piercing my flesh.

Piercing Soh'fee.

The sight of her falling still in Adira's arms. My anguished cry.

I...failed.

I drift in and out of consciousness, my mind a haze of pain and regret.

I failed her. My light. The one being who saw past what I was to who I could be. Soh'fee brought me back to life when all I knew was vengeance and death. And now she is gone, snatched from this world because I couldn't protect her.

The fluid surrounding me is meant to heal, to regenerate torn flesh and broken bones. But it cannot heal the ragged hole in my soul. My body may survive this ordeal, but the part of me that was patched together by the one thing I came to love in this universe will remain shattered.

Images flicker through my mind on an endless loop.

Soh'fee looking up at me, her eyes filled with curiosity, not fear. The feeling of her in my arms, her lips on mine. The sight of her still form after the Gryken pierced her heart.

I never got to see joy light up her eyes. Never got to see her carve out a life of happiness in this new world being built.

She never got the chance to.

A roar builds in my chest but comes out silent, soaked up in the fluid surrounding me. I slam a fist into the side of the tank, uncaring of the pain. Physical pain means nothing. This anguish is so much deeper.

For the first time, I wish for death. An end to this suffering and the chance, however small, to see my light once more. She deserves so much more than the violence and darkness that was all I could offer her.

I was never meant for someone so pure.

Floating to the bottom of the tank, I set my feet on the floor and the fluid begins to drain. I stagger out before the tank has receded completely, driven by the need to see her. To hold her one last time.

How long have I been floating there?

Minutes? Days? How many cycles have passed? How many—

I stop short, staggering to a halt, my body swaying with the demands I'm placing upon it.

There, in the next tank, Soh'fee floats as if only sleeping. For a moment, I can only stand staring at her still form, something shattering to pieces within me.

Consciousness clicks and I move with staggered speed to pull up the light matrix attached to the chamber. But there are no neuron signals. Her life organ does not beat.

Her skin is pale. Even paler than before.

The scans show what I already know to be true.

My Soh'fee...is gone.

I press a hand to the transparent surface, wishing with all that I am that I could turn back time. That I could trade this worthless life of mine for hers. Soh'fee deserved so much more. But not this. Never this.

My legs give out and I crumble to the floor. A howl tears from my throat, calling on the gods of Edooria to come to my aid even as my fist slams into the unforgiving floor until my claws leave smears of lifeblood behind.

Rising, I force myself as I stumble over to my workstation.

The battle that happened in this room erased, it seems like nothing happened here. As if I didn't lose the very thing keeping me whole in this very space.

The body of the Gryken is gone. The evidence of our fight removed.

Activating the files, my claw trembles as I force my digits to move.

There. Documented right there is my attempt at saving Soh'fee.

A new creation completely. A modified version of the ba'clan. Something I'd theorized on Edooria. Something I'd worked on but could never make a success. The ba'clan are not easily changed. They resist it. But I had hoped...

I'd hoped that my ba'clan's will for survival was as great as my will to see Soh'fee live.

Back on Edooria, my attempt to change them had been a last resort for myself.

But for Soh'fee it was her only hope.

This genetically edited symbiote might have been able to disrupt the network's hold and establish a new form of symbiotic control—one that she could coexist with, rather than be enslaved by.

The formula had almost been complete. Where did I go wrong?

And then I remember. The Gryken attacked her before the serum was ready. I rushed. Forced it to complete the process. I could think of no other way to save her. And in that simple moment, my entire existence was shattered.

Slipping to the floor, my gaze moves back to my mate.

There are no words for grief such as this. It shreds my soul into ribbons and fills the jagged, aching holes left behind. I cling to the faint hope that this is some nightmare I will wake from. That my light's eyes will open once more and she will grace me with her radiant smile.

But nightmares end. This will not.

Crawling over to her tank, I lean against it. I would crawl inside too if it would not disrupt the tank's mechanics.

I remain there, crumpled against Soh'fee's tank, unwilling and unable to face a world without her in it.

She brought me back to life. Made me see new purpose. And now, with her gone, that life is over once more. There will be no second chance. No redemption from this.

The door to the lab opens silently, and Fer'ro steps in.

I'm thankful he is alone. For I do not think I could bear more than his presence.

I threatened his mate for my Soh'fee, and I wouldn't be surprised if he decided to rend me here. But even as he approaches, I know I would do it again. And again.

"Welcome back, brother," he clicks, sliding to the floor beside me. "You have not fully healed."

For a few moments, all we do is sit in silence.

"It does not matter," I finally click back.

He doesn't reply.

There is nothing to say.

I may not have claimed Soh'fee in the way most Vullan do. We did not share a colony of ba'clan. But she was mine in every other way. And losing a mate...

Every Vullan knows that leaves a hole that cannot be mended.

"I am sorry, brother," he finally says, and I tilt my head back against the tank, gazing up at Soh'fee.

More moments of silence pass.

Where do I go from here?

"In the end," I finally say, "You were right."

Fer'ro remains silent.

"I kept that beast for some reason not yet known to me. Captured it. Sealed it away." I pause. "And now, my thirst for vengeance...cost me the one thing that gave my own life meaning. I destroyed the very thing I sought to protect."

Fer'ro stays with me for a few more minutes...or maybe hours. I do not know.

Time passes without much care before he finally rises and leaves.

And when I fall back into unconsciousness, I allow the darkness to take me.

My light is gone, and with her, all traces of the male I might have become. I am adrift once more, and this time there will be no guiding star to lead me back.

CHAPTER THIRTY-FIVE

MINA

The silence in the camp is eerie.

Since we broke ground here, naming this new place Unity, there has always been laughter. Chatter. A new beginning.

Now, the air stands still…and I worry that this new hope we were nurturing—survivors of an apocalypse, the rebuilders of Earth—was all just that…pure hope. Never to be made into reality.

Shifting on my feet, my ba'clan shiver all across my frame. For the last few hours, it's all they've been doing. Ever since I exited the ship and came back to the ground.

For there is danger here now. An enemy we didn't expect.

One we aren't sure how to fight.

The Corrupted stand like silent sentinels in the center of Unity, unmoving. Unblinking. They haven't eaten or drunk in days, simply standing and waiting.

Waiting for what?

None of us know.

Sophie, that woman with the intelligent eyes, was their leader. And she is no more. So why are they still…waiting.

I swallow hard, gaze flicking to the young girl by my side. Asha. The child He'rox and Sophie brought back with them. The one with abilities like Sophie's. Powers neither of us asked for or wanted. Powers that now control the Corrupted.

Or do they?

"Hey, honey." I crouch before the child, trying my best to control my ba'clan that want to rear back. The last thing she needs to see is spikes rising from my back. "Can you try again?"

Asha shakes her head, tugging at her dark hair, and it hurts my heart that I have to ask this of her.

"They won't listen to me," she whimpers, sounding every bit like the scared child she is. Her head turns as she looks across the camp, her gaze skipping across the soldiers lining the perimeter of the tents. And behind them, the Vullan stand guard, ready to defend if needed. All eyes are on the Corrupted.

We've had to keep Asha away from everyone else, still unsure of just how this thing spreads. There are no marks or lesions on her palms. How she gave the parasite to Sophie is still unclear.

Pressing my lips together, I glance around the settlement. The half-built homes and community structures were abandoned after the Vullan urged everyone to retreat to the safety of the ship for now.

And even though most of the civilians are now within the ship, I could cut the tension on the ground with a knife.

My gaze flicks to my mate, and unsurprisingly, I find his eyes locked with mine. No matter what, I always have his attention, despite that he's aware of any and everything happening around us.

I shake my head slightly, letting him know that it's a failure. Asha can't control them…and that makes them an even greater threat.

San'ten snarls enough that I see his fangs. I know he and his brothers see the Corrupted as too dangerous. Anything tainted by the Gryken as dangerous.

They want to purge them.

But we can't. Not yet.

They're humans. Victims. Just like us. And if we destroy them, we destroy any chance of learning how to free others from the Gryken's control.

If that's even possible now.

I rise from where I crouch before Asha, worry gnawing at my insides. Something isn't right here. I can feel it, like an itch beneath my skin. The Gryken genes embedded within me, as much as I despise them, sense things the human part of me does not.

And right now, they're screaming that I'm missing something.

Nodding at Deja, she takes Asha in hand and leads her toward a tent.

Adira steps up to me, eyes somber. We've been through so much together, enough to last us lifetimes.

"If this...thing is spreading as fast as it seems..." Her gaze flicks to the Corrupted and that sick feeling in my gut tightens.

"Then those people out there that survived..."

"We have to save them somehow." She turns to me and I can see the resolution in her gaze. "Everything is at stake."

Everything.

She's right.

Unity, this new city, the hope of continuing to live in peace, it's all at stake.

"What do you think they're waiting for?" she whispers.

"I...don't know."

Adira's ba'clan spikes at her shoulder and she releases a shuddering breath.

"If we don't do something soon, they're going to kill them all. And I'm not talking about our mates. I'm talking about the soldiers. The general gave them specific orders before he left here. Alongside the Vullan, their task is to help us rebuild while eradicating all threat." She takes another breath. "And this is a threat if I ever saw one."

For a moment, silence descends between us.

"You saw them out there." Sam moves to stand beside us. "When they first arrived, they acted normal until Sophie screamed for them to stop. They weren't mindless like this. She..."

"She suddenly controlled them," Adira whispers. "And now they're waiting."

"*For what?*" Sam's worried brow dives further, her ba'clan becoming increasingly upset as they move like a wave over her skin.

That feeling in my gut increases.

"They're waiting..." I whisper. "For her."

My heart thumps hard in my chest as I turn, striding through the settlement as I pass the Corrupted. They don't move, don't react.

I swallow hard as I call the lift, waiting for it to get to ground level and take me up into the ship.

Because whatever I missed, the clue is with Sophie.

My breaths come in shallow inhales as I clench and unclench my fists as the lift rises, eyes on the other women who have come to be my closest family. Sam and Adira watch as I go and I pray to God that whatever compulsion is sending me to that place is good.

He'rox's lab is not a place I like to be in. The human woman still trapped there, floating in darkness and silence, could've been so easily me, if He'rox hadn't been able to save me.

Once the lift touches down, my feet move against the smooth floors of the Vullan mother ship as I head toward the lab.

The wall opens and I slip inside the clean white space, heading toward the back where He'rox lies.

As soon as the wall opens, shivers go through my ba'clan.

They hate this place almost as much as I do.

My gaze moves to He'rox first. In the darkened room, he looks like a strange creature floating in the liquid. Comatose, he has been that way since he'd awakened and staggered from the regen tank.

His brothers can find no reason for it. His body is healed, but he simply will not wake.

I hesitate in the doorway. We were never close, He'rox and I.

I don't think he was close to anyone.

Seeing him now, in all that he is, I understand why.

His thirst for vengeance against the Gryken and his hatred of what he was, reminded me too much, even subconsciously, of what I'd become. Of the effects of having one of those creatures spawning inside me.

It's a reality I still fight every day.

But Sophie loved him. That was clear.

Their bond bloomed in much the same way mine did for San'ten. A scorching, all-consuming passion that burned away all doubt and darkness.

And if my suspicions are right...

I step into the room. He'rox's tentacles don't react, remaining limp. His chest rises and falls with steady breaths, but his eyes remain closed. Shut off from the world.

From everything he's lost.

I imagine I would do the same if something ever happened to San'ten. How could I go on...

Shaking my head, I take another step forward.

"I know you can hear me, He'rox," I say softly, moving closer. "I need you to wake up now. Sophie...I don't think she's gone. The Corrupted, they're waiting for her. I can feel it."

Not a single twitch or flutter of his eyelids. I clench my jaw, releasing a slow breath.

"Do you know," I whisper, "your brothers...they never told us what you did. All that you sacrificed on Edooria. How you..." I gulp, coming face to face with the fact this Vullan had been prepared to sacrifice himself for the good of his people. And that I...not so long ago, had been prepared to do the same.

Except, San'ten came after me. San'ten saved me.

Just like Sophie saved him.

It's selfish to ask more from someone who has given their all. Yet, here I am. We need him. We can't fight this scourge without him. He's the Vullan's greatest mind.

He can't give up. Not when we still need him. Not when Sophie needs him.

My hands curl into fists. "Sophie wouldn't want this, He'rox. She saw the good in you. She wouldn't want you to live like this."

Still nothing.

I release a slow breath. Perhaps it's too late. He's too far gone in his grief. But we have to do something. The Corrupted are a threat as long as they remain unmoving in the center of the camp. More than that, if there's a chance, any chance at all that Sophie is alive...

We have to take it.

My gaze slides to her, watching her float in the still liquid.

Something deep within me is telling me I'm right. That she's still in there, somewhere. That part of me the Gryken gave me, the only blessing in this madness, might be right.

I have to stall the others. Prevent them from striking and cutting down the Corrupted. Get them to wait.

Because they are just the first of a wave that will come against us. And this can't be how it ends.

A world like this, an insidious threat eating right through it, is not the Earth we all risked our lives for.

CHAPTER THIRTY-SIX

SOPHIE

Do you know what happens when you die?

For a moment, there is nothing.

No thoughts, no sensations, no sense of self.

Nothing.

When the Gryken tentacle pierced my body, I felt *life* slipping away. I saw He'rox's anguished face as he held me in his arms. Then darkness swallowed me.

Now, I feel as if I'm floating, surrounded by a warm light. The pain and fear that consumed me in my final moments are distant memories now.

This place of light is a place of peace. So different from the new world as I know it. Not destroyed and desolate. Not dangerous and filled with terror. Here it is safe.

Is this what people call the afterlife?

A part of me longs to stay here. It would be so easy to just...remain.

But another part tugs at my spirit, calling me back. I see glimpses of the people I loved—my father and then...He'rox.

His pained cry as I faded comes back to me like a dagger to my chest.

This light may comfort me, but my place is with those still fighting in the darkness.

Reluctantly, I turn away from the warm glow and my eyes flutter open.

Liquid.

I'm underwater. Only this time, panic doesn't set in.

I've been here before. In this tank. Only this time, my body isn't fighting for me to exit.

My chest expands and I take a deep breath, only realizing the moment I do that I shouldn't be able to breathe. And yet, I can.

I take another breath as I spin slowly, vision clearing to reveal more of the room and my heart arrests the moment my eyes land on the being in the tank beside mine.

He'rox?

I swim closer to the barrier, pressing my hands against it as my heart hammers in my chest.

Is he alive? His tentacles float so still, his face at peace.

"He'rox!" My fist slams into the tank, a dull thump vibrating through the water as I stare in horror at him.

He can't be dead. He...he can't be.

As my panic rises, somehow through the fog overtaking my mind, I notice the barely perceptible rise and fall of his chest. He's breathing. And the wounds in his chest the last time I saw him? Gone.

He's asleep, not dead.

And... I'm not dead either.

But how? I *should* be dead...

My gaze drops to my frame, skimming over my nakedness.

Nothing is different.

Nothing, except for the fact I can breathe underwater.

Turning back to face the male before me, thoughts race through my head.

He'rox tried to save me. He *did* save me. But how...

Lowering myself to the base of the tank, the mechanism reacts the moment my feet touch the floor. The water drains as the tank lowers, and soon, I am standing in cool air.

I step out on unsteady feet. My body feels weak yet alive, defying all logic.

Blinking, I look around.

Everything seems sharper than before. More vivid. I can even hear the dim hum of He'rox's cylinder.

And there is something else. Something thrumming through my veins that I feel now that I'm no longer in the tank.

For a moment, I freeze, the horror of before coming right back to me. The parasite. The network. It was taking over, flooding through my veins.

I glance down at my arms again, but only my pale skin meets my gaze.

It's...not there.

And yet I can still feel a pull to *something*. The source of which I cannot yet determine.

I move to He'rox's tank on legs that feel new, and place my palms on the glass. "He'rox, wake up. Please wake."

His tentacles remain still yet I sense a connection between us, faint yet undeniable. What he did for me, how can I ever repay him?

I owe him my life.

I owe him *everything*.

I can only stand and stare at him floating there, some part of me screaming for him to open his eyes while another part wishes to break the glass just so I can touch him again.

A shiver goes through me, the cool air finally getting to me now that the warm water's evaporating off my skin, and a wave moves all through my frame.

I'd felt it before. Once. That time when I had He'rox's ba'clan on me, trying to save my life. But this time, it's different.

Far more powerful, like a thick cloak spreading all across my skin, and a gasp comes from my lips as I stagger back, eyes wide as I look down at myself.

Black ink's flooded all across my body. And I can see them.

For the first time, they're clear.

Right before me, they move and sway across my body, organizing themselves into an impenetrable shield. A new version of ba'clan. Dark now, not white like before.

"He fixed you," I whisper.

A pulse goes through my entire frame as the ba'clan respond.

My heart thumps hard as I move back to the cylinder, pressing my hands against it once more.

"He'rox," I whisper. "Please wake up. I need you."

Still, he does not stir.

Gaze flicking to the ba'clan that's covered even my fingers, I stare at them.

"He gave me this gift," I whisper again, more to myself than to them, but they pulse against me once more. Their knowledge floods into me in a way I don't know or understand. Memories of He'rox's experiments, his hopes for a way to fight the Gryken threat from within. A genetic modification that could be shared, not forced.

Yet in desperation to save me, he did the unthinkable. And against all odds, it worked.

As the ba'clan pulse over my entire body, I feel their alien consciousness merge with my own. Almost as if we are now one, working in harmony.

And still...something else.

"Did you..." I gulp, wondering if I want the answer to my next question. But the ba'clan aren't evil. If they were, I'd be dead already. They would have used my body without me having a choice in the matter.

Like the network wanted.

"Did you get rid of it?" I whisper.

There is no pulse and I wonder how much direct speech they can understand.

"The Gryken parasite. The network. Did you..."

My hands pulse against the regen tank—or rather, the ba'clan pulses so hard against my palms that I feel even my bones vibrate. And then...

My eyes widen as threads of black ink spread like veins across the glass.

Frozen in terror, I don't even think to pull my hands away.

The veins spread so fast, they almost cover the entire surface.

Like an alien entity with unknown power, they network and web together, stretching out from where my ba'clan-coated palms rest upon the surface.

Instant panic rises within me and I start to pull my hands away.

But they're glued to the surface, only coming an inch away from it as the veins continue to network over the transparent material.

"He'rox," I say his name, eyes locking with his closed ones, praying he'd wake up. "He'rox!"

Nothing. No response.

And as the veins network higher and higher up the cylinder, I lose all semblance of control.

"HE'ROX!"

Darkness arrives as he suddenly opens his eyes, locking with mine instantly.

A sob mixes with a laugh in my throat, only to be replaced with a lump that stops me breathing as the network spreads so fast it almost conceals my view of him entirely.

I have no clue what they're about to do, and I slap my palms against the tank again.

"He'rox, you have to get out of there. I don't...I don't know what's happening."

But even as I say this, the ba'clan pulse soothingly across my skin, as if to calm me. As if to say this alien entity is not a threat.

But nothing can stop the fear going through me. Not as I watch the veins network along the tank. Heading for the top as if intent on heading inside the tank itself.

Panic wells in my chest and I can hardly breathe.

I don't know how to stop this. I don't know how to stop *it*!

The ba'clan pulse again and I press my palms harder upon the glass, trying to calm my breaths and trust in the one thing that's kept me alive thus far. The veins immediately slow their advance, fading back towards my hands, and my eyes widen.

I can control it?

I can control *them*?

The ba'clan's memories flood my mind then. They show me how they purged the Gryken parasite from my cells, merging with it, creating something new. Something undefined.

And now they wish for He'rox. To be with him again.

I swallow hard, heart hammering an unsteady beat as the veins slowly fade back toward my hands, and when He'rox is fully revealed once more, his eyes are still on me. He hasn't moved. Hasn't sunk to the bottom of the tank to engage the controls so they release him. Not even his tentacles move.

He simply floats there, staring at me, and for the first time since waking up, I wonder if something else is wrong.

He was hurt. I remember that. But he's healed now, as if nothing happened before. But is he alright? That I don't know.

"He'rox, it's me." I smile at him as the veins slowly disappear and I blink away tears welling into my eyes. "It's me. Sophie."

The only indication he even hears me is the sudden flicking of his ears off the sides of his head.

A sob mixed in with a soft chuckle leaves my lips.

"Cute," I whisper, and that's when his tentacles move.

They wave at his back almost like four tails wagging as he floats closer to me.

Dark eyes move over me as if in disbelief, because my He'rox, the

He'rox that I know, reveals nothing on his face. And in that manner, he reveals nothing now.

"*Sophie?*" His voice sounds in my mind and I blink a few times. Still flat, devoid of emotion, but undoubtedly his voice in my head. "*How are you alive?*"

My chest heaves as the last of the veins disappear behind my palms as if they were never spreading across the tank. As if they don't exist.

My palms look undisturbed as I turn them to face me.

"You saved me," I whisper.

His gaze meets mine as one of his hands comes up against the interior of the tank, pressing directly against my face if the tank wasn't between us.

"You did it. You saved my life."

Again, only his ears flick as he stares at me and I wonder what's going on behind those dark eyes.

"*It worked,*" he finally says. "*I succeeded.*"

It's almost as if he doesn't believe it.

"Why don't you come out here?"

Those dark eyes stare at me for a few beats before his feet settle on the floor. The tank immediately engages and begins to drain, and soon, we are standing before each other.

"Sophie," He'rox says my name again, as if in prayer. "How is this possible?"

I take a step toward him and he doesn't move. "You saved me. Against all odds, you saved me."

His gaze flicks over the symbiotes covering my body. "The ba'clan. They healed you."

I nod and he blinks at me, nictitating membrane sliding across his eyes.

"This is…what you humans call…a miracle."

I smile, unable to help it as more tears well in my eyes.

The way he stands there, not one thing moving except his lips when he speaks, is making something deep inside me ache with a pain that can only be soothed if I am in his arms.

"I knew you could do it," I whisper. Taking another step forward. He'rox stiffens. His muscles growing hard as he forces himself to remain still. I swallow hard, forcing myself to remain still too, although everything within me wants me to rush toward him.

I must give him space.

It's clear he thought the worst had happened.

"I'm real, He'rox. I'm really here."

He blinks at me.

"Why don't you come over here to me?" I whisper.

He'rox blinks, the nictitating membrane sliding over his dark pits like a thin curtain once more.

"I fear that if I touch you...you will vanish back into my subconscious."

His utterance makes me choke on a sob and another laugh, and before I realize I've moved, I'm throwing myself into his arms.

He'rox staggers back, tentacles curling around me to keep me steady. For a moment, he simply stands there, frozen. Then his arms wrap around me and he crushes me against his chest with a strength that would hurt were I still human.

A shudder runs through his powerful frame as he buries his face against my hair, breathing in deeply, and the ba'clan pulse against me as if content with where we are. I cling to him, tears streaming down my face as joy and relief flood my senses. He's alive. We're both alive. Against all odds, we survived this.

"You came back to me," he rasps, voice thick with emotion. His large hands trace over my back as if reassuring himself I'm real. "I thought I lost you forever."

"You saved me," I whisper, leaning back to meet his gaze. A light twinkles in his dark eyes, chasing away the hopelessness I saw there. He stares at me as if I'm the only thing in this world, the only thing that matters.

Slowly, as if afraid I might break or disappear, he lowers his head.

His lips skim over mine in a kiss filled with reverence, passion, and promise. My body trembles at the feel of his lips against mine as I whimper and tilt my head back more, hungry for the taste of him.

The connection between us ignites, searing into my soul as the air crackles around us. I cling to him, pouring all the love I feel for this male into our embrace.

We have survived the impossible. We have been given a second chance. And this time, I will not let anything tear us apart.

A slight sound behind us has me stiffening and before I can stop it, my ba'clan spring out, forming more tentacles than I can count at my back, the edges hardened into sharp spikes.

Stiffening, my breath catches in my nose as I pull away and turn, eyes wide as they land on whatever threat is at my back.

Mina's wide eyes stare back at me. At us. Her own ba'clan form spikes all along her arms, one particularly dangerous one pointed forward, ready to slice the tentacles if they come too close.

"Sophie?" she calls.

But her expression holds no joy. Only shock.

"You're alive," she whispers, swallowing hard. "Are you...are you still Sophie or something else?"

As if recognizing she is no threat, the tentacles lower, sinking into my back in a way that should creep me out, except it feels completely natural.

"I'm me." I think.

Tears well in Mina's eyes, and she promptly shakes her head.

"I want to congratulate you. Shit, I want to hug you and cry and toast and celebrate but..."

A pit falls in my gut because I just know that whatever she's about to say, it isn't anything good.

"But...I came here as a last resort. To try and wake He'rox because we have to stop them."

"Them?"

"The soldiers...they're going to kill the Corrupted. With you and He'rox gone, the general didn't want to take any chances. They're preparing to fire as we speak..."

Something tells me there's more...

"And?"

"And there's another group heading this way. Bigger than the last one. They've got vehicles. Weapons." She releases a breath. "They have anti-Vullan flags...we don't think they're corrupted, but one thing is clear. They're coming to destroy the base."

CHAPTER THIRTY-SEVEN

SOPHIE

Mina's words send shards of ice through my veins.

Without another moment's delay, He'rox and I race from the lab, through the halls of the ship toward the lift. My senses feel sharper than ever before, acute enough that I can pick up the sounds of activity below even from within the ship.

I want to ask him about it. Ask him if he can hear the sounds too or if I'm the only one experiencing them, but now is not the time.

I'm scared, terrified even, that this new me has more power than ever before. I feel stronger, faster, more invincible than I have ever felt in my life. As if I could grasp time itself and make it bend to my will.

I glance at He'rox moving in tune beside me.

Is this how the Vullan feel all the time? Holding such indescribable power at the edges of their fingertips?

They could be gods here on Earth...and yet they came to save us. To rebuild with us. To live alongside us.

I feel them too. Like a constant pull there on the ground and even within the ship.

"I can feel them," I whisper, and Mina's eyes dart to me. She looks away then, focusing on the path ahead of us.

"My brothers..." He'rox says and I nod.

"It's the effect of the ba'clan."

"And I can feel something else, too."

Mina's gaze darts to me again as we turn a corner, and I see when her throat moves. "This way," she says.

I only realize then that I can sense something within *her*. Faint. Almost as if it isn't there. Not as strong as He'rox's or those Corrupted on the ground. She's been tainted by the Gryken too.

I give her an encouraging nod as we continue on. The reality that humanity is changed more than we realize a heavy thought on my mind. Pushing the thought back, I extend my senses to the ground. Half-amazed I'm able to. Half-terrified by this new power.

My consciousness snags on the soldiers below as they prepare to fire. But even more alarming is the approaching threat Mina described.

As we come to a halt and step into the lift, my chest heaves with extended breaths.

"This is a bad idea," He'rox suddenly says, dark eyes swallowing me whole. "You should have remained in the lab. There are tests I must perform and you need rest."

I smile at him, gripping his arm with one hand. Against the contact, the ba'clan pulse, crawling along my skin as if ready to go to him. "I've never felt more alive."

He'rox's ears flick as his gaze studies my face. "I've only just gotten you back. I cannot lose you again."

There's a deep intensity to his words that makes me know, without a doubt, how genuine he's being.

"I'll be fine." I lean closer to him, resting my forehead against his bicep as I breathe deep.

That sweet vanilla fills my nostrils and I have the sudden urge to crawl him like a pole. Pulling back, I swallow hard as I stare at him.

The ba'clan pulse against me again, as if urging me to continue.

"To be honest," Mina breathes, cutting through the path my thoughts had taken, "neither of you should be outside the lab. You've both been through a lot. Your bodies need rest." She pins me with her gaze. "Especially yours." She takes a deep breath. "We all thought…"

"That I was gone." I say it with a soft smile before I force myself to release my hold on He'rox. Memory of his thick cock sliding inside me almost makes my eyes roll over.

The longer I hold on to him, the more the urge to climb him grows deeper. As if I need to meld myself to him. As if I want every bit of him inside me.

As if I want to *claim* him.

The ba'clan pulse at that word and I swallow hard as that space between my thighs throbs in response.

This shouldn't be happening, should it? I just woke up. We're in the middle of a war. I should not be thinking about fucking him.

But the more his scent floods my nose, the more intense the feeling gets.

Turning my head slightly, I force myself to take shallow breaths.

"Sophie?" Mina asks and I shake my head.

"I'm okay. I–I'll be fine."

But I can't deny there's a pull toward He'rox. An urge, no, a *need*, to continue where we left off, the ba'clan whispering that I must bond further with him. That our connection will make us stronger, better able to face what is to come.

When the lift doors open, I force myself to focus as we rush out into chaos. The soldiers have their weapons trained on the eerily still Corrupted humans in the center of camp. But in the distance, the roar of engines grows louder as the unknown group approaches.

"Don't shoot!" I shout, raising my hands. The soldiers hesitate, thrown by my sudden appearance and probably the fact that I'm alive. I must be a sight.

Unruly red hair blowing in the wind while covered completely by ba'clan so dark, they suck in the light of the sun.

The Vullan around us snap their gazes to me, their attention almost unnerving if my ba'clan didn't pulse against me in support. I watch as spikes rise along their arms and fall, only to rise again, as if their ba'clan can't decide whether I'm a threat or not.

"Lower your weapons!" They probably won't listen to me. I hold no power here. I'm just a civilian. But before they can decide to ignore my order, black tentacles erupt from my back, slamming into their weapons and ripping them from their hands.

I expect the Vullan to move, to come at me, but not one of them even shift. As the soldiers stumble back in shock and fear, eyes wide and curses leaving their lips, I take another step forward, eyes on the Corrupted and their eyes on me.

I don't know what I'm doing. Heck, I don't know what I *should* do. But I know these people don't deserve to die. Not when there's a chance to save them.

The whole camp is watching me now and I stand alone, swallowing hard, the weight of what I just did on my shoulders. I attacked the soldiers. But just when I believe this is all on me, He'rox steps up beside me, his own tentacles writhing in a display of power.

"We have stopped you from making a grave mistake," he says. "The Corrupted are not the threat here—the true enemy approaches even now."

As if on cue, several large vehicles smash through the perimeter of Unity, skidding to a stop amidst a shower of immediate gunfire. Men pour out, firing indiscriminately at anything that moves.

"Fuck!" someone screams and my eyes widen as before me, one, two, three Corrupted fall to the barrage of bullets.

Anger rises within me at the same time that He'rox wraps his arms around me and I realize he's pulling me back, away from the chaos.

"No!" I scream. "We have to help them!"

"I will not lose you again!"

His face meets mine, presses into mine till all I can see is the darkness in his eyes, and my heart aches. I clutch on to him, hands grasping his head as I crash my lips against his.

At first, he doesn't respond, and then he's kissing me like I'm the air he needs to breathe.

"Then come with me," I whisper.

I know he won't deny me. I know that despite all this, he won't tell me no, and I feel some shame for using his love for me like this, but there are lives at stake.

He'rox growls at me, enough that my ba'clan form spikes, irritated at his aggression.

My gaze snaps the way we'd come and I realize the devastation that's occurred in just a few seconds.

The sound of gunfire erupts across the space, hitting the Corrupted, taking them down one by one, and the soldiers, now having grasped their guns, are firing back, taking down some of the attackers, but not enough. They aren't shooting to kill.

Enough of humanity has died.

That's when I see Vullan moving. Like dark shadows, they move with speed among the group of attackers, snatching away guns and splitting the weapons in two, but there are too many of them. Over two hundred, maybe.

These people must have traveled for miles. Met up. Organized this.

That's when I see the flags. Soiled white cloth raised high above their vehicles. Crude alien faces drawn with red Xs slashed through them and my belly bottoms out.

This is all because of ignorance. Hatred. Fear.

It's clear we don't want to kill them, but they're giving us no choice. Some of them will die.

In the chaos, the first sail of smoke going through the air catches my attention as a bottle bomb smashes into one of the tents and I scream as it bursts into flames.

They're destroying everything.

I struggle in He'rox's arms, willing him to let me go. "The people! We have to get them to safety." But as soon as the words leave my lips, I realize the tents are empty. I sense nothing inside them.

"In the ship..." He'rox says, reading my mind.

I nod, meeting his gaze before I smash my lips against his in a kiss that tells him that he means everything to me. "We have to stop this."

He'rox stiffens, clearly not agreeing, but he nods anyway.

And so we turn. Together we move like one unit, racing back across the ground toward the fray.

A few of the attackers break through, raising their guns to fire at He'rox and me. Before they can pull their triggers, black veins erupt from my back, ensnaring them in an unbreakable grip and I stagger to a halt, blinking at the sight before me. It happened even without me really thinking, but I embrace it.

The people struggle helplessly as I stride toward them, my expression grim.

"Find cover!" I scream at the Corrupted and they finally move, scrambling on weak legs to various sections of the camp.

Dropping the attackers in my grasp, I ignore their whines and cries of pain as I move through the conflict, tentacles grabbing and snapping guns in two in a move that stuns me at the raw stretch in my grasp.

Some of them run. Some get on the vehicles and retreat, while others stay and fight.

I hear one scream, abandoning their useless gun as they race at San'ten with double knives. He allows them to sink the blades into his chest before he snarls down at them, so many sharp teeth baring over their face that they go pale. Taking hold of their wrists, he snaps the bones, huffing in disgust as the man's screams fill the air.

Looming behind me, He'rox's tentacles form a cage around me as I move through the chaos, rendering those attacking helpless.

There is so much destruction, but it ends soon, and I see the moment they realize they'd lost the fight even before they'd arrived.

As Mina steps on the last gun, the sound of it cracking under her feet echoes in the air. Only the sound of whimpering remains, those attackers injured on the ground, some trying to crawl towards the woods, some who can run already on their way.

He'rox must read my mind because he opens his cage and says, "Go."

I move. Faster than humanly possible, I dash across the camp, He'rox and the Vullan at my back as we corral the attackers.

"Have mercy!" one screams.

San'ten rips the blades from his chest, and I swear his eyes roll back as if he's enjoying the pain. "Mercy?" he says. "We know no such thing."

I cringe at his words but the ba'clan pulse against me and it's almost as if I can *feel* them communicate with his ba'clan.

His gaze snaps to mine immediately and I nod.

He may be vicious. Scary even. But he isn't about to hurt these people. He just wants to scare them shitless.

"You're monsters," one woman spits. She has a nasty gash across her face, probably from before judging from the scab across it. "All of you."

Her gaze locks with mine and for a moment, I pause.

She's talking about *me*.

I look at the tentacles writhing around me and then He'rox's, which enclose mine as if they're mates.

He moves forward, one tentacle snatching the woman from the ground.

"Which monster?" he growls, voice chilling the air. "Tell me you refer to me and not my mate."

Warmth swims inside me. *His mate.*

I am his. And he is mine.

"I can see inside your soul, human," he continues, "and I see nothing but darkness there. You are the real monster here."

He drops her to the ground as if she's trash and she scrambles backward, eyes darting to her companions, most of whom are either staring at us with defiance, or hiding with their gazes averted, tremors racking their frame.

"There is a bigger threat here," I say, loud enough for everyone to hear. "Our world is still under attack, and instead of working with us to rebuild it, you've come to destroy the start of something good. Something great. The Gryken, those beings that used those huge machines to destroy this planet, *they're* the enemy. They and what they left behind."

My gaze skims over the group of wounded people, and I check to see if any of those dark veins are present. I see none. At least not yet. There's a chance these people are untainted, but that doesn't solve the problem of the Corrupted we have in the center of the camp.

And as for me...I walk amidst the people before us, noting how they cower and move away from me. The tentacles at my back wave, my ba'clan on full display, and I don't try to hide it. Not only for myself, but for him.

I turn to face He'rox. My beautiful monster.

He needs to know that what he did to save me wasn't a mistake. That I'm not ashamed of what I now am.

I hold his gaze as I continue speaking.

"Look at them," I whisper. "They're beautiful."

All around me, the Vullan snap to attention. I can feel their collective thoughts. The warmth that spreads through them at my words.

On the ground, another woman snarls. "Monsters. All of them are monsters! And you're one of them." She glares at me, Mina, and the other Vullan in the clearing.

"I'm human, just like you," I say.

"*Bullshit.*"

"Yes, I've changed a little, but in here," I touch my heart, "I'm the same." I turn to the others, some still pinned under Vullan arms. "All of you came here to attack the camp. You believe the Vullan are your enemies but *you're wrong*. We need each other if we want to survive and rebuild in a new world."

"You fool!" The woman who'd called me a monster stands, cowering a little as He'rox comes and towers behind me. I step back, my back brushing against his chest and just that simple contact grounds me. "You think something that looks so evil, so demonic is on our side?! *Open your eyes before our entire world is gone and we have nothing left!*"

Someone else stands. "If they're so good, if they really came to save us, then why are they still here?!"

My ba'clan pulse. The definite sensation of a blade going through me hits me all at once, and I realize the wound is not my own. It isn't even tangible. And my attention snaps to the Vullan around us.

They might not show it. They remain expressionless. But I can feel it. Feel how the words stab them worse than any weapon could.

"Why don't they leave? They killed the other aliens but they're still here! This is not their home! It's ours!"

Again, the ba'clan pulse, that wound going deeper.

"If they're so good they will listen to us, right?" someone else stands, nursing an arm that's obviously broken. "Tell them to leave. We can rebuild on our own. We don't need any aliens to help. They've done enough to destroy everything!"

Their words shoot through me too.

"What are you saying?"

My gaze snaps up as Adira walks toward us. At her back, Sam, Ga'Var, Fer'ro, Deja, and Fi'rox.

The woman's lip curls as she sets sights on Adira and the others, her disgust, her hatred clear. "This world is ours. Let them go back to theirs. They don't belong here."

"Tell them to go back, or there'll always be war here. We will *never* accept them," her counterpart says.

"*We will do no such thing.*" The words tumble from my lips with such force the women startle. I stand at my full height, tentacles swaying behind me as I study the group. "The Vullan are going nowhere."

I can almost feel when all of the Vullan look at me and I glance at

Adira. She's the one in charge here. She should be the one speaking, and yet, I can't stop myself from continuing. Because something tells me that what I'm about to say, Sam, Adira, Deja, and Mina will all agree.

"This is their home," I say. "They may have come from somewhere else, but this is their home. Will always be their home." My gaze shifts to the Vullan in my midst and I almost feel their ba'clan respond, sizing me up. "They're welcome to stay with us. Heck, we want them to stay with us." I shift my focus to *my* Vullan. *My* He'rox, and tears well in my eyes. "Never before have I ever met a species so selfless. These males you see before you lost everything, and they still came to our world, to help pieces of shit like you." I turn my gaze on the females and then on the other people cowering here. I probably should leash my anger, but I can't. "They didn't have to come and you know what, maybe they shouldn't have. Maybe they should have let our world burn and allow us all to perish."

My gaze flicks to the camp. To the billowing smoke as the remaining Vullan douse the fires these people set.

"You're deluded," I whisper, feeling the fury in my eyes as I cast my gaze on the people before me once more. "You think we're better than them..." I almost laugh. "You have no idea what's out there...do you? You think we could have survived this on our own...or maybe," my gaze shifts across their faces, some of them averting their eyes once I focus on them, "maybe you're happy they came here but now that they've helped us eradicate the threat, you want them gone."

The moment some of them dip their heads, I know I'm right.

Disgust fills me. And anger, on behalf of the Vullan around me.

"*They stay*," I say with finality. "This is their home now, as much as it is yours."

This time, my gaze shifts to the Vullan and several of them perk their ears off their heads. The action makes me smile. "We will share this planet. We will live here. Make families. Friends. Grow. Populate."

One of the Vullan growls, one that isn't the least bit aggressive, and at the sound He'rox snarls and steps closer to me. My cheeks heat the moment I realize why.

The idea of them being welcomed. Them staying here. Mating with us. Making families. That's what caused that sound.

Because...and I didn't realize it till now...I haven't seen a female Vullan. The only mates they could have would have to come from us.

The thought makes me smile even wider.

They really are big marshmallows. Just like Mina said the first time I came to this camp.

"I know you're afraid of what's different. The Vullan look strange and have powers you don't understand. But inside, they have the same hopes and desires as us. The desire for peace, for community."

There is silence and I can see some of the people before us slump their shoulders.

He'rox steps up beside me, his tentacles gently caressing mine. "She speaks the truth. We Vullan came in peace, to help humanity against the true foe."

More silence before a man who is being held hostage by one Vullan speaks up. "You killed some of us already. How can we trust you?" Murmurs of agreement arise from the group.

"You gave them no choice," Adira snaps.

I turn to the Vullan holding the man and nod. Dri'ro, my ba'clan supplies, telling me his name. With a jerk of the chin at me, he slowly releases the man, and one by one, the Vullan let the others go. My ba'clan pulse. Communicating. Urging unity and peace.

As the man rubs his wrists, reddened from the grip Dri'ro had on him, he stares at the Vullan for a long moment.

I step closer to the group, feeling like I've had to preach this message once too many times. But something tells me that I'll have to do it again and again, until what's left of humanity finally understands.

"Let's start again." I smile. "Hello, I'm Sophie."

CHAPTER THIRTY-EIGHT

SOPHIE

The sound of my footsteps pounds in my ears as I pace. Here in a sterile room, I wait, watching people come and go through the transparent wall before me.

Only one thing remains constant. One person.

He'rox.

As work on rebuilding Unity began, I knew it was only a matter of time before his patience ran out. As soon as we gave the new arrivals an ultimatum—stay and help us, or leave and not return—He'rox whisked me into his arms and headed for the ship. Now I watch him work, aware of almost everything around us.

There is much I don't understand about this new ability I have, but one thing is certain. I am forever changed.

He'rox's concern over my well-being and the changes that happened to me warm my heart so much. It's only because of his love and care that I sit waiting patiently on the floating bed in the room, watching him work. Watching him go through massive amounts of data as he runs scan after scan.

On the ground, things should be progressing. Some of the attackers had stayed to help, but I suspect others will return with more violence.

And all these hours later, He'rox has worked tirelessly. I fall asleep and wake, and he is still there, focused on the light matrix. Focused on me. And I feel he's checking and rechecking things just to make sure he doesn't miss anything.

Just to make sure I'll be alright.

Far behind him, in the room beyond the wall, every Corrupted that survived the attack float in suspended animation. Even Asha too. Induced comas, their bodies preserved as He'rox attempts to find a cure, and my head tilts slightly as I watch him work. He's a genius, the way he moves. His attention focusing on things I couldn't even begin to understand.

"What are you doing right now? What part of this are you working on?" I move closer to the transparent wall before us, pressing a palm against it. Tendrils of dark veins move out before coming back into my hand, evidence of the urge within me to touch this male.

"I need a compound," he says, gaze moving from the matrix to me. "Something that will either fully reverse the corruption or give the Corrupted control over the parasite."

My throat moves as I watch him. A few moments of silence pass between us as he studies the data before him.

"And do I need to be here? Behind the wall, I mean."

He'rox's gaze moves to me once more. "Until I know you are safe. Until I know you will be all right. Until I am certain..." He releases a breath. "I will run the tests one more time."

"How many times have you run the tests now?"

He doesn't answer immediately.

"One hundred and ten times."

My eyes widen a little. "And the result?"

"One hundred percent integration." His gaze bores into mine.

"What does that mean?"

He'rox pauses again before answering. "You are at peak health. Even healthier than you were before and...your ba'clan..."

"You succeeded in creating something new."

His ears flick. "I succeeded in creating something new."

"You succeeded in saving me."

He does not reply to that. Instead, "I will run the tests one more time. I need to know you are safe."

My heart warms while at the same time, my ba'clan pulse with impatience.

My gaze slides to the tentacles writhing at my back, and I consciously move them. I still haven't gotten used to them. To the way they move on their own if I let them, or the way I can create them from thin air.

And yet...it also feels like this was all meant to be.

"And if the cure is the serum you gave me?" I ask. "The one that's granted me all these powers..."

"If we give humanity the same powers you've received...it could do more harm than good."

His words hang in the silence that envelops us because I can't argue.

He's right.

Just what happened to Unity is proof enough.

So I wait. I watch him do the tests. I allow him to realize that it's over now. That we're on the right path. That the Gryken haven't won.

I know he feels responsible for what's happened to all those people. For what's happened to me.

It's the only thing keeping me on the other side of this wall as I watch him and wait.

Because ever since we left the ground, that intense need to wrap myself around him has returned.

With no ba'clan, the shadows that play underneath his ridges look smooth enough for me to run my tongue along them and I lick my lips, wanting to taste his skin.

Hours or minutes pass as I watch him work, never seeming to tire as he does test after test. Until finally, I press my hands against the barrier between us once more.

"He'rox." My one word is like a command, and he lifts his head and looks at me. "Come to me."

A moment passes between us and I think he will not oblige, and if he doesn't I intend to break the wall—or at least attempt to do so.

But He'rox suddenly stands at his full height, hands hanging limp at his sides. His ears flatten against his head as he stares at me. So I repeat my request.

"Come to me."

The ba'clan pulse in anticipation as He'rox moves away from the light matrix and accesses the barrier, an oval hole opening as he steps into the room.

Slowly turning, I face him.

We stand there, looking at each other before my body moves. The tentacles and my ba'clan disappear as I throw myself in his arms, my body melting into him, molding against his.

As soon as our lips touch, a shudder of delight goes through me, shooting straight to my core and I whimper as I flick my tongue into his mouth.

An answering purr comes from his chest, vibrating against me as I wrap my legs around his waist.

"What took you so long?" I tease.

"I cannot make a mistake," he growls against my lips, tongue flicking out to lap at the skin on my neck as my head tilts to the side. "I can never lose you again."

"You won't," I whisper, a whimper leaving my lips as he runs one of his fangs against my sensitive flesh.

My hands roam over his muscular back, feeling the ridges along his spine and the play of his muscles as he moves against me. His scent fills my senses, musky and sweet, and I find myself inhaling deeply, wanting more.

I writhe against him, my body betraying its needs and He'rox growls against my skin.

He breaks away from my lips, his eyes burning with an intensity that sends shivers down my spine. He pulls back for a moment, his eyes locking with mine, and at that moment, I know he's about to do something new. He leans in, pressing his lips to my neck, and I feel the tentacles on his back slither up my body, holding me against him as he slides to the floor.

Tilting my head, I capture his lips again even as a tentacle writhes between us, brushing over my nipple and teasing it to a peak. When my breath catches and I whimper, the other nipple is suddenly caught by another tentacle, both now writhing and curling in unison.

My pussy clenches, my clit throbbing with anticipation of what is to come.

"Fuck," I murmur against him. "You have no idea how long I've wanted to do this."

He'rox growls, only making me throb harder.

"From the moment you exited that regen tank and I could smell you, I've been going nuts."

He growls again.

"An urge to claim," he says, and I whimper when something hot and thick erupts between us.

My eyes widen as I see his cock extrude from his pouch, the movement so sudden and so hard, it slides right through the center of my lips. It's pure white tapered thickness that makes my eyes roll back before I bite my bottom lip, forcing myself to focus on his words and not the sweet honey flowing through my channel.

"Yes," I whimper.

"*I should be claiming you.*"

I want to huff a laugh through my nose, but then he continues. "I've wanted to claim you ever since you followed behind me into that forest. But I could not. My ba'clan...I had no ba'clan to do so. And my curse..."

I take his face between my hands, pressing my lips against his as I meet his gaze.

"Your *blessing*." Kissing him, I suck the tip of his tongue into my mouth and He'rox purrs against me. "And I have ba'clan now. *I* can claim *you*."

Those dark eyes look at me as he stills.

"He'rox," I whimper, even as his cock pulses against my clit. "Will you be mine?"

His ears flick and I giggle, kissing him again. "I'll take that as a yes."

He'rox grips my ass so tight, I swear there'll be an imprint of his hands when we are done, and I watch in amazement as the tentacles at the base of his cock begin to writhe and pulse, as if they have a mind of their own.

A rumble goes through him as he shifts with me in hand, tentacles holding me tight, and before I know it, he's crouching over me.

I tighten my legs around him, pussy clenching on air as he grips his cock and guides it to my wet entrance. His fangs bare and my eyes roll back once more as the cock-tentacles rub against my pussy.

"Fuck me, He'rox. I need you to fuck me. *Hard*."

He'rox's growl vibrates the air around us as he thrusts his hips, his cock sliding between my lips, and I lean my head back, the anticipation almost too much for my body to hold as he pulls back, grips my ass tighter, then slides inside me.

My eyes fly open wide.

The sensation is overwhelming. The tentacles at the base of his cock writhe around my pussy, my ass, as if trying to find a way inside.

He'rox snarls as he thrusts deeper, taking more of my pussy with each stroke. I try to fight for control, but his cock pulses as he pounds me hard and deep, and my body begins to shake. This time, I know it's not from an orgasm. It's from the pleasure of him fucking me as hard as I asked him to, his cock pulsing in me and touching every nerve ending I have.

He'rox pulls back until almost all his cock is out, his growl vibrating the air around us, and I feel the tip of his cock pushing against my clit. My pussy clenches and I draw in a deep breath as he slides back before pushing forward again, this time the tip of a tentacle stroking against my clit as he fills me.

"Fuck, that feels good." I gasp.

He'rox rumbles deep in his throat again, and the tentacle on my clit vibrates, matching the pulsing of his cock as he thrusts. I cry out as my pussy tightens.

He'rox pulls back and thrusts deep, over and over again, the tip of his cock reaching my farthest areas and just when I think I can't take it anymore, my pussy clenches on something new. Burrowing in alongside his cock, one tentacle moves as if searching for something. My eyes widen as another enters, making my eyes roll back with the impossible stretch.

"Tell me, my light. Do you like that?" He'rox rumbles.

"Fuck. Yes." I gasp out.

"Because I would like to try something else." His voice is like rumbling thunder in my ears.

"What?" I barely manage to say. What more could he possibly do?

His breath is ragged and loud in my ears as he says, "Would you like my sazi inside you? Or my tentacles? Or both?"

I glance back at him, my eyes rolling back into my head at the shock of the feeling, but I'm unable to come up with an answer. I'm too damn lost in the sensation of the tentacles moving, pulsing inside me and the cock fucking me in long, slow thrusts.

Electricity zings through me, and I cry out again, my pussy clenching and quivering around his cock.

His lips wrap around my ear and his breath is hot and heavy against my neck. "Say it, my light. Allow me to mate with you how I want to."

"I...I...Y-yes." I manage to grind out.

His cock and the tentacles in my pussy are stretching me as wide as they can and He'rox's hips rock back, dragging all three of them out of me until I'm completely empty. I cry out as he thrusts forward again and the tentacles extend inside me before the stretch becomes even tighter, forming a knot around the base of his cock, right inside the entrance of my channel.

He rocks back and forth, not able to pull out all the way as he pulls me closer, grinding our pelvises together as he begins to click words in Vullan. Words I don't understand until I focus, the ba'clan nestled at my spine translating the sweet nothings he's whispering and probably not aware I can understand.

"I claim you as mine. You are mine." His fangs press against my neck and I shiver with every word as it resonates in me, the tentacles in my pussy pulsing with his heartbeat, my pussy spasming around them with each pulse of my clit.

"He'rox." I gasp his name as I feel him, feel the heat and the love.

"You are mine." He grinds against me, a deep growl vibrating through his chest. "You are my light."

"Oh fuck." I gasp as I feel him swell even bigger and harder inside me. My vision blurs as pinpoints of light begin to dance in front of me. Gasping for air, I'm not able to hold back any longer as my spine tightens, my pussy spasming as I shatter all around him.

His teeth sink into my neck and I feel him in my head as my world spins out of control. I scream his name, my pussy emptying a gush of liquid all over his cock and the tentacles as they pulse and groan as I milk them dry.

"My Sophie." His voice is a growl in my head as I feel the warmth of his seed explode deep in my womb. The warmth of his seed combined with the warmth of his tongue as he laps at my neck makes me feel euphoric. I'm distantly aware of his cock still rigid and pulsing as he groans low in his throat before the cords of his neck strain and he collapses against me.

Knees weak and trembling, I catch us, not letting go of his head, his mouth sealed to my neck, his cock still pulsing, still pumping his seed into me as I lie back against the floor. Circling my arms around his shoulders, I give in to the exhaustion. It's as if all the worries in the universe have been eradicated from my life with that one act. That one bond.

"You are mine." He groans against my neck as I feel his cock pulse one last time, emptying one last wave of hot seed before the knot that binds us together begins to relax. Still slicking his cock with my fluids, his tentacles still curled inside me, I moan, kissing the top of his head as he breathes deep, both of us exhausted.

"I love you, He'rox." My eyes drift shut, sleep pulling at me.

There's a moment of comfortable silence before He'rox speaks. "That is not a word we Vullan use," he says. "All I can tell you is I will not be able to continue existing if you are no longer here with me, Sophie. I hope that is enough."

I smile against him. "More than enough."

He releases a breath, his lips finding mine. I kiss him back, loving the feel of his mouth claiming me as I drift off to sleep, comfortable knowing that he is here and we belong together.

And when I feel a smooth warm wave moving over me, I smile again before my eyes flutter open.

For a moment, I'm left speechless.

It's not the haze of sleep that's creating the vision before me. This is real.

All across my arms, the ba'clan flow like a thick wave. They travel from me to him, swirling from my fingers to cover his skin, flicking from black to white the moment they touch him.

"He'rox..." I whisper, stiffening with alarm as I watch the event unfolding before me. "What's happening?"

He'rox lifts his head only slightly, looking at me and not the ba'clan that's currently flowing over him.

"They are returning," he simply says, and my brows furrow a little.

"You mean they are leaving me." I'm surprised at the level of disappointment that immediately blooms, but the ba'clan pulse against me as if in comfort.

"Never," he says. "They are yours now, too. Belonging to you, as you belong to me."

I blink at him, confused, until I realize something.

His eyes flick from black to blue then back again, before the darkness slowly disintegrates and those ice-blue eyes of his return.

At his back, the tentacles that writhe slowly retreat, releasing me as they disappear into his spine.

"They're healing you?"

He shakes his head slowly. "I am forever changed."

For the first time since it began, he looks down at himself, ears flicking off his head as he watches his entire frame flood with white ba'clan. When he looks at me again, those ice-cold eyes aren't so cold anymore.

"You have given me a gift more precious than you can ever imagine," he rumbles. "Saving you has created a change in them. They have returned to me. No longer dying, but alive."

As if to test this theory, spikes rise all along his back and arms and for the first time, I hear a rumble of a chuckle in his throat.

My eyes tear up as I smile, wrapping my arms around him tighter as I pull him into me.

"Think we can do this now?" I whisper against his lips. "Save the world, you and me?"

"With you, my light. I can do anything."

EPILOGUE

HE'ROX

The pure white lights of my lab flicker as I peer into the lens, adjusting the magnification with trembling claws. After so many failures, have I finally done it? Beside me, Sophie squeezes my shoulder, her eyes tired but hopeful. "Is it working?"

I will never tire of hearing her voice within this space.

All of my existence, I have worked alone. Now, I have a partner by my side. One filled with curiosity and loyalty that matches my own.

My gaze slides over her beautiful face, slipping to her lips. Lips that have been wrapped around my sazi on just this morning's light, and a growl rumbles in my chest.

Soh'fee giggles, leaning in to kiss my cheek, and a thrum rises in my chest. The rumble turning into a purr at her show of affection.

I will never tire of this.

Taking a deep breath, I soak in her scent as I focus on the lens once more.

The corrupted tissue sample is transforming before my eyes, the dark, twisted strands unfurling and turning healthy and pink.

"It's working," I whisper. "On some samples."

I glance at Soh'fee, wondering if I will sense disappointment.

"That makes sense," she nods, brows furrowing, but there is no disappointment in sight. "The network seemed to affect them differently. Some had tentacles. Some didn't. Some seemed more aggressive while fighting. Others weren't." She leans closer. "I wondered if it was just different stages of the illness. Possibly, it was just variable presentation."

I rumble as her scent gets sweeter the closer she leans.

"We can fully cure some of your people. That is certain."

Sophie throws her arms around me, nearly knocking me from the stool on which I sit. I cling to her, overcome with emotion. Never have I felt this much for one being.

On Edooria, I believed my sacrifices for my world put my planet at the height of things I cared for.

I was wrong.

Everything Soh'fee and I have endured, all the failures and setbacks—they have led us to this point. I have saved my mate. And she has saved hyu'manity.

"We shouldn't wait," I say to her. "We must distribute the cure to those trapped in isolation. The sooner—"

"The better." She smiles at me and I am once again caught in the brightness of her light.

We work for two straight cycles, injecting the Corrupted and watching the cure do its work, freeing them from the grip of the parasite that has for so long rendered them prisoners.

The last of our regen chambers are emptied as the hyu'mans emerge, blinking in the light, frail but with a spark returning to their eyes that had been absent. My life organ swells at the sight of their relief.

We have given them back to one another.

Returning to the ground, Soh'fee and the other hyu'mans work to rebuild Unity. Carbon from our ship is repurposed to create living quarters that will tower from the ground.

Flame-resistant, as Soh'fee demanded, and as she directs one of my brothers in how to build them, I approach her from behind.

She smiles even before I touch her; the ba'clan alerting her to my presence.

And when I reach around her and fasten a gem around her neck, she pauses, eyes widening.

"What's this?"

"To my kind, this gem's eternal flame is a symbol of undying devotion." I pause. "My bond with you is eternal, as enduring as the flame within this stone." I bring her closer to my chest, reveling in the feel of her softness against me. Her eyes glisten with water as she reaches back and embraces me. I close my eyes and lose myself in her warmth, her touch, memorizing everything I can.

When I open my eyes again, I take in the events happening around us.

The Vullan and hyu'mans now talk of integration and perhaps, my brothers will not return to what's left of Edooria.

Five thousand years...

I look down at Soh'fee.

I have found my home.

We watch my brothers work alongside the hyu'mans, erecting the living structures that Soh'fee described, and she smiles.

"Every Vullan will have a home here."

Close by, some of my brethren's ears flick, and a chuckle rumbles in my chest.

Hyu'manity talks of home, but all they hear is talks of finding "mates". And perhaps, that is fine, too.

More hyu'mans will arrive. And perhaps some, like my Soh'fee, will not fear being mated to one like me. My brothers have a chance.

More hyu'mans come each day, their eyes lifted skyward in search of the vessels that defeated the darkness. And though there is only one, they still come amazed.

Those against us are present still. But word of our victory against them has spread. And for now, they keep their distance.

My gaze shifts to my Soh'fee. To her smile, her happiness flowing from her in waves, and I am content.

No longer staring into the void, I am present.

My mate, your light has kindled the flame of hope in my cold, dying soul. Our work is not yet done, but the future is ours to forge. Together, we have ensured hyu'manity's survival.

My bond with you is eternal as the flame—and it has saved us all.

AFTERWORD

Thank you so much for reading!

I received many messages about wanting He'rox's story and though I had it in my head all along, it took me a while to start putting it on paper.

He'rox has always been different from his brothers. From the start in book one, Arrival, you might have noticed this fact. His story was so intricate though, his character so reflective, so deep, that I waited to tell his story.

I wanted it to be just right or not write it at all.

Then came Sophie. When she developed in my mind, I knew I was ready to put He'rox's story down because he found the right heroine that was exactly what he needed.

Sophie's adjustment to He'rox, the way she jumped right in and accepted him for who he was even when he couldn't see the truth pulled at me (I know this might be strange to hear because I'm the one writing it, haha. I promise, I'm not crazy.)

This is for all my lovely readers out there. I truly hope you enjoyed this fifth book of the Captured Earth series.

♥ A.G.

Scan the QR code below if you want to ☞ Join my mailing list ☞ Find me on Facebook ☞ Join my Patreon (access NSFW character art, ARCs, quarterly mailouts and more!)

ALSO BY AGWILDE

Xul: Captured by Aliens Book One
Athena wakes up in hell.
Well…it's an alien slave ship, but it might as well be hell because she only has three choices.
Mate. Become a sex slave. Or be killed.
Great options.
Desperate for freedom, a chance for survival is presented in the handsome rogue alien called Xul.
But Xul is caught up in problems of his own and a mission he cannot afford to let fail—one that could be easily compromised if he dared open his heart.
That doesn't leave her with many options and it doesn't help that she finds him utterly frustrating…
…and strong, hot, irresistible…
She shouldn't really be thinking about him like that. Should she?

Other books in the series: Crex, Yce, Kyris, Kyro

Riv's Sanctuary: Riv's Sanctuary Book One

Abducted from Earth over a year ago, Lauren spent most of that time getting accustomed to her new life as one of the "animals" in an alien zoo.

When she's sold by the zookeeper, her life takes a turn she wasn't expecting. She has no idea where she'll end up till she's brought to a sanctuary owned by a tall blue hunk of an alien called Riv.

Riv's life is quiet and peaceful in a place as far away from civilization as he can manage. So when an annoying chatterbox of a human ends up on his doorstep, he's less than pleased. The human disrupts his life and his solitude and he can't wait to get rid of her.

He's not interested in helping her, and he's definitely not interested in love.

Except...she's managed to wheedle her way in and suddenly those barriers around his heart don't seem so strong anymore.

He has two options: Let her go.

Or let her in.

Other books in the series: Sohut's Protection, Ka'Cit's Haven

---

Ajos: The Restitution Book One

She didn't move to the big city just to be kidnapped by aliens.
That wasn't even possible...
Right?
WRONG.
When Kerena wakes up, she's not on Earth anymore.
Heck, she's not even in the same galaxy, and the face hovering so close she can make out every detail? That face is definitely...not...human.
But before she can really figure out what's going on, Kerena realizes she's caught in the middle of a war—one she was thrust into as soon as she was ripped from Earth.

She's surrounded by aliens in a rebellion, but there's one—the one with the strange golden eyes, minty-teal skin, and rippling muscles—that holds her attention.

His presence is magnetic and his heated gaze makes something stir deep within her.

He's battling something that has nothing to do with the war and his warning that she should stay away does not go unheeded.

He's a dangerous rebel fighter. She gets that. So...why is he still hovering so close? And why is he growling at everyone that so much as looks in her direction?

Most of all, why does he keep looking at her like she belongs to ... HIM?

Arrival: Captured Earth Book One

ADIRA
The machines came, and they trampled us all.
I have nothing left. No family. No friends. No home.
They harvest us. They breed us. They feed from us...
There is no hope...Not until one fateful moment when my eyes open and I see something streaking across the skies.
What appears is like a demon before my eyes...
But can they be worse than the evil already upon us?
I will just have to wait and see.

FER'RO
Sailing across the stars for what feels like eons...we have followed our enemy to a little blue planet.
We had wanted to arrive before them...now I think we may be too late.
But when we kill the first Scrit and I see the being drowning within its depths, I know I have to save it.

And *it*...turns out to be a *her*. **A female.**
This planet has hope yet. I will save her and her kind.
...Little do I know...she's the one who ends up saving me instead.

Dark. Steamy. Gritty. A thrilling romance intertwined in a plot that will give you chills.

Other books in the series: Base Zero, Cataclysm, War

Scan the QR code to view all books

ABOUT THE AUTHOR

A. G. Wilde is an avid reader, a gamer, a lover of all things space, alien, and sci-fi.

She is addicted to intense romance, irresistible heroes, and deliciously naughty things.

♣☆✳☆♣

patreon.com/agwilde
facebook.com/agwilde
twitter.com/authoragwilde
instagram.com/authoragwilde
amazon.com/author/agwilde

Made in the USA
Columbia, SC
09 June 2025